Highland Archer

HILDIE McQUEEN

PINK DOOR PUBLISHING • 2016

Highland Archer

Copyright © 2016 Hildie McQueen

Pink Door Publishing
Augusta, Georgia

Editor: Scott Moreland
Cover Artist: Dar Albert
Interior Formatting: Author E.M.S.

ISBN-13: 978-1-939356-50-5

Published in the United States of America

Chapter 1

The Archer

Air rasped in and out of Valent's lungs as he raced through the thick forest near his humble home. Low branches slashed his arms and face, yet, undeterred by the pain, on he sprinted. Fear coursed through him while tears streaked down his cheeks as he jumped over a fallen tree and cut to the right upon spotting the road back to the cottage where he lived.

Footfalls nearing from behind forced Valent to run faster.

A hard hit to the center of his back sent him stumbling forward. He let out a scream when a second hit landed on the back of his head and he slammed to the ground tossing his bow and quiver to the side.

It was impossible to count the blows that followed. Kicks and punches continued until he faded in and out of consciousness. Finally, his attackers ran off and he curled into a ball, willing the pain to go away. If he didn't get up and make it home to get his wounds tended to, he'd not make it to the archery competition the following day and surely lose his spot as apprentice archer.

Valent dragged himself to sit and winced while trying hard to keep from sobbing. His sides ached when he breathed. Blood from his nose dripped down the front of his tunic.

"Valent!" a deep voice called out. "Get on with it, boy. I've yet to see what ye accomplished in the hunt." Old Tavish came in to view, mouth falling open. "Not again."

Tavish hurried to him and bent down peering at Valent's face. "Who did this?"

Not that it mattered if he named his assailants. There was nothing to be done about it. "Donall, Ceardac, and Beathan."

"Ah," Tavish said as he wrapped an arm around Valent's waist with care. "Come on. Get up slowly boy. Let's get ye home... I will send for Meagan to come see about ye."

"No." Everything ached, from his face to his calves. Valent shook with pain at standing. "Not Meagan."

It took longer than it should've to get to their cottage. Tavish couldn't help him much. The man was riddled with discomfort every day from old battle injuries and walked with a pronounced limp.

Once inside, swaying side to side, Valent dragged his right leg across the dirt floor of his home to his cot. Each movement brought a groan as Tavish helped him lower to the bedding.

"I have decided to speak to the laird in the morning," Tavish announced with a huff. "'Tis time he does something about his sons. Could 'ave killed ye, lad."

At six and ten years of age, Valent knew he was much too old to have an old man speak for him. "I will do it. Do not be speaking for me, Tavish. If the laird gets angry, let it be with me."

"Drink this," Tavish forced a cup of vile smelling liquid to his lips. "All of it."

Within moments of drinking the tonic, Valent could barely keep his eyes open.

"Do not send for Meagan, please..." his word were slurred and he fought not to sleep. "I beg ye, Tavish." He hated it when a tear slid down his face. "I must compete tomorrow or any chance for me as an archer is gone."

There was doubt in Tavish's gaze. "Ye will be fine, lad."

"My God, Valent, what happened to you?" Meagan's worried eyes took in his bruised face. A sad sight he must be. Valent groaned, squeezed his eyes shut and prayed she did not bring her daughter. The fair Lora would never look upon him with admiration, not after seeing him like this.

Meagan placed a wet cloth on his brow. "One day you will grow to be broader and bigger than whoever did this and you will take your revenge. Poor thing, look at you."

"You won't be able to compete for the archer guard now." Lora's familiar singsong voice made Valent cringe.

Tavish coughed and cleared his throat. "Of course, he will. And teach the lot of them how much better he is."

Even though there was pride in Tavish's words, they angered Valent. It was doubtful he'd be considered. Especially since losing his prized kill when running from Donall and his brothers.

The next day, each step brought a streak of pain up Valent's right leg, but he refused to use a walking stick for support when going to the main keep. He entered the dark interior ensuring to take measured steps.

Just inside a small antechamber, a high-pitched voice called out.

"Who assaulted you?" Ariana, the laird's daughter's

rounded eyes met his before taking in the rest of his face. The girl didn't move from the chair where she lounged while continuing to study him.

The color of autumn leaves, he'd never seen eyes like hers. The first time he'd seen her up close, he was seven years old and she a child of about four. He'd never forgotten when she came to him and took his hand, attempting to get him to play with her.

"Your brothers," he replied to the young girl who gasped, her mouth forming an "O".

"They are no better than the beasties they hunt," she told him. The laird's daughter stood and neared to inspect his injuries. "Da won't do anything to them. Ye may as well just go back home." She shrugged as if no longer interested and returned to her seat.

Footsteps sounded and he whirled to find the laird standing in the doorway. "What are ye doing in here?"

"I called him in," Ariana piped up behind him. "He was limping and I wanted to know what happened."

The laird's gaze was cold and distant when meeting Valent's. "You're the boy Tavish took in are you not?"

Valent bowed his head. "Aye, my laird."

"I hear good things about your archery skills." The laird's comment surprised him. Once again, the shrewd gaze went from his face to where he held his arm protectively around his waist. "I suppose your injuries will stop you from competing tomorrow."

"Nay. I will compete still." Valent's eyes rounded at realizing the lack of proper address. "I beg forgiveness, my laird, you did not ask the question of me."

"'Tis fine." The man waved his apology away. "How did you become injured?"

Realization dawned. It was best not to confess the truth of his injuries. If the laird became angry with him, it would be impossible to win a place with the archer guards. He'd remain a stable boy with no aspiration to ever defend his people, his laird.

The laird lifted a brow in question. "Well?"

Ariana got to her feet and stood beside her father. "Donall, Ceardac, and Beathan beat him."

Of course, the girl would enjoy seeing her brothers punished. The fact the boys would then take it out on him was not something she'd ever consider.

"Go to your chamber, Ariana." The laird let out a weary breath before addressing him.

"So the hunting prize, the doe, presented yesterday was not Donall's kill?" The laird waited on his reply, his gaze without warmth.

Valent knew his best chance at the laird allowing him to compete without a kill would be based on how he answered. "I was not at the presentation of the kills, as Tavish was tending to my wounds. Therefore, I canna say, my laird."

The McLeod nodded and looked away. "I see."

He hoped the laird would allow him to compete, but when permission was not forthcoming, he waited to be dismissed. Instead, the laird turned away from him. "I've always wondered." The laird paced with his hands grasped behind his back. "Who took you from your home to deposit you at my doorstep and why? You were but three or four at the most. When the housekeeper found you, it was as if you'd just been promptly deposited. Not overly malnourished, nor mistreated, barely able to speak as you were too young. And you don't remember anything?"

Although he wanted to leave and immediately see how well he could work with his bow, curiosity kept him planted.

Tavish discovered him when he'd been fighting for food scraps in the courtyard. The old man had taken pity on him and brought the wee lad to live with him. Valent had already been at the keep for a few weeks by then.

"Nay, my laird. I would one day like to know where I came from. Why I was abandoned. I only vaguely remember a brother, a boy."

"You may compete tomorrow. Without a kill to your name, it will take great skill to beat out the others." The laird eyed his bruised face and bandaged left wrist. "With your injuries I doubt ye will overcome."

"Thank you, my laird." Valent bowed his head. "By the end of the day, I hope to pledge my bow and myself to ye."

The laird's slight nod was enough lift his spirits.

Chapter 2

Fourteen years later

Valent wrapped his hands around the woman's waist as she straddled him. Lisbeth lifted and lowered her hips, breathing harsh, breasts bouncing from the exertion. He closed his eyes and allowed the sensations to take control.

To ensure she climaxed, he reached between her legs and caressed her until she cried out and trembled, her sex constricting around his hardness.

When his release neared, once again he took her by the waist. "Get off me." He easily lifted her and rolled to his side to spend his seed onto the dirty blanket.

"Stay with me, Valent," the woman begged as she ran her hands down his chest. "I want your strong arms around me all night."

Every time he came to her, the same invitation, and Valent always replied that he could not. It was best he stopped visiting her, as she cared more for him than he ever would for her.

The woman was older than him by ten years, a kind person whom he brought small animals for her supper, provided wood in winter and completed repairs to her cottage.

Although he never asked, it was apparent Lisbeth had other lovers. Not that he blamed her. It was the only way for her to survive the harsh life of a widow.

"I cannot. Tavish is not well and I do not like to leave him alone for long."

She sat up on the bed and smiled in understanding. "You are a good son to him."

Valent didn't bother to correct her. Tavish was, indeed, the closest thing to a father. The man could barely move about now, his legs so crippled, many times Valent had to carry the old man outside the cottage for fresh air.

The old man spoke more and more of dying, preparing himself and Valent for what seemed to come soon. "I am at the end of my days here," he often said. "Too tired to tarry about much longer."

The sun was setting as Valent walked to his cottage; he looked toward the tall walls of the McLeod keep. He'd fought with the head guard many times over his decision not to live in the guards' cramped quarters. Even now that he was head archer, they had insisted he move to live within the walls.

Yet he refused to leave Tavish on his own. He vowed to care for the man whom he owed life to until the very end. If not for Tavish, surely Valent would have died while young.

His mind went to the laird who'd not made an appearance in the last few weeks. It was rumored he was very ill and would not make it through the next winter. The clan would see a new leader soon.

With quick tempers and reckless attitudes, any of the laird's sons could very well be the downfall of the clan.

Of the laird's three sons, the eldest Donall, was the

most like his father. No friend to Valent or anyone of lower ranking, the soon to be laird rarely deemed it necessary to speak to the guard. Interesting, since they were sworn to defend his life, one would think the man would find a way to endear himself to them. At least the elder McLeod was smart enough to invite the guardsmen to dine with him and often attended their competitions.

It was not an easy time in the northeastern Highlands. Too many clan clashes. Even within the larger clans, family struggles had caused rifts that divided them.

Although the McLeods were rarely challenged and remained strong, there were rumors of an imminent attack by rival Clan McKenzie.

The ongoing clashes between the two clans had ceased years earlier and Valent hoped that the passing of the current McLeod laird did not lead the new McKenzie laird to think the McLeods weak and attempt a takeover.

That night, he settled onto his cot and the sounds of the wind outside lulled him to a deep sleep.

The mist of the mountains swirled thick in the air. The fog made it hard to see more than a few yards. Valent narrowed his gaze and strained towards the trees. It was out there, looking at him. Red eyes in the distance took in his every move. Fear sent an icy trickle down his spine. It was escape or die. Although he understood he could never outrun it unless he hurried, his legs refused to budge.

"Find it. Kill it," a raspy voice demanded.

His mind screamed that he run when the huge claws appeared out of the darkness. Large enough to cut him in half, the huge hand paused in midair. "You or him?"

The voice, while familiar, struck as much terror as the thought of death. All he could do was tremble. His right hand was squeezed. Someone held it tightly, refusing to let go. In desperation he reached toward whoever stood next to him with his free hand.

The hand slid out of his grasp and Valent fought with all his might, flaying his arms in an attempt to find the person, but instead of flesh and bone, there was only air.

He began to cry and then scream in frustration. They did not understand him. He could not speak. Could not communicate his wish to remain, to not lose whoever held his hand. Then he was lifted into the air. He struggled and cried out, his arms extended over the beast's shoulder.

On the floor lay a small boy crying, his mouth wide open. When the child opened his eyes and looked to him, Valent went limp. It was him, a boy child torn from his family.

But no, it wasn't. He was being carried off by the beast.

Gray mist gave way to darkness and terror at what came next and his body shook uncontrollably. The beast threw him down and he scrambled to a tree and huddled under the low branches.

"Time to pay," the beast roared.

Valent jerked awake, his breathing harsh. The same dream that haunted him for years. Each time the same frustration. In the midst of the terror-filled events, there were bits, hints to his past. Who he was and what happened when he'd been torn from his family. If only he could see more, understand more and not be overtaken by fear.

He raked a shaky hand through his tangled, shoulder-length hair and got up. He checked on Tavish, who slept soundly, and went outside. The brisk air would help clear his mind and slow the beating of his errant heart.

Once outside, he inhaled deeply. The forest was lightened by the full moon and he stared at it. "Who was that beast? What did it mean?"

Why did he see himself both taken and left behind? What could it possibly mean? He remembered a brother. Seemed to be older than him, but who knew. Someone he played with as a child. A secret he'd kept, never revealing to anyone the sparse memories of his short childhood before coming to Clan McLeod. There was a woman as well, with dark hair like his and the same gray eyes as he and his brother. The woman had kissed him often, hugged him to her and sang soft songs. Had she decided to keep his brother and send him away because he was not good enough? What cause would a mother have to send her child to live with strangers?

"I will find you," he vowed as a falling star crossed the sky. "One day, I will find you, mother and brother, and learn the truth of why you didn't keep me."

At a soft sound, he flattened against the wall and searched the darkness. A deer walked out of the trees and continued its trek without seeing him. Valent's right hand itched. If he'd had his bow, the animal would be their meal through the winter. No matter, he had plenty of time to hunt. No other archer could boast to be as good as he.

Yes, he was proud of his accomplishments, always winning competitions both standing and on horseback. Valent was not apologetic as he trained hard and often.

After a long time, Valent made his way back inside. The cottage was quiet. Too quiet. Tavish usually snored like a boar while asleep. His chest constricted and he ran to the small cot where the old man slept.

"Tavish!" Valent shook Tavish. Tavish didn't respond; the old man's body already turning cold.

"No!" Valent shook him once again without result. "Do not leave me. I have no one."

Valent's hoarse cry floated over the forest.

Once again, he was alone.

The arrow whizzed past Valent's leather wrist bracing, arching gracefully through the air. There was a collective hush as he hit the center of the target. He'd bested Donall McLeod and the new laird glared at him, not hiding the hatred he felt.

Ignoring the man, Valent pulled a second arrow and aimed. Once again, he hit the target dead center, right beside the first. Applause and cheers erupted from the guardsmen as he helped the McLeods win over the visiting clan.

The laird stalked away, not bothering to congratulate him. Valent didn't pay him any mind. As he was now head and shoulders taller than Donall McLeod and the laird had stopped tormenting him years earlier, there was no need to worry about the petty annoyance.

It didn't bother Valent not to be invited to feast in the great hall later that day, nor did he care if the laird was angered over losing to him. If he was to be honest, there was little he cared about those days.

Valent walked to stand beside the guards enjoying their revelry.

"I knew you would do it," cheered Cullen, a fellow archer, smiling widely. "Ye're the best archer in the land."

"Congratulations." They turned at the sound of the deep voice. Laird Munro came forward, his guards flanking him. It was comical to watch Laird McLeod rush to stand before Valent and push Valent aside to shake the visiting laird's extended hand.

"Your archers are impressive," the Munro told Donall, his gaze moving past to rest on Valent. "I will ensure my men practice more before we meet again."

"They do well" was Donall's reluctant response. "You are welcome to return, of course. Now come, let us celebrate. A feast has been prepared in the great hall."

The Munro nodded at Valent. "Please join me at my side."

Donall's eyes bulged when he met Valent's. "Do you not have to go see about Tavish?"

Being Tavish had trained them as boys to hunt, the laird remembered the old man well.

"Tavish died four weeks past." Valent couldn't stop the pang in his chest at mentioning the old man's name.

"Right, of course," Donall replied, motioning for everyone to follow as he and the Munro made their way toward the keep.

The meal was like nothing he'd ever had, flavorful and with so many choices, Valent was overwhelmed. From the corner of his eye, he noticed the Munro watching him closely. Finally the man leaned closer.

"What is your surname? Are you a McLeod?"

"No, Laird. I have no name. I was abandoned here as a child. A man named Tavish named me Valent, saying I'd be very brave one day." He attempted to keep his tone neutral. Admitting to being a bastard with no name was not something he'd ever become accustomed to.

"Is that so?" The laird studied him. "You remind me of someone I once met. He is a McKenzie." The laird whispered the last name, being the McLeods and the McKenzies were near to warring over borderlines.

"I would rather die than be one." He could not keep the hatred from his voice. "I am sure I come from the south. Tavish says there is a small clan, the McRae, who are known for sending off young children with traveling men in hopes of finding them better homes."

"It is possible. Have you gone to seek them out?"

"Nay. I couldn't leave for long as Tavish remained ill

for many years. Now that he is gone. I am considering it."

"One should know from where one comes." The laird picked up his goblet and drank from it. "I wonder, however, at the familiarity of your face. If only I could remember who exactly it was."

Valent held his breath, but the Munro did not speak of it any longer. He wanted to ask a favor of the laird, but didn't dare with Donall obviously straining to hear what they spoke of. If only the man could try harder to remember who he favored. "Thank you, Laird, for thinking of it. Maybe one day ye will remember."

He looked to other side of the high board where Donall sat, his mother on his left and his first on the right. Next to the laird's mother was Ariana. A finer looking woman he'd yet to see. She'd grown to be breathtakingly beautiful with a heart-shaped face and dark amber curls that fell to the center of her back. She wore a thin-jeweled headband across her forehead and green jewels at her ears and throat. Her amber eyes scanned the room until resting on him.

It was not in his nature to remain at the high board. That was not where he belonged. Excusing himself, Valent moved to sit with the other guards when the Munro's head of guard came to see about his laird.

Once seated, he could not force his gaze away from the beautiful Ariana. It would be easy to spend hours admiring her. It was said she recently returned after losing her husband to illness. She'd been in mourning for a long time. By the color of her forest green gown, she was no longer.

The air left his lungs when she smiled at him. The corners of her lips lifted and he fought the urge to look behind him to learn to whom she really smiled. He was content to pretend it was him who she graced with such a gift and he bowed his head in return. When he lifted his head, she spoke to her mother, the soft smile lingering on her lips.

Yearning for her touch was something he didn't dare aspire to, yet most nights he pictured her face before falling asleep. When she'd married, he'd been part of the procession escorting her to her new husband. A McLeod of the south, who was much too pompous, was the groom.

No one, in Valent's opinion, deserved her. He'd begrudged her husband for years, barely able to keep from rushing after her to ensure she was well. Ariana McLeod would never be his. Of course, he knew that and had accepted it long ago. But no one could stop him from dreaming and admiring her from afar.

"Valent." He started and his friend, Cullen, laughed. "You look in a daze. I just saw Lora sneak off. Is she finally succumbing to you? If not, then I am considering following."

It was rumored she was Donall's lover, but he'd never seen any indication of it. "Nay, I'll go see what she's doing, perhaps helping in the kitchens." He pushed away from the table. Although he had no responsibility for Lora, he'd known her his entire life. Even after outgrowing his infatuation, he cared for the woman.

The hallway was dark and Valent stepped carefully to not make any noise to avoid anyone in the household catching him about. A moan sounded and he moved faster toward it.

"Always ready for it, are you not, Lora?" Donall's voice was hoarse. "You are a randy wench."

Valent stopped at hearing Lora's reply. "Only for you, Laird. Yes. Yes!"

She was bent forward over a table, her skirts thrown over her back. Donall took her from behind, ramming into her with force.

Stumbling backward, Valent turned away. How to handle the situation? He contemplated making noise, but then there was a possibility he'd attract more not needed attention. He let out a huff and walked away. Not his business. When he turned the corner, Ariana crashed into him and gasped in surprise.

"Ouch. You are crushing my foot." She pushed at his chest and he moved back, too startled to speak. Ariana was more stunning up close than he could have imagined. With creamy skin and of delicate bone structure, she resembled a lovely field flower. She studied his face. "You are pale. Did you see a ghost?" On her tiptoes, she tried to look past him.

"Lady McLeod, you should return to the great room at once." He finally found his voice. "Please."

She pushed her hair behind her shoulder and he could feel his eyes round at the view down her bodice. His mouth became dry. Unaware of her effect on him, she tapped her foot. "Move aside, archer. I am going to the kitchen to speak to cook."

"Is there not another way you can go?"

"What? Why are you keeping me from passing? Are you hiding something?" She placed her hand on his arm and attempted to pull him aside. Her fingers were warm and soft on his skin and he almost closed his eyes and prayed she'd never remove it.

"A large rat."

"Oh." She took a step back. "A rat?"

"Aye." He held his hands up about shoulder width apart. "Huge."

Ariana giggled. "That would be a cat if it was that big."

"What goes on here?" Donall McLeod approached from behind Valent and pinned him with a pointed glare. "How dare you stand here and speak to my sister."

"He was protecting me, it seems," Ariana responded and shook her head at her brother. "Don't chastise him. It was my fault for arguing over it."

"Protecting you how?" The laird looked from her to him. "Explain."

"He said there was a huge rat just down a bit and that I shouldn't go past," Ariana informed him and pushed past them both. "I am too exhausted to care about a rat the size of a cat. Goodnight, gentlemen."

After she left, Donall moved to stand in front of him and pulled out his sword, pushing the tip under Valent's chin. "I've never liked you. No reason really."

The steel cut into his skin and he felt the trickle of blood trail down his neck. Valent didn't move nor did he meet the laird's gaze.

"Whatever you expect to gain from stopping my sister is lost on me. As I would not have cared if she saw me with your precious Lora. You have wanted her all your life have you not? That is the only reason why I take her. I took the whore harder when you came around the corner. I needed you to see how much better I am than you."

Hatred at the man spread through his body. "She is not a whore."

The sword inched deeper into his chin and blood trickled freely down the front of his tunic. Finally Donall pulled it away and Valent held his hand to the cut to staunch the flow.

Donall wiped the blade on the hem of Valent's tunic and leaned forward, his lips to Valent's ear. "Yes, she is."

Chapter 3

Ariana knew exactly what the archer tried to protect her from seeing. When she turned the corner, a peasant girl stood in the hallway, her dress askew and her lips swollen.

The young woman bobbed a quick bow and attempted to straighten her frock. "Milady, is there anything I can get for you?"

Often, she wondered if the women her brothers joined with agreed to it or were forced. This lass didn't seem upset. "No, I do not. You do not work inside the keep, but I've seen you. What is your name?"

The girl flushed a bright red. "I am Lora, milady. I am the healer. Took over for my mother, Meagan."

"Yes, I remember now." Although weary, she felt a need to find out more. "My brother, Donall, just walked past me. Are you acquainted with him?"

Lora's eyes widened. "Yes. What I mean to say, milady, is that he is kind to me."

The answer was sufficient to allow her to give the young woman leave. Ariana made her way to her chamber.

"Milady," Lily, her handmaid, said and rushed to her. "You look about to fall over. What happened?"

"After months of mourning, being restricted to these chambers, it's hard to get used to a long day of activity." She sunk into a chair. "I should have rested during the day. I can barely keep my eyes open. Mother is cross that I left the dining hall too early, but I almost laid my head upon the table."

Lily removed Ariana's shoes and stockings and then went behind her to pull the pins from her hair. "Ye will get plenty of rest tonight. There is not much to do on the morrow, is there?"

A picture of the archer she'd spoken to in the hallway appeared forefront in her mind. "Can you find out when the archery competition will take place?" She kept her gaze on the flames in the fireplace. "I would like to see it."

"Archery?" Lily frowned down at her. "Are ye sure," the maid asked, not taking her gaze from Ariana. "Ye've always said ye hate the games."

"I'm interested in archery, you know that. Plus, I want to know what happens this year."

"It's too late, milady. The archery competition was today. The games are over."

"Oh." She let out a sigh. "Who won?"

Lily smiled and poked out her bony chest. "The McLeods, of course, milady. The archer, Valent, cannot be beaten. He is the best in the land."

The maid grabbed a brush and began to untangle Ariana's hair, entertaining her with details of the archer's feats. Seemed he had many an admirer, her maid amongst them.

"Are you being courted by him?" Ariana asked feigning indifference. Since a young girl, she'd stood on the high balcony and watched the archers practice. Valent, the bastard, was always a sight to see. Since the day her brothers had beaten him, she'd kept a vigil for him. If she noticed her brothers goading him, she'd come up with a reason to get their attention. Once, when she was ten and five, she'd followed Valent on horseback to see where he lived.

Although she could never hope for more than admiration, as he was only an archer and she the laird's sister, she often daydreamed of how it would feel to be kissed by him. When she'd married, what she missed the most were the rare glimpses she caught of him.

Valent.

"Milady? Did you say something?" Lily watched her with a curious expression. "It sounded like you said the archer's name."

"I did," she admitted. "I was thinking of a time my brothers beat him rather badly."

Lily's expression changed to serious and she cast her eyes down.

At once, Ariana was aware something was amiss. "What is it? Why do you react this way over my comment?"

"I overheard a plan to do so again because he beat the laird at the archery competition. Your brother is sending Fergus to beat Valent when he leaves tonight."

Fergus was a mountain of a man. The giant rarely spoke to anyone and angered easily. It was common to hear about him beating someone to near death merely for not moving out of his way fast enough.

Ariana got to her feet. "We must warn him. I cannot believe my brother has not outgrown this vendetta or whatever it is he has against the archer."

"Everyone talks about it, milady. No one knows why he hates him so." Lily let out a sad sigh. "Do not worry yourself. I will go find him."

After Lily left, Ariana made her way to her mother's chamber. Her mother slept just down the hall from her, having relinquished the larger set of rooms on the floor below to Donall once he became laird. The flickering candles in the hallway gave an eerie glow and a trickle of apprehension slid down her spine, like a premonition of something horrible on the horizon. She pulled her robes tighter to dispel the chill.

"Mother?" Ariana pushed the door open and found her mother by the narrow window looking out. "Is something amiss? You seem sad."

Her mother shook her head and extended her hand. "Nay, I am just enjoying the quiet of the night. Come, Ariana, look at the moon. It is huge in the sky tonight."

Together they peered at the night sky. The huge moon hung low in the sky, illuminating the empty courtyard below. Ariana studied her mother's peaceful profile. "We have an interesting bond of sorts now, Mother," Ariana said. "Both widows."

"A sad one I never wished to have with you," her mother replied. "Is there a reason you came, dear?" Her mother took her hand. "It is rare you come to my chamber at night."

If only she could confess to her mother her true feelings, how lonely she felt, at odds with the world. Wishing for a man who could never be hers. But her mother had always insisted on doing things perfectly, according to their standing within the clan. "Did you ever love anyone except my father?"

They moved to chairs before the fireplace and her mother's expression became wistful. "A young lass' infatuation at most. Every girl dreams of a handsome man. I once considered myself to be wildly in love with my cousin, Malcolm. He was so much older than I and always had a stern expression. Yet he always had a kind word for me."

Ariana pictured the still attractive man. "Aye, I can understand that."

"Is there someone you've taken notice of?" Her mother smiled at her.

With a shrug, she dismissed the question. "I notice several handsome men among the guards, but they are beneath me, of course."

"Very much so. Your brother would never allow a union with a guard. Do not even speak about it." Her mother looked to the doorway as if expecting one of her sons to be lurking there. "What about the Munro's eldest son. He is not married."

"Mother!" Ariana could not help but laugh out loud. "He resembles a toad."

Her mother covered her mouth with both hands. "Aye, he does. He will remain single unless his father arranges a marriage without him present."

They laughed harder until Ariana's sides hurt. "Do they leave in the morning?"

"Aye." Wiping tears from her face, her mother went to the door when someone knocked. Lily looked to Ariana and then to her mother.

"Oh, there you are, milady. I've delivered the message."

"Message?" Lady McLeod looked to Ariana. "What message, Ariana?"

Ariana's chest constricted at Lily's blunder. "I asked Lily to tell my brother I needed to speak to him when possible." Ariana blurted the first thing that came to mind and gave Lily a pointed look, hoping the maid kept her mouth closed about her message to the archer.

Her mother's eyebrows rose. "What do you wish to speak to him about?"

"About my place here. I wish to remain and not marry again."

Her mother came to her and took her hands. "You are young still and should marry. Being a widow gives you more choices; perhaps you should ask your brother to allow you to pick your next husband. I'm sure he will understand. We do not have a need to join with another clan as we are strong enough with our current allies."

Finally, she was able to leave her mother's chamber. Ariana hurried back to her bedroom, Lily on her heels. "I am sorry, milady. I shouldna spoken freely like I did."

"Do not worry. I am sure Mother believed me."

Lily waited for her to remove her robe and placed it at the foot of the bed. "Milady, are ye really planning not to marry again? Ye're still young and can look to a future of wee ones to raise."

"Not to an old man who my brother decides to pawn me off upon. Like Mother said, as a widow, I have choices now. And I choose to remain here, taking care of my mother and looking after the household." She thought for a moment. "At least until Donall marries."

"Aye, milady. Very well, then. Into bed you go."

Ariana lay in the dark, her mind wandering back to the archer. She'd forgotten to ask Lily if she'd spoken directly to Valent or how the message had been sent. If her brother got wind of it, she was sure his reaction would be harsh. Hoping she'd not made things worse for the handsome man, she attempted to sleep.

Standing in the brisk morning air, Ariana held her bow and quiver and approached the training site. Valent was there. He was not harmed, looked to be fine. He held up his bow while looking to a younger man. She admired his stance and the width of his back as he pulled back on the string while explaining what he did. Her eyes traveled down his back to his taut bottom. A very well formed one, indeed.

"'Tis a beautiful morning, is it not?" The voice made

Ariana jump. The Munro's son stood next to her, his bulging eyes focused on her chest. "Do you often train with the archers, Lady McLeod?"

It was hard not to step away at noticing his lips resembled two earthworms sliding against each other. Instead, Ariana forced a smile. "Aye, at times I do. Excuse me for asking, but I thought you and your father were to depart this morn."

"Aye, we will be leaving soon. But I saw you from the balcony and came to seek a private word. Bid my farewell."

"Oh." Ariana let out a breath. "How nice of you. I wish you well."

He took her arm. "Could I ask for you to walk with me for a bit?"

When she looked to the archer, he turned to them. Locks of his dark hair had fallen over his face making the contrast of his light gray eyes even starker as he looked to them. His gaze moved to where Munro held her arm.

Ariana met his gaze hoping to convey her distress at being asked to spend time with the toad of a man. He looked away and she wanted to scream in frustration. "Of course." She placed her bow and quiver down and allowed him to lead her away.

The man was shorter than her by a few inches. To make up for it, he stretched to his full height as they walked. "I am a man of few words. Therefore, I will not mince them. I find you quiet attractive and would like to ask that you consider becoming my lover."

At the man's words, Ariana stumbled and put her hand out to a tree to steady herself. "What?"

He didn't seem to notice her distress managing to look down his nose at her, his lips curved. Dread filled her as she realized they were away from the view of others. "I know you to be widowed. You can take a lover and it would not be frowned upon." The dreadful man pushed her against a tree, his face only inches from her. "The nights can be very lonely, can they not?"

When she pushed against him, he did not budge. His face darkened and he glared at her. "You cannot hope for a better lover than me." His attempted to kiss her, but she turned her face. Not discouraged, he began to kiss her neck. Ariana shoved at him while attempting to kick him. "Stop!"

Just then an arrow impaled the tree directly above their heads. Munro jumped back, cursing. He whirled around to find a very menacing Valent behind him. "Sir, I believe your father is seeking you."

Standing head and shoulders above Munro, Valent made the horrible man crane his neck to look at him. "How dare you shoot at us? I will have you whipped within an inch of your life."

"On the contrary," Ariana interrupted. "Once my brother learns about your attack on my person, he will reward Valent." It was a lie, since Donall hated Valent, but the vile little man did not know.

"You are not worthy of my time." Munro attempted to push Valent aside. When the archer refused to move, he rounded him and stalked away.

The archer did not move, his almost translucent gray eyes on her face. "Are you well, milady?"

His beauty took her breath away. Dark, sable brown hair that fell to his wide shoulders in waves blew in the light breeze. His lips were sensual in a manner that made a woman lean forward in anticipation of tasting them. There was an aristocratic air about him that made her wonder of his lineage. "I am well. Thank you for your rescue. I do not know how far he would have gone, otherwise."

He nodded and turned away. "I will walk you back."

Ariana reached for his arm. "Why does my brother hate you so? You have been the target of his disdain since childhood."

With a one-shoulder shrug, he tried to dismiss it, his gaze on where her hand landed. "Just doesna like me, I suppose." He tried to take a step forward, but she held him back.

"Valent? I wish something of you. Would you kiss me if I asked?"

His eyes flew to her face and his lips parted. For a long moment, he looked into her eyes until, very slowly, his gaze lowered to her mouth. "Aye, milady, I would."

"Come," Ariana said, sliding both hands up his arms, amazed at the strength of them. "Kiss me." She grasped his shoulders.

His left hand trembled slightly as he lifted it to her face. He cupped her jaw and moved toward her. When his lips fell over hers, Ariana could not help but close her eyes at the soft, yet wonderfully innocent, kiss. He didn't push further, but remained still, his lips on hers, his hand at her jaw, their bodies apart.

Just as she was about to pull him closer, he stepped back. He didn't speak, instead, waited for her, his hands to his sides. In the right one, his bow and quiver, the other relaxed against his thigh. His expression remained void of emotion.

It was then she realized he only kissed her because she'd asked him to. An obedient servant of her family's. "Valent. You didn't have to kiss me if you didn't wish to. I asked because I've wanted to kiss you since I first saw you when I was a young girl. It is the first time I am alone with you. This was not a request of the laird's sister, but of a woman who finds you attractive."

His beautiful eyes softened when looking at her. "I am honored then, milady."

She wanted to kick him in frustration. But, of course, it was not his fault for standing on formalities. More than anything, she wanted him to slam her against the same tree Munro had and take her. How she wished he would thrust his hardness into her and make her his. She wanted to know what his bare skin felt like against her own. Needed to hear the sounds he made while losing control of his body.

She smiled up at him. "Thank you for it. Now, I will wonder about other things about you." His eyes rounded and she began walking toward the keep.

He fell in step beside her. "Did you plan to practice today, milady?"

As much as she wanted to spend more time with him, at the moment, she was much too distressed at everything that she doubted she would be able to shoot straight. "I did, but not any longer."

He nodded and remained silent. She slid a glance at him from the corner of her eye. His movements were graceful, his gaze straight ahead. Wearing only a tunic and breeches, it was easy to see the lines of his impressive body. "Do you still live at Tavish's cottage?"

"Aye, milady, I do."

"Alone?" When the words left her lips, she almost groaned out loud. He must think her desperate for a man's company.

"I have a dog."

"Do you really? Where is he now?"

"There." He pointed to the deerhound that rushed to him as they came out of the wooded area. The archer lowered to one knee and the dog sat before him waiting for attention. "Arrow, bow to the lady," Valent commanded, motioning to her.

The dog lowered its head at her feet. "Hello, Arrow." Ariana petted its head and smiled at Valent.

Neither moved nor spoke, but looked at each other. The surroundings vanished in that instant. All she could see was the handsome man who she wanted more than life itself.

A horn sounded and the trance was broken. "The Munro leaves," she said, stating the obvious. "I must go."

Making her way to the keep, she turned to look over her shoulder. Valent remained on one knee, his frosty eyes on her, his hand on the dog's back.

Chapter 4

Valent was glad for the excuse of Arrow's presence, as he wasn't sure how much longer his wobbly legs would contain him. Maintaining a neutral expression had been almost as hard as keeping himself from ravishing Ariana McLeod.

That she'd asked him to kiss her astounded him. Her confession of wanting him for years even more so. Although he'd admired the beautiful woman from afar and found her stunning, he never dared to even dream of such a thing.

He stood when the young man he'd been instructing approached, ready for the task at hand.

It was best he continue about things. The sooner he forgot the feel of her lips under his, the better.

"Archer! You there, come here." The younger of the laird's brothers, Beathan, called to him. "Get your mount, we must ride at once." There were several others with Beathan. Four guardsmen and one other archer.

Soon, they rode towards the northeast. He wondered at the stoic expressions, but didn't dare ask.

They climbed a hill and brought the mounts to a

stop. Below, they could see for many miles. In the distance was a camp. Beathan cursed. "The McKenzie dogs are, indeed, encroaching upon our lands. Just as you reported." He spoke to a guardsman to his right.

The guard peered straight ahead. "Looks to be only about ten of them. What do you think they do?"

"Scouts," another guard said.

Valent doubted it. The men were probably unaware of having trespassed. A common mistake, he mused. They looked to be hunting and not hiding, camped in plain view.

"Kill them. Send the McKenzie a clear message. We do not stand for encroachers."

It was hard not to give the man an incredulous look. The McKenzie Clan was a powerful one. Not one to be crossed. "Sir, it would be wise not to kill any of them," he dared to say.

Beathan ignored him. "Leave one alive."

They rode towards the camp, pushing their steeds to a run. Valent and the other archer raised their bows and let arrows fly toward the men who scrambled to find weapons. They didn't have a chance. All were dead within minutes except two.

Valent dismounted and met the gaze of an injured young man. He motioned to the boy with a flat hand to stay still and blocked him by positioning his horse in front of him.

The other man, an older one, stood by a tree, head held high awaiting his demise. The guardsman looked down on him. "Go back to your clan and let them know not to encroach on our lands."

"We didn't know," the man stuttered. "Out for a hunt is all. They didn't deserve to die for it."

"Stop speaking or you will join them." The guard lifted his sword. "Go now. Leave."

The man hurried to his horse and did just that. When the guard turned to where the young man lay, Valent let out an arrow, piercing an already dead man. The guard turned to the body, his attention driven away from the young man on the ground. Valent let out a relieved breath.

They rode away after driving the horses off. Valent hoped the injured one would survive and make it home.

He found Arrow upon returning to the keep and called the dog, deciding it was time to head to his cottage. Just then, the same guard caught up with him. "The laird wishes to speak to us." The guard did not meet his eyes and apprehension traveled down his spine.

They entered the courtyard where the other guards and archer were already standing in front of the laird. He motioned for Arrow to stay back and he joined the men. Donall's cold eyes flickered from him to the dog. "Come forward, archer."

Valent stood before the laird, his head bowed. It was a good stance as far as he was concerned since it made it easy to hide his hatred for the man. "My laird."

"You allowed a man to live who you were ordered to kill." The words made the blood in his veins freeze. "Why?"

"He was but a young boy. They were hunting, unaware to have trespassed."

A blow to his face with the back of the laird's hand only made Valent angrier. "You are not allowed the luxury of thinking!"

The laird paced before the men lined up behind him. "And you also failed as you did not complete my brother's mission." He looked to the guard who'd fetched Valent. "Except you."

The men shuffled in discomfort, awaiting their

punishment. Valent would not give the laird the satisfaction. Instead, he stood still, his head bowed, rage boiling through his body.

"Five lashes." The men let out audible sighs of relief at the low number. The laird moved to stand in front of Valent. "You will each give him five lashes." There was a collective gasp.

Valent was dragged to posts and his arms spread, his wrists tied to each. They cut the back of his tunic open. Arrow barked at the men and one lifted his sword to the dog. "Arrow, go!" Valent yelled and the dog gave him one last look before dashing away.

Valent didn't fight the men, knowing it would do no good. Instead, he looked to the guard who'd turned him in. "Is the boy alive?"

"Nay, I went back and killed him."

All air left his lungs and he allowed his head to hang for a moment.

"Begin!" the laird called out and the first lash was like fire to his skin. With each lash he made a promise. He would leave; go as far as he could. Although he'd pledged his alliance to the McLeod Clan, it was a fruitless thing.

The whip was passed to another man. Valent heard the shuffling of feet. A new lashing began. Soon he lost both count and his footing, allowing his legs to fold under him.

"Enough!" A woman's voice permeated the ringing in his ears. "What are you doing?"

"Do not interfere, Mother. His punishment must be done or I'm sending a message that you can stop it at any time." Donall's voice sounded bored.

The woman walked up to Valent and lifted his head; it was the laird's mother. "How many lashes has he received?"

"Twenty," someone replied.

"Then it is enough," the woman said while looking into his face. "I must speak to you at once, Donall. It is important."

She let Valent's face drop.

"Cut him loose," the laird ordered as he followed his mother inside.

Two men helped Valent toward the guard's quarters. Each apologizing for what they'd done. Movement caught his gaze and he looked up to the balcony. Ariana McLeod stood watching.

He couldn't help the hatred. How he hated the McLeods. Each and every one of them.

Once he was laid upon a cot face down, a healer came with cool water and cloths. He ground his teeth when she poured the water over his back. The woman was silent, other than a command she gave to another to bring more water. He couldn't concentrate on the sound of her voice, didn't actually care who it was at the moment. His sole purpose became to heal so he could travel. His body shook, the tremors making his teeth chatter.

"He's getting feverish," the woman said in a low voice. "Bring the cot closer to the fire. Do not cover him. The blankets will cling to his wounds." He couldn't help but continue to shake until the warmth of the fire began to permeate. Slowly, a fog descended, whether it was death or slumber did not matter to him as he succumbed.

"Valent?" A woman's voice sounded as if far away. "Can you hear me? Open your eyes."

The first attempt to lift his eyelids failed. When he opened his mouth to speak through his parched throat, it wasn't possible. Everything was too difficult, he preferred to remain asleep. "It's been three days. You have to try to open your eyes. I have broth for you."

Lora's face came into view, blurry at first and then clear. "You have to eat something."

When he moved, the skin on his back pulled and he let out a groan. "Can you help me sit?"

Together, they managed to get him upright and she held the bowl up to his lips. "I cannot understand why the laird would do this. Why you took the punishment for everyone."

He didn't bother replying. Long ago, he wondered why the hatred from Donall. But as the years went by, he gave up caring. It didn't matter, it just was. "Where is Arrow, my dog?"

"He's here." She motioned to his dog that lay under the cot. "Hasn't left your side."

The broth was tasty, a few bits of meat in it. He drank it down and held up the bowl to Lora. "More."

She eyed him. "Let's see if it stays down. If it does, I'll get you something else."

Several other guards entered the tent. At once, they noticed the pretty woman, their attention on her. Lora ignored them, looking at Valent instead. "In a few days, you should be able to return to your cottage. For now, your wounds remain raw."

"I would rather leave now." He looked around to find his tunic and then remembered it had been torn from his body. "I need a tunic, is there one about I can wear?"

One of the guards brought one. "It's old, but has only a few holes."

Lora helped him dress while frowning. Each movement of his arms brought more stinging to his back.

"Hold it there." Before he could lower the tunic over it, she went around to his back. "I'll wipe the blood and add some bandaging to keep it from soaking through your tunic." He nodded and waited.

Moments later, with bow and quiver in hand, he headed to his cottage. He walked slowly, barely able to keep from stumbling. Finally, his cottage came in to view, a welcome sight. He pushed the door open and had to blink several times to ensure he was not dreaming. In the middle of the room stood Ariana McLeod.

Chapter 5

He looked about ready to faint. Ariana motioned to Lily and they rushed to Valent, taking his arms and guiding him to his bed. "I didn't think you would be here for a few more days."

They helped him lower to the bed and then moved back. When she came with Lily to his home, to bring two new tunics and ointments, she didn't actually plan to find him. They'd cleaned the small cottage and brought several blankets, dried meat, and cheese.

Lily went to the fireplace and began to build a fire, while Ariana poured some of the mead they'd brought for him. "We came because I felt I should do something. I feel terrible about what my brother did. The other archer explained what happened. That you tried to save a boy's life."

He remained quiet, his attention on the fireplace. "You should not have come, milady."

Her maid went to the table and took the bowl of salve and clean cloths. "You need to remove your tunic so I can apply this salve."

There was pleading in his gaze meeting hers. "I cannot do it. It has stuck to my back."

"Oh God!" Ariana rushed to him and confirmed that,

indeed, it had. "Heat some water Lily. I'll cut away what I can. The rest we'll have to soak off."

She placed her hand on his shoulder. "Please, lay on your stomach."

"No. I ask that you both leave. I will take care of it myself. Thank you for bringing the...items. But I would like to be alone...milady." He was obviously in pain, could barely speak.

Of all the stubborn things to say. Ariana wanted to kick him in the leg. Instead, she forced a neutral expression and rounded the bed. She pushed at him and he winced. "Get on your stomach and stop being a stubborn goat."

His dog whined and went to hide behind Lily, who stared at them wide eyed.

"Bring the items, Lily. I don't have all day."

Valent gave up and they helped him lie down. He groaned with each movement, telling of how much pain he was in.

An hour later, he slept soundly. Lily peered down at him and then to Ariana. They'd covered his back with a thick salve and wrapped his torso. The calming herbs would soothe the wounds and help the pain. Tomorrow, she would send Lily back to remove the binding, wash the salve and reapply it.

"He seems to be resting soundly, milady." She gave his dog a piece of bread and chewed on the other half. "I think we should go back before your brother misses ye."

"Good idea. Go outside and wait for me. I want to pray over him for a moment."

"You are kind, milady." Lily took the basket and went outside.

Ariana kneeled at the side of the bed and bowed her head. Once she finished the quick prayer, she brushed the hair back from his face. In slumber, his face relaxed and he took her breath away. "I wish I could know you better, Valent. Be well, my brave archer." She kissed his brow and stood, tears burning her eyes at how he'd suffered for his good deed.

"The Munro sent a missive asking that you visit," Donall told her over his goblet at the evening meal three days later. "I can't think of a good reason why you shouldn't."

Ariana's stomach lurched. "I can think of many. I will not go."

Donall studied her. "Why?"

"I have other matters to tend to. I've already promised to visit our cousins, did you forget?"

"No I have not, but it is an honor for them to ask you to come. Perhaps the Munro seeks you as a wife for his son."

She looked to her brother. Unlike her two other brothers who had auburn hair and green eyes, he had straight light brown hair and dark brown eyes. Donall was pleasant of face, but not handsome. Her other two brothers were both taller than he and broader of shoulder. Of them, Donall favored their mother the most. "Donall, I do not wish to marry again. I prefer to remain here with you and Mother."

Until he turned to her, she held her breath. Of course, as the eldest and laird, he could send her away. If he were to insist she go to the Munro's, Ariana wasn't sure what she'd do, but one thing she knew for sure—she would not step foot inside the Munro keep.

Her brother's gaze was cool, without any kind of brotherly affection. He'd never been close to her; she always mused it was because of their difference in age, he was ten years older. "It's up to you, of course. The messenger has not been sent back. I will let them know you are predisposed." Donall peered at her for a moment longer. "We should discuss your plans."

"Yes, of course." This was not the time for the conversation, so she let it drop. Donall soon became distracted and she was grateful. Once the meal was over, she would speak to him in private. She looked to Lily, who stood at the entrance of the room. The maid motioned to the stairs and she nodded. Lily had gone to see Valent. The maid went daily during the middle of the day. She reported that he'd sent her away each time and he was surly and unlikable. Lily had managed to change his dressing twice. Hopefully, he allowed it this day.

When the meal was over, she made her way up the stairs toward her chamber. Ceardac stood in the hallway. She wondered at his presence. "What brings you here, brother?"

"Where does your maid go daily? Is it an errand of yours?" Ariana grew tired of men. Always questioning, not giving her any peace.

"What does it matter to you, Ceardac?"

He studied her for a moment. "She goes in the direction of the archer's cottage."

"Aye, I know. She asked me to allow her leave to see about the man's wounds. From what she told me, he was very badly whipped."

Ceardac had the decency to flush. "Aye, he brought it on himself. If she has your permission then I have nothing to say on it further."

He walked away and she couldn't help but wonder. Was Ceardac worried that she was interested in Valent? Or was he annoyed that Lily might? Interesting. Lily was a slight, young woman, with wavy, brown hair and pretty. The maid had arrived a young girl and been her companion since. Although they'd grown up together, she'd never noticed any interaction between her and Ceardac.

Then again, her brothers had been horrible boys and she and Lily spent most of their time avoiding them.

Chapter 6

It had been a week since the lashings and Valent could finally move about without the constant reminders of his injuries. He'd bathed in the loch earlier, removing the remainder of the salve from his back. It was good to be back to normal. Earlier that day, he'd used his bow. A bit sore, but he'd been able to kill a small rabbit for his evening meal.

Hurt and anger filled him. All his life, he'd been the object of Donall's scorn. The man hated him and never wasted a moment to show it. Now that Tavish was gone, Valent had no reason to remain, no alliance to anyone in the clan.

The only one who'd care for him was Tavish. After years of serving the McLeod, he owed them nothing more.

He sat the small table his mind awhirl. It was obvious that Lady Ariana felt guilty over what her brother had done. She had a kind heart; it had to be the only reason for her sending her maid every day to check on him. Finally, he'd sent the woman away the day prior, telling her he was well enough to return to his duties. She'd not returned that day.

At the sounds of shuffling outside the door, Valent

strained to listen to what it could be. It was too late for the maid to come see about him. Perhaps another of the archers was stopping by. The knocks were soft and rapid.

When he opened the door, a hooded figure holding a basket stood before him. With one hand she pushed the hood off to reveal a beautiful face.

"Lady Ariana. What are you doing out in the dark? Are ye in trouble?" Valent looked past her only to see a horse tethered to a tree, nothing else.

"Nay. I came to see you. Brought you something to eat." She looked past him, awaiting his invitation to enter.

Valent stepped back. He stood rigid at the doorway. Now that he wasn't beaten and bleeding, her attention would not be diverted from his humble home. The lack of rugs on the floor, simple furniture and drafty walls suddenly made him uncomfortable.

She moved to the center of the room and placed the basket on the table. "It seems I am too late. You have already eaten." Like a flower in the center of a patch of weeds, she stood out in her fine dress, the plush cape falling from her shoulders.

"I thank ye for it." Feeling daft for not inviting her to sit. He closed the door and went to the table to pull out a chair. "Please, sit milady."

Her eyes, the color of the rich, autumn leaves took him in, the corner of her lips lifted. "I make you uncomfortable. I should not have come."

She smelled of fresh meadow and he inhaled deeply before answering. Yes, she made him uncomfortable. The stark difference between them too tangible to ignore while, at the same time, he would rather be lashed again than have her leave so soon. "I am wondering why ye take so much interest in me. I am but an archer in your brother's service. You are a lady who should not lower herself to be here."

Instead of sitting, she removed her cape and laid it across the back of the chair. The soft fabric fell over his hand and he looked to it only to be startled when her hand cupped his face. "Valent. You are a brave, strong man. I am but a woman who wishes to know you better. Whether we are lady and archer is secondary."

He swallowed at the feel of her soft hand on his skin. "In this room right now, yes, we are a man and a woman. Out there..." he motioned toward the door, "things are very different."

"Then let's remain in here for now. As a man and a woman." Ariana closed the distance between them and ran her hands up his arms. "Will you allow it?"

The question in her eyes made it impossible to not react. Valent cupped her face and lowered his own. When their mouths met, he was not gentle like the time before. Tonight he wanted to remind her who he really was. A man with emotions, needs, and if she allowed him, he would take her fully. Whether a folly of a woman who had everything easy or truly caring for him, either way he was going to plummet into the experience.

She let out a soft moan and parted her lips. Valent plunged forward, his tongue delving into her mouth while he untied the fastenings of her dress. There would not be any procrastination. Ariana came to him without pretense.

When Valent slid her dress past her shoulders, the warmth of his mouth on Ariana's neck immediately overtook the coolness of the cottage. His lips traveled to her shoulder while at the same time he palmed her breast with one large hand. With the other, he pushed her dress past her hips.

She ran her hands under his tunic and almost wept at the feel of his hard chest and rippling stomach. The contradiction of the smoothness of his skin over the taut muscles was intoxicating and she lifted the hem and watched in fascination as he pulled the tunic over his head.

Ariana waited for what he'd do next. His gaze fell over her. The beautiful gray eyes darkening when looking at her breasts and then traveling downward to between her legs. "Open your legs for me, Ariana." The husky command took her by surprise. She complied and waited to see what he would do.

He unfastened his britches and pushed them down. Valent was magnificent. With slender hips and long muscular legs, he was built to be a warrior. His thick sex jutted up from the juncture between them, a heavy patch of dark hair above it.

Closing the distance between them, he lowered to the floor and pressed his mouth onto her stomach while his hands slid down her legs and back up to the inside of her thighs.

Never had anyone explored her like he did. His lips traveled across her body pressing kisses to each place. When his lips moved to her sex, she trembled in anticipation. "Oh!" She placed both hands on his shoulders to steady herself.

Valent looked up at her and smiled. "You are beautiful." He straightened to full height and she fell against him, needing to touch as much of him as possible.

"Look at me." He lifted her chin. "Think on what is about to happen between us. If you chose to walk out I understand."

"Is that what you want?"

"Nay. I want you in my bed more than life." He took her hand and guided it to his hardness.

Ariana curled her fingers around it and slid her hand to the base and back to its tip. The skin was velvety as silk surrounding the hardness. He gasped and her lips curved. "Take me to your bed, Valent."

He pulled her against him and took her mouth with a hunger that astounded her. She suckled at his tongue and tentative to touch his back, she held his waist and slid her hands around to his taut bottom pulling him tenderly against her.

Valent smiled against her mouth. "I am not a boy. You don't have to be gentle. My back no longer hurts."

He lowered her onto the bed and looked down at her. "I will never forget this night."

Unable to wait for him any longer, she held her arms to him. "Come to me now. I need you over me."

There was a flicker of something in his expression and she worried for a moment he'd not comply, but he moved over her and took her mouth again. His lips traveled from her lips to her neck. The roughness of his hands over her skin created a delicious friction when he spread her legs and settled between them. He slid his hands under her and lifted her, pressing against her, his thickness sliding between her folds. Ariana dug her fingers into his shoulders and lifted to kiss his throat. The strong-corded muscles of his neck made for a perfect place to nip and lick.

He was a forbidden fruit and tasted of earth and danger. So many things to pull them apart, too many differences between them, but in the moment, Ariana realized she was in love with Valent. The realization did not surprise her as much as it enriched the fact that he was about to be her lover.

Valent's sex nudged at her entrance and Ariana

looked into his eyes. He was beautiful, his sensuous lips parted as he looked down to where he guided himself into her. His locks fell forward curtaining his handsome face.

She inhaled sharply at the intrusion when he finally drove into her body. The thickness both welcome and enticing. Ariana wrapped her legs about his waist as he pulled out and thrust back in.

"Love me, Valent." The words came from her heart, but she knew he would think it meant only her body.

His lips curved and his darkened eyes raked her face. "Ye are so beautiful." He closed his eyes and thrust into her, then pulled out almost completely before driving back in. The motions continued while Ariana clung to his shoulders, her nails digging into this skin.

"More," she cried out. "I want more of you."

He took her mouth and pushed his tongue in, while his hand slid under her buttocks and he lifted her and drove in deeper, taking all of her.

The sounds of their lovemaking intermingled with the flickering of the flames in the hearth and the sounds of the night outside. A more beautiful night she would be pressed to remember.

An hour later, Valent helped her dress. He was subdued, but attentive, kissing her shoulder as he fastened her bodice about her. She cupped his face. "Thank you for such a precious gift."

When he smiled, her heart melted. "I am honored that you found me..."

"Stop. We made an agreement. In here, we are but a man and a woman. You are more deserving than any man I know. You are kind and brave and very strong."

She giggled when he took her by the hips and pulled

her forward. "Is that what you will think upon after this night?"

"No." She kissed his jaw. "I will think of how wonderful you made me feel. And you?"

"I will think of how soft your skin is. How beautiful you look when lost in passion."

He ushered her to the door and helped her atop her horse. He rode beside her as far as the edge of the woods and then whistled to his dog. "He will accompany you to the keep. Once you are there, just say *go* and he will return home."

They locked gazes and Ariana wanted to beg him to run away with her, but instead, she only smiled. "Goodnight."

"Where have you been sister?" Donall stood just inside the great room, his face hidden by the dimness. "I saw you ride from the woods' edge with a dog as your companion."

Her heart hammered hard against her chest. She looked to her basket. "I went to hunt for night blooms."

"Alone?" He grasped her arm none too gently and she stumbled forward. "I do not believe you." His eyes pinned her and she could see only darkness.

Through gritted teeth, she spoke to him while attempting to get free. "Why would I lie, Donall?"

"Perhaps you are visiting someone."

"If that was the case, I would bring Lily with me. I had the archer's dog to keep me safe."

"Tomorrow I will have him brought forward. You better pray he tells the truth. The twenty lashes will be nothing compared to what will happen."

"Why do you hate him so? What is it about the archer that makes you want to hurt him always? Since we were children, you have always been cruel to him."

She let out a breath. "He's a bastard. A man with no clan. He has nothing."

"You are correct and should always remember that, sister. He is nothing. Which is why, if I find you have laid with him, he will die." He lifted a brow at her. "Your basket is empty."

She didn't dare look at the basket. Before arriving, she'd purposely placed night blooms in it. "Do not embarrass me by summoning the archer in and asking him questions when all I did was hunt for flowers." Ariana met his gaze without blinking. "I tire of you and our brothers constantly questioning my every move. I know who I am and in which manner to conduct myself. I am not a simpleton nor a whore."

Finally he seemed to believe her. "Very well, I will not. But from now on when hunting for...blooms, take a guard."

Instead of fleeing from his side, she decided to, once again, question him. "Is the reason you dislike the archer because he bests you at everything?"

Donall's jaw clenched. "He does no such thing."

"I am trying to understand the basis of your dislike."

His gaze traveled past her. "I must attend to other things." Donall walked away.

Loud booms sounded, hooves pounded the ground and battle cries rose. The violent noise rumbled through the thick, stone walls.

Startled from a deep sleep, Ariana jumped from her bed and dashed to the window. There were alarmed screams outside, men rushed around with torches, teams leaned thick beams against the main gates. She couldn't see anything past the courtyard. It was much too dark.

Ariana raced to a smaller window on the opposite wall. The sun barely peaked in the horizon. An arrow flew toward her and she ducked. It bounced against the side of the window and was followed by another that made it inside.

Lily barged into the room, tears streaming down her face. "Milady, we are under attack. They're storming the gates now."

"Lower yourself, Lily, an arrow has already made it in here." She grabbed at the maid's hand. Lily huddled next to Ariana on the floor.

"What happens? Why are they attacking?" Lily's voice shook.

"I do not know. Did you hear which clan it is?"

"No. Milady, I was awakened when they began ramming the gate. The laird and the guards who slept in the great room were rushing out as I came to find ye."

Another boom sounded and both jumped. She wondered how much longer the gates would hold. Ariana crept to the window and peered out. There were rows of warriors on horseback. Swordsmen were in the front and behind them were several rows of archers.

The sun rose in the horizon, enough to give her the cover of darkness being indoors. The tartan colors became clear.

The McKenzies.

"Why would the McKenzies attack us?" She looked to her maid, not expecting an answer.

"The hunters that yer brother, Beathan, had killed. They were McKenzies, milady."

Ariana fell to the floor, her hands over her mouth. "Oh no. What has he done? Their clan surrounds us on all sides. They are strong and powerful. I canna believe Donall allowed it. Has he become so arrogant that he'd not consider this outcome?"

"Aye, and bloodthirsty those McKenzies are. They willna stand for killin' of their kind."

"God help us."

"Yes milady, we have to pray hard."

Her brother, Ceardac, burst in with sword drawn. "The gates won't hold much longer. Go out through the cellar, to the back exit. Wait at the boat. I will join you there." He turned to the door.

"Mother!" Ariana went to him and clung to his arm.

Ceardac looked down at her. "I will find her."

"Where is Beathan?" she asked, referring to their other brother.

"He is a warrior. Refuses to go. Donall stays as well."

"Come with us, then." She did not let go of his arm. "Please, Ceardac, we can't get away alone."

"Aye, I will ensure to get you to safety." He looked to Lily. "You as well, Lily. Hurry, then, get dressed. I will fetch Mother." He left.

She and Lily dressed in a hurry, the maid wearing some of Ariana's clothes as there was no time to go to her own chamber. Ariana pulled on breeches under her dress and Lily helped her pin some of her jewelry onto the inside of her coat.

Once that was completed, they did the same to the coat Lily wore. Ariana grabbed the maid's shoulders. "Listen to me, Lily. If we get separated I want you to say you are a lady and keep the jewelry. Use it to purchase passage to the McLeods of Skye. Promise me."

"Yes, milady." Lily's eyes were bright from fear and unshed tears. "But we must stay together. I canna bear the thought of being apart from ye. Not after all these years."

They went into the hallway. The noise from the great room was deafening. "What happens?" Lily screamed. "What are they doing?"

"Never you mind, let us run." They grabbed hands and raced to the passageway at the back of the stairs and went down to the lower level. Once they exited the back, they'd be in caves by the ocean. Ariana looked behind them. "Where are Ceardac and Mother?"

"I do not know, milady." Tears spilled down Lily's cheeks. "We cannot leave without him...and your mother. Please."

"We will not. I promise." They scampered down another set of stairs. The salty air permeated once they opened the last door.

"Come, Lily, step carefully. The stones are always slippery." Ariana moved with caution, one hand on the wall.

"We must go. We cannot wait any longer. The McKenzies are inside the gates and will round the keep at any moment."

"Hurry." Ariana yanked Lily's hand and they went down the stairs as fast as they could. The drizzle made the stairs treacherous and she could see the men pushing the boat upon which her mother and brother were. She couldn't yell for them to stop. Not without alerting the McKenzies.

Instead, she waved.

"They are leaving! Hurry, Lily." Ariana pulled the maid just as angry yells came from the opposite side of a short wall.

"The McKenzies," Ariana gasped and took a step forward only to be stopped by Lily.

"We must go back, milady, and find a place to hide. They will catch up to us, otherwise."

They rushed back up the stairs and entered the keep once again. Once inside, Ariana pulled Lily down a short hallway just as the two groups of men clashed. Her lungs burned from the combination of holding back sobs and terror. She felt for the almost invisible door and they ducked into a storeroom. The doorway was hard to find unless one lived there. They'd hidden there many times when they were children and hiding from her brothers.

Huddled together, neither said a word. Both were lost in thought and straining to hear what became of their clan.

What felt like hours later, footsteps sounded and the women held their breath. Whoever it was moved closer.

Chapter 7

It didn't take long to pack his few belongings. Valent took one last look around the tiny cottage and lifted the bundle he planned to tie to his horse's saddle. The dwelling had been his home for most of his life. The cot, table and chairs, would have to be left behind. Hopefully, someone would make it their home. Perhaps one of the village families would be happy there.

"Are you ready to face our new adventure?" He spoke to Arrow, who tilted his head to the side. "I am. Although it is not a good idea to revoke a pledge and I did give my fealty to Laird McLeod, I can no longer do so." Of course, the dog didn't understand what he said, instead it pawed at the ground as if it, too, had to say goodbye.

On the bed was the blanket Lady Ariana had brought when she'd first visited. The fine material was softer than anything he'd ever owned. He picked it up. He would use it for the cold nights when he would need the memory of her beauty to keep him warm.

It was hard to sleep in that bed, to look upon it, without picturing his night with Ariana McLeod.

No matter, he could not remain there any longer.

It would be too much of a temptation to be with

Ariana again. No matter how wonderful the time with her had been, he knew she only wanted his body. A lady like her could not give up all for the humble life he offered. It was for both their sakes that he left.

After tying his bundle to the saddle, Valent mounted and urged the horse forward. A few minutes later, he stopped at the sounds of hooves. Inside the woods' edge, he spotted a large number of McKenzies heading toward the keep. *What happened?*

A horrible thought struck. Had the McKenzies attacked seeking revenge? Of course, how could they not? It had been reckless and stupid for Beathan to order them to kill those men.

There was no other reason for such a large number of warriors cutting through McLeod lands. Stuck between McKenzie lands, the current situation was dire. Valent considered the McLeods of the north and those of Skye. The only way to get to either would be to travel through McKenzie lands and it would take days.

Valent didn't wear the McLeod colors, perhaps it would help him get through and get a message to the other McLeods. Immediate help was needed.

At a sound behind him, he drew his bow, set an arrow into it and pulled back the string.

"Valent." The young man he'd been training came out slowly from behind some bushes, his entire body shaking. "The k-keep is under attack." Face flushed and eyes wide, the boy was clearly terrified. "What should we do? I tried to go there, but it's completely surrounded. There are so many of them. Too many to count."

"Aye, I just saw. We must go to the village and warn them. Get men together to defend it. Come, let us go through the forest and avoid the attacking clan."

He eyed the young man. "First, take your colors off. Put them with my things." He dismounted and took his bundle and opened it. Into it, he placed Lady Ariana's blanket and then hid the bundle in the bushes. "Put your tartan there as well. Come, let us hurry."

The village came into view. People scurried about carrying items to carts or rushing their children indoors. Obviously, news of the attack had reached them. Several wagonloads of women and children were already being driven away. Valent hoped they'd find a place to hide until it was over. By the sheer numbers of those surrounding the keep, it was doubtful the McLeods would survive.

"Go to the McLeods of Skye. Take a couple of the younger men with you." His apprentice nodded. "Aye, Valent, I will ride hard and fast."

Valent dismounted and joined a group of men that had come together in the center of town. The blacksmith was handing out swords and Valent looked to the older men and young boys who held the weapons with determined looks. None of them had ever fought. If the McKenzies attacked, by the end of the day, most would lie dead.

He held his hands up and called to the group. "I have seen the invaders. They are many in number. The keep will fall soon and most of the guardsmen will perish." There was a collective moan amongst those gathered.

Valent got their attention again. "When they get here, let me speak to them. We don't stand a chance unless we reason for some kind of truce." When the men began to grumble, he hollered at them. "Did you not hear me? If you fight, you will die. It is more important to live and protect the woman and children. Which laird governs us is secondary."

One of the men, the ironsmith, came to him and placed a beefy hand on his shoulder. "Verra well. If we trust ye, do not fail. We will await the outcome of your talk. If they strike you down. We will fight."

"There will be no choice then," Valent replied, meeting the man's gaze. "Honor be with ye."

"And with ye." The man looked toward the ill-equipped group of men who stood ready to defend the town. "And may God help us."

At the pounding of hooves, everyone turned to a wall of horses heading toward them. The men grouped together and Valent motioned for them to remain and mounted. He went to the edge of the village, his bow strapped to his back, and broadsword sheathed.

The McKenzies neared and slowed until stopping at the edge of the village. One man flanked by two others rode closer. The man looked to the group of weakly-armed men and then to Valent. His eyes widened slightly, but he did not sheath his sword. "Who are you?"

"I am Valent. An archer for the McLeod."

He exchanged looks with the other men. "What say you, McLeod?"

Valent resented being given the name of the man he hated. "I am not a McLeod. I have no surname."

Once again, the men looked to one another. Finally, a second man moved closer and peered at him. "Unless your people lay down their weapons, we will slaughter every one of them. You, however, must come with us."

He looked over his shoulder at the townsmen who watched the interaction with avid curiosity. They didn't seem frightened. But like him, they were curious as to why the men kept exchanging questioning looks.

"Very well, I will come with you. Do I have your word no harm will come to the village people?"

"Aye, unlike you McLeods, we do not kill innocents."

Valent looked over his shoulder. "Lay down the weapons. They will not harm you."

When they neared the keep, his heart began to pound at seeing the devastation. The dead lay strewn about while several of his fellow guards were tied at the wrists and guided to where they'd be imprisoned. He searched for the laird and his family, but only saw the younger brother, Beathan, who was tied to a post in the center of the courtyard. The same place he'd been lashed days earlier. The man screamed to be released immediately. Threatening death once the rest of his clan arrived. Valent wondered how the man could be so stupid. If anything, his death would be precipitated by his hollering.

The McKenzies surrounded Valent when he dismounted. "Come." The man who'd spoken earlier pushed at his shoulder. "Our laird will want to speak to you."

Just as he took a step forward, a man went to Beathan and speared his shoulder. "Shut up."

Beathan growled. "I will kill you."

"Why is he still alive?" the leader of his escorts asked.

"The laird wishes to kill him himself."

The leader looked to Valent and motioned his men, who pushed Valent forward toward the inside of the keep.

"Why me? I am but an archer." Valent refused to budge another step. "I will go with them." He pointed to the bound guards.

Someone poked a blade into the center of his back. "Move."

They walked into the keep. The room was empty. He heard crying in the distance. No doubt, the maids were huddled in terror.

In the center of the room, several of the McKenzies were gathered around a table. They all looked up at their entrance. One stood. "Why are you bringing an archer in here? He should go with the others..." the man stopped midsentence and his eyes rounded. "Who are you?"

Valent looked at the ceiling. "What does it matter? I prefer to be with my men."

"So you are the head archer?"

"Aye." Valent gritted his teeth when someone yanked at his bow. "Don't touch it."

Surprisingly, they did as he demanded.

"Valent!" He turned to see Ariana and her maid being tugged into the room by two men. Immediately, he searched her body to ensure she was unharmed. Her wide eyes met his and she took a step forward only to be yanked back. "I fear they killed my mother. I don't know where my brothers are." Tears streamed down her face.

Enraged, he let out a growl and moved toward her, only to be dragged back and held by four men. One man placed the tip of his sword at Valent's throat. "Unless you wish for the ladies to watch you die, don't move."

"What is it?" Someone entered the room. Valent ignored him, focusing on Ariana and attempting to convey to her that he'd do all he could to protect her. She calmed and blinked, then reached for her maid's hand.

"Laird, we brought this man. Ye need to see this." The leader spoke while bowing his head. "The archer..."

"Take the archer to the courtyard. And damn it, unarm him. Why is he still armed?"

The voice, it was eerily familiar. Like his own almost. Both he and Ariana turned to the man who spoke. Time slowed and all the air left Valent's lungs.

The man who'd spoken wore McKenzie colors. Valent took in the man's face while the laird did the same, neither able to look away.

It was as if looking in a mirror.

Ariana rushed to his side. Valent didn't know if she'd been released or fought to get away. Instinctively, he pulled her to his side and drew his sword. His attention remained on the man who looked identical to him.

Joined by Ariana's maid, they moved toward the doorway.

The laird narrowed his eyes. "You cannot go. You know as well as I there are too many of my men outside."

He ignored the McKenzie, not wanting to think on what awaited beyond the doorway. Valent needed to get away. He needed time alone to absorb that he'd finally found his brother, the one he'd been taken from so many years ago. The one his family had preferred over him.

His brother motioned to his guards to stay back and he approached Valent and the women. "We must speak. It is obvious you are the brother we all thought long dead."

With the women huddled against him, Valent continued to move away. "There is nothing to be said."

"You cannot leave. You cannot hope to fight against so many while protecting two women." The McKenzie looked to Ariana and the other woman with distaste. "Would you prefer McLeods over your own family? Your clan?"

"I have no family. Nor do I have a clan."

"There is much you do not know." There was little warmth in the laird's gaze and he was reminded of the same look he'd received all his life from the McLeod. "Return to McKenzie lands with me. You will be treated better than if you go out there." He motioned to the courtyard. "How do you think they will respond once they realize we are brothers?"

Valent looked toward the courtyard. If he went with

the McKenzie, then Ariana would be left unprotected. She clung to him and Valent could only wonder how well he would be treated once the McKenzie learned Valent was one of the men who'd killed his people. "I will remain."

The laird stalked to the doorway and pushed the doors open then called out to his men. "Allow them to pass."

Chapter 8

The Battle

"Allow my brother and the women through. Let them go." Valent's twin brother signaled to the guardsmen in the room and two came forward. "Escort him to wherever he wishes to go. Ensure no harm comes to either him or the women."

Valent struggled to remain upright. At thirty years old, it was unfathomable to finally meet the boy he remembered in his dreams. His twin, identical, no less.

So many times, he'd considered what would happen if they finally came face to face. His answer was abundantly clear by the tightness in his chest and lack of ability to breathe.

However, this was not the time to show weakness.

His brother was the laird of the McKenzie Clan who'd just attacked and taken over the McLeod keep. Valent had grown up on McLeod lands after being abandoned there as a three-year-old foundling.

For the second time, identical eyes to his met Valent's stare and, for an instant, he saw a flicker of warmth. "Your name is Darach. Mine is Steaphan."

It was as if someone punched him in the stomach. The air left his lungs and, for a long moment, Valent could not move. He swallowed past the large mass that formed in his throat. It took thirty years to finally learn his given name. "My name is Valent." He blinked away the moisture in his eyes. "I am no longer that boy your family gave away."

His twin shook his head. "One day you will learn all that is the truth. For now, I will not push the issue." Steaphan McKenzie stormed past him to the courtyard.

Valent finally understood the reason for his mistreatments by the previous two lairds. His entire life, both McLeod lairds, father and son, were barely able to hide their hatred whenever he was present.

Rage coursed through him not just at the McLeods for never telling him the truth, but also at the man who just walked away for what he represented. The family that had thrown him away like rubbish.

Ariana trembled against him bringing his attention to their current situation. On his other side, her maid, Lily, pressed against his side, as well.

The McKenzies had invaded the keep after he and other guards were ordered by Ariana's youngest brother, Beathan, to kill McKenzies. An innocent group of McKenzie clansmen out hunting, not aware of having trespassed on McLeod lands.

They'd killed all but one, who Beathan sent back with a message warning the McKenzies against trespassing. That was all the proof the McKenzies needed to attack. That they'd waited almost three weeks to do so was what caught the McLeods off guard.

Donall McLeod, the laird, Ariana's eldest brother, was presently hanging in the courtyard.

On his way in from the village, Valent saw Beathan, the younger brother, tied to a pole, a prisoner, his immediate future uncertain.

The third brother, Ceardac, may have escaped. Valent had yet to see him about.

Right now, the pressing matter was to get Ariana and her maid away from the disaster that was their home and deal with the situation at hand at the village.

Valent wished he could protect her from the sights outside the keep. There was utter death and devastation of her people.

"Come. Let us go to the village. We can find you a place to stay until they leave," Valent whispered to her while giving Steaphan's retreating back a pointed look. "They will not remain on McLeod lands for long," he said louder.

The guard who stood beside them clenched his jaw, the dislike for them palatable. "Do not be too sure."

They walked through the familiar courtyard and Ariana let out a cry at spotting Donall's body. "I must go to him." She took a couple steps only to stop when McKenzies blocked her path. There was pure pain in her eyes when she looked to Steaphan who stood in the center of the courtyard. "Will you at least allow us to bury our dead?"

The laird looked to the body and then to her, his face as if made of granite. "My dead were left in the open for animals to feast upon. Their families were not able to give them a decent burial. Yet, you ask it of me? For the man who ordered innocents to be killed?"

"Please?" she asked one more time her hand outstretched toward her brother's body. "I cannot leave him like this."

Steaphan looked to his guardsmen. "Follow them as far as the village."

"Come." Valent took her arm pulling her, once again, gently against him.

Lily took her other arm. "Yes, milady, we must go."

With one last look to her brother, she allowed Valent to guide her away. Once outside the gates, he assisted Ariana and Lily to mount his horse. Valent whistled for his dog. Arrow came running from somewhere near the gates and they set off.

He and the dog walked alongside the horse toward the village, which was about an hour's walk away. The guards followed at a distance, seeming almost as if they were more interested in a conversation than ensuring their safety.

Valent figured they spoke of the resemblance between the brothers. How Steaphan and he were mirror images of each other.

Some of his lifelong questions were answered. The boy he'd dreamed of over the years. Now he understood why, in his dream, both he and the boy who remained behind crying looked the same. Each time, he'd been confused at it seeming to be the same boy. He thought it was he, both taken and left to remain behind.

The walk to the village allowed him to ponder Steaphan's words. He'd said there was much he didn't know. Valent wasn't sure he wanted to know the truth any longer. Now that he knew he was a McKenzie, bitterness took the place of the previous curiosity. The McKenzie Clan was not far away. They could have come looking for him. Even if enemies over the years, that should not have stopped them from searching for so young a boy.

From what the McLeod, Ariana's father, said to him once, the McLeods had not taken him, as the laird had often wondered how he'd been deposited there as a child without anyone noting a stranger at the keep. According to the late laird, he'd been well fed and cared for prior to being a foundling for whoever decided to take pity.

The village came into view and Ariana looked down to him. "Looks like most of the dwellings remain."

Although surrounded by McKenzies camped on the outskirts, the village was eerily back to normal, smoke coming from the inn's chimney, the market set up in the center where many gathered around a bonfire, talking.

Upon spotting them, several people rushed to greet them, eyeing the McKenzie guards with distrust.

Valent assisted Ariana and Lily to dismount. Ariana turned to look at him. "We must talk." Her gaze roamed his face as if assuring herself he was still the same person.

"Aye. Get settled. I will find you."

Ariana and Lily were bustled away by the villagers to the inn.

Valent wasn't quite sure what to do other than to see what, if anything, the village men planned. Other than guess the McKenzie's next move, there was little to be done.

Once the McLeods of the north or from the Isle of Skye came, it was sure they'd battle against the McKenzies. By killing the laird and taking over the keep, the McKenzies declared war on Clan McLeod.

Valent found the blacksmith just inside his shop along with ten men. "Ah, there you are." The man motioned him over. "Tell us, what did you find out? Why were you allowed to return unharmed?" Every face turned to him with various levels of expectation.

Not ready to disclose information on his identity, Valent reached for a cup and poured ale into it from the nearby pitcher. "They have killed the laird and captured the younger brother, Beathan. Most of the surviving guardsmen are kept as prisoners." Everyone began asking about relatives and whom he'd seen. Valent tried to remember as best he could, the irony that if he were one of the dead or captured, no one would be asking for him. He touched an older man's shoulder. "Your Keddy is alive. I saw him with my own eyes. He is held prisoner, but well."

Tears sprung to the man's eyes and he nodded, relief evident. "Thank ye for telling me so."

"What news do you bring? Are we to fall under a new laird?" another man asked.

The room became quiet and Valent met the men's gazes. "The McKenzie did not say anything other than to instruct me to bring Lady Ariana to the village." He took a breath. "They block any way into the keep. They know if we travel north we cannot escape without entering another of McKenzie Clan's lands."

Sidigh, the blacksmith, pounded the table. "They know we cannot get away or send word to the McLeods of Skye, either."

"My apprentice went. He left earlier upon realizing we were under attack. I pray he makes it," Valent informed them.

"And us, what are we to do now?" Everyone looked to him as if waiting instruction. Valent wasn't sure when it was decided he was to lead them. But he knew it was imperative someone did.

"We must gather weapons, bring them here to store. Get all the men together and prepare for when the battle begins. They will not leave the lands without one last attack, I can sense it."

The men began to talk at the same time. Most had very little battle training. He wondered if they'd be able to provide more than a feeble opposition if attacked by the seasoned McKenzie warriors.

He moved away and paced, going over different

battle plans he'd learned over the years. The men, seeming to sense he needed to think, kept away, their conversations soft. Finally, Valent went to them and looked to each face.

"Gather all the men in the village. Have them come here after dark. We do not want the McKenzies to suspect we gather."

He'd devised a plan, not a very solid one, but, hopefully, one that would work.

It was time to find Ariana and ensure she was well. There was little he could do for her at the moment. Her world had been turned upside down on this day. She'd lost her entire family and home. However, there was a chance, although small, that the McKenzie would abandon the keep without destroying it before returning to his home. If so, she could return and reclaim it.

However, her life was forever changed. If all three of her brothers were dead, she'd have to find a husband and soon. When other McLeods came, her relatives would want to find her a husband right away to become laird.

His gut clenched at the thought of her married to another. He knew a lowly guardsman, an archer like him, had no right to feel that way, even after a night of passion when she'd come to his cottage.

A Scot with no name or clan of his own could never aspire to marrying a lady like her. His heart, however, did not understand logic and it clamored for her to always remain with him.

The lowering sun brought a chill to the air. He pulled his tartan around him. It was of muted colors, no clan affiliation, just a garment to keep him warm. He walked around the edge of the village noting where the McKenzie's camp started and ended.

At the inn's entryway, he was greeted by the smell of food and warmth from the fire in the large hearth. Ariana sat in the corner. Next to her sat the ever-present handmaiden, Lily. He could not bear to stay a distance away so he moved toward them. When she looked to him it was obvious Ariana felt the same way.

She held out her hand. "I wondered if you would come. I am not sure what to do."

He sat next to her, but did not take her hand, aware the other people in the room watched them. A bowl of food was placed in front of him and he began to eat. Between bites, he looked to the bowl in front of her. Ariana's food had become cold. "You should eat. There is much to be done and we need to maintain our strength."

It was good to see her high spirit remained by the angry glare she gave him. "I can't possibly eat, right now. How can you act as if nothing happened?"

It was best to ignore her question, as his answer would only anger her further. The fact that he felt nothing for the dead McLeods was not something Valent needed to admit. Not just the dead did he not care about, but also the clan who inhabited the keep. All of them could rot in hell for all he cared.

Just before the attack, he was set to leave, to go far away and not return. Now that he knew where he came from, which clan had allowed him to be taken as a child, there was little reason to remain any longer.

He ate another spoonful of stew and pondered the situation. Until someone came to defend Ariana and keep her safe, it was his duty to remain on McLeod lands. The already difficult decision to go elsewhere would be compounded the longer he remained there.

Her heavy sigh conveyed her sadness. The situation was dire, indeed. Of course, once the other McLeods arrived, they'd be better matched against the McKenzies.

Clan war was imminent. With her future so uncertain, he understood why she could not find the desire to eat. At seeing her so defeated, Valent knew, until she was safe, he could never leave her.

"Eat. Ye have to maintain your strength. There is much to be done." He dipped a chunk of bread into his broth and gave it to her.

Ariana ate the bread, but nothing more. "You are a McKenzie." Her statement was flat. "What will you do now?"

"Nothing different. They are not my clan." As an archer, he'd been too far from the front lines in battles against the McKenzies to see his brother's face. How had none of his fellow guards ever mentioned it? Perhaps, too enthralled in the battle, they'd not stopped to look at faces. He rarely did when fighting, not wanting to remember the face of those he felled with his arrows.

Two men neared the table and awaited permission from Ariana to sit. When she kept her gaze down, he motioned for them to sit.

Tiobald, an old guard, lowered his bushy brows. "We number less than thirty. That is counting the injured men at the stable." He scratched at his long beard. "How many of the McKenzies are there?"

"You cannot be thinking of fighting," Ariana exclaimed, taking in the older man. "They number ten times as many."

"However, they are divided," Valent told the men. "We can strike at the ones just outside the village."

"Aye," Tiobald agreed. "What think ye, Sidigh?" he asked the other man, the blacksmith.

Sidigh studied Ariana's face. "Lady Ariana, we cannot wait for them to attack first. That they've waited thus far is a good thing. It gives us a time to plan. I don't understand why they have not attacked the village, other than they expect us to yield without a fight, perhaps."

"Then do so." Ariana leaned forward, her eyes shiny with tears. "If you fight, too many could die. They are a ruthless people."

"Not any more than the McLeods," Valent couldn't help but add. "We killed unarmed men. Just for hunting."

No one spoke for a few moments. Finally Tiobald looked to Valent. "We meet at nightfall. Tonight would be the best time to attack. We'll follow your plan. It is our best chance. From the restlessness of the McKenzie men, they will strike soon."

Chapter 9

Death had become an unwelcomed, familiar entity to Ariana. Her father not long passed, her husband dead within months of their marriage, and now her older brother. If the McKenzie killed Beathan, she wasn't sure how she'd withstand it.

Ariana clung to the hope that her mother and other brother, Ceardac, had managed to escape the day before, during the attack. They'd boarded a small boat with hopes of making it to the Isle of Skye. When Ariana and Lily were cut off from making the boat, they had been forced to leave without them. In her heart, she maintained the hope they made it and would return soon.

Valent continued talking to the men. They'd moved away from her to stand by the hearth. No doubt, not to further upset her. She found it strange, but she understood the motivation behind the McKenzie's attack now and did not blame them for retaliating. It was true; Beathan should never have ordered his men to kill those poor hunters. How had her brother not considered the repercussions of his actions? Now, they all paid for his stupid mistake.

As far as her oldest brother, Donall, he was not the

strong leader he should have been. Too arrogant and brash. He had been eager to take the lairdship although he wasn't prepared for the responsibility. Yet no matter his faults, it was hard to fathom never seeing him again. No matter his faults, he was too young to die.

She brushed at an errant tear and looked to the pale Lily who had yet to say much more than necessary. Her ever-faithful maid wore Ariana's clothing, as they'd planned for the young woman to pretend to be of higher breeding if they'd been successful in escaping and separated. Thankfully, they'd had the foresight to sew Ariana's jewels inside their clothes. At least that was something the McKenzies did not acquire.

Valent shifted from one foot to the other and she couldn't help the pang of want. Needing to be with him, against him. In the shelter of his arms, finding some sort of solace. No matter what anyone thought of her, he would spend the night in her bed. The last thing she cared about was social standing. More than anything, she needed his comfort and touch.

As if sensing her regard, he looked to her, his somber gray gaze sending a clear message. He wanted the same from her.

"Lily, I'm going to retire. You should do the same."

"I'll help you undress then, milady." Lily yawned.

"No, don't. You are just as tired as I am. Go on now. They have prepared a room for you."

The innkeeper's wife came to them and placed her hands on her ample hips. "Aye, Lily, you will stay in the room next to ours. It's been empty since our Meagan married. Come on now, I'll loan you a shift."

Lily looked at Ariana one last time, not used to the treatment, and then acknowledged the woman. "No need, I still have my bedclothes under all this. Lady Ariana and I had to dress in a hurry."

"We'll talk tomorrow," Ariana told Lily and then stood. Valent watched her and gave her a slight nod. Relieved he'd come to her, she went upstairs.

From the bedchamber, she could make out the McKenzie camp just outside the village. There was a bonfire and men milled about. The sun was setting, but she could make out how heavily armed they were. How could the few McLeod men think they had any chance against them?

When Valent came to her, she'd tell him to instruct everyone to surrender. It was better. Too many children would be left fatherless and women without husbands.

Ariana had been so deep in thought she didn't hear him enter. Valent pulled her near and she placed her cheek against his broad chest. "You came. I need you with me tonight. Stay please."

The steady sound of his heartbeat reminded her of the possibility he could die and she clutched at his tunic. "Don't fight, Valent. Please surrender to them. No more death."

"We have a plan to try and save the guards who are imprisoned. There is a chance it will work with little bloodshed."

She doubted it, but remained silent, not sure what to do or say that would matter at this point. The men had already made up their minds and would not change directions at her request. If the McKenzie gave an order for all of them to be killed, then they had to be prepared. It was understandable. What they did made sense; but she could barely breathe at the thought of losing anyone else. Especially Valent, so soon after realizing she loved him. Every single part of her heart belonged to him now.

His large hands cupped her face and lifted it to him. When his lips fell over hers, she let out a sigh at the wonderful feel of want. Life. Yes, that is what she wanted. To feel alive and know that Valent lived, too.

The fabric of his tunic was thick and rough as her fingers curled into it to pull it up. He sensed her need to touch him, or felt the same, because he pulled it off over his head.

Frantic movements brought them to finally discard all the clothing and he lifted her away from the pools of her dress and coat upon the floor and carried her to the small bed. He placed her upon the bed with a gentleness that touched her heart.

He brushed his hair away from his face in an impatient gesture that almost made her smile. If not for the immediate need of him, she would have offered to cut it for him. Instead, she raked her fingers through the soft tresses and brought him to kiss her.

The softness of his lips on hers contrasted the hungry suckling and nipping of his teeth at her bottom lip. She arched under him, needing more.

Valent understood her message and his rough hands moved over her skin, touching from her sides down to her hips. "You are so perfect. So beautiful," he mumbled at her ear. The huskiness in his voice sent her to want him more.

"Make love to me, Valent. Stay with me always."

He lifted and peered down at her. His lips curved, a rarity for the mostly somber man. "I am with you now. All we can ask for is the now, darling Ariana."

Her heart ached and she almost blurted how deeply she felt for him, but something told her it could prove a mistake. "Love me."

Ariana reached for him, sliding her hand down his long shaft, her breathing hitched at the silky skin covering the hardness.

"Mmmm," Valent moaned and bucked into her hand,

his hips moving back and forward, encouraging her to stroke him. "I could spill just from this."

After several minutes, he pulled away and moved down her body, his tongue trailing from her throat to her breasts. He circled each tip and laved at them until her breathing came in pants. "I need you." Ariana attempted to reach for him, but he took her hands and held them over her head.

"Let me get my fill of you, Ariana. I want to touch every inch of you." He took her mouth, his tongue delving in, keeping her from responding. Still holding her hands with one of his, his other reached between her legs, his fingers parting her folds until reaching the center.

Ariana's hips lifted and he accommodated her need by sliding his fingers into her body. "Ahhh!" She let out a gasp when he released her mouth. "Yes."

Valent's lips curved as he watched her come undone, his darkened eyes fixed on her face.

Finally, when she couldn't take any more, he settled between her legs. His sex nudged at her entrance and she held his hips. The thickness of his shaft made her breath hitch as he slid in slowly.

Both moaned once he was fully seated.

"Take me, Valent." Ariana clutched at his hips.

The soft glow from the fire in the hearth accentuated Valent's beautiful body when he came over her, the flames countered and shaded muscles that moved and bunched as he made love to her, bringing her to the brink of madness. His head fell back as he, too, neared the fall to the abyss that was passion.

The sounds of their breathing, sighs, and soft moans intermingled as, once again, she began to soar. He was everything at once, a delicious assault of beauty and strength.

She wrapped her legs around him, bringing him deeper, and he plunged into her then shuddered with his release.

Valent maintained enough control not to crush her, but fell beside her onto the bed, bringing her against him. She threw her leg over his hip and clung to him, not ready to lose the connection and intimacy that came from being joined. "Stay like this for a moment," she whispered. "Don't move away. Remain connected with me."

Valent pulled her against his broad chest and Ariana cradled her head on his shoulder.

"You are not staying are you?"

"I cannot. We plan to strike once the moon is high. I must go."

All air left her lungs and fear resonated through every part of her. At once, the devastation that was now her life rushed over Ariana like ice cold water and she pushed away from him and curled into a ball. "I cannot lose anyone else. How can you do this to me?"

The words were selfish and made little sense, she knew it. But didn't she deserve to be so? To not want to lose the first man she ever loved, so soon after discovering the magical feel of it?

"I will be back for you. I promise." He pulled her back to him and tilted her face to his. "Look at me, Ariana."

His eyes were dark, his face stoic, but there was warmth in his gaze. "I promise you. I will fight to be with you again."

"And after that?"

A resigned sigh left his large body. "You know it will be impossible for us to be together. Much will happen in the next weeks. Your clan will be changed forever."

The truth of his words shook Ariana. Of course,

things were to be different. If only both could fathom how much so.

The high moon gave Valent enough visibility to aim at the McKenzie camp. Other than a few who stood guard, the majority slept. They were too complacent. Much too trusting of the small village.

Perched atop the roof of the stables, Valent and another archer lowered their arrows to a torch and lit the tips, then loosed them toward the camp. Arrow after arrow they shot while the armed village men waited below.

There were shouts of alarm when the McKenzies woke. As they dashed from the blazing tents, the McLeods cut them down, killing some and taking others.

The men's screams clashed with the sound of weapons, metal striking metal. Smoke filled the air, giving the atmosphere a surreal look as the battle ensued.

Even with the element of surprise, the McLeod men had a hard time containing the McKenzie warriors. Their sentries had managed to let out an alarm just after Valent and the other archer had begun, but not soon enough to save most.

Valent and the other archer scrambled down to assist. Valent jumped to the ground landing on his feet and immediately pierced a man who held a sword over Sidigh. The blacksmith had the advantage of strength and took a man from behind, wrestling the sword away. He held him down while another villager tied him up.

Valent scrambled to a better vantage point and, once again, loosed an arrow felling a warrior who howled at the pain of the arrow entrenched into his upper thigh.

When the man reached for his sword, Valent stood over him. "I wouldn't move if I were you."

The man's eyes widened when seeing his face. "Who are ye?"

Valent motioned for men to come and tie up the fallen man. Once it was accomplished, he shoved the arrow through his thigh, ignoring the man's shouts. Then he broke the tip off and pulled it out of the leg. "Bind it so he doesn't bleed to death. We need him."

The entire time, the man's gaze bore into him. "Ye are a McKenzie. Why do you do this?"

"I am not a McKenzie." Valent stormed away to see how many other prisoners they'd taken.

Twenty men in all were bound and tied by the end of the fight. It was enough for what they had planned.

"Liam is injured badly," Sidigh told him. "He's being carried to the inn. I do not think he will survive to morning."

The fires were dwindling, the haze with it. The older men and women of the village emerged and began throwing water from pails on the last of the blazes to keep them from spreading to the village. The prisoners were lined up and made to sit in a row, while the McLeods stood over them with swords and bows.

"Do we wait until morning?" the other archer asked Valent. "We don't want word to get back to the keep and they send the other warriors here. We cannot survive it. Our numbers are too few and with the prisoners to look over..."

"You fret more than a woman," Valent snapped. He stalked to where the blacksmith stood. "Are the wagons ready?"

"Aye. Look, they bring them now."

"We must ensure they cannot get free, or reach one another and untie the bindings." After ordering the men to ensure the prisoners were well contained with both hands and feet secured together, the McKenzies were loaded onto two wagons.

Horses were brought and Valent rushed to his just as Ariana tugged at his arm. She searched his face then her gaze fell over his body. "Are ye hurt?"

"No, I am fine. You should go inside." He looked over her shoulder to note several of the village people watched them with interest. "Ariana, you must go away from me."

Instead, the infuriating woman fell against his chest. "Let them talk. I do not care. Please, do not go. They will kill all of you." Tears slid down her cheeks.

Every part of him ached to embrace Ariana and make promises to soothe her, but he wouldn't lie to her. There were no promises to be made at the moment. He motioned to a village woman and two came for Ariana. She didn't fight them as they pulled her away.

She locked gazes with him. "Don't you dare die."

Instead of a reply, he mounted and urged the horse to the front. Valent raised his bow over his head and motioned for everyone to follow.

Word must have gotten to the McKenzie, for they were already mounted and lined up just outside the keep. The laird, sitting tall on his steed, was in front of his guard making an impressive sight.

Dressed in the McKenzie tartan of blue and green with his family crest on his shoulder, he looked equal parts leader and warrior.

Valent waited for the reaction of the men with him and, one by one, they looked from the McKenzie to him. "What is this?" Sidigh asked. "You are brothers."

"I am not his brother," Valent replied, not giving any other explanation.

Valent held up his sword and looked over his shoulder at the McLeods. "Remain here with the prisoners."

Valent and Sidigh moved forward, as did the McKenzie and his lead guard.

Steaphan's gaze raked over him, hesitating on his bloody arm. It took Valent by surprise that anyone would care enough to ensure he was not injured. Of course, it could just be morbid curiosity. "Are ye hurt?"

The words further shocked Valent. Sidigh looked to him, his concerned expression annoying Valent more than anything.

Valent spoke next. "We want our men. Will exchange with yours. One man is badly injured. He will die soon if not tended to." He motioned to the two wagons. "We bring twenty."

Steaphan narrowed his eyes. "I do not make bargains."

"Then you will die today," Valent said, his eyes locking with his brother's eyes.

"I doubt it." Steaphan turned to look over his shoulder. "We outnumber you and are better trained."

"Not by much."

"If you persist, it is you who will die today." Steaphan looked to be worried. "Is that what you want, Darach?"

The name was not his. It felt foreign to be addressed as such. "Matters naught to me."

Steaphan's gaze focused on the wagons, searching the prisoners.

"I suggest you discuss the matter with your men before deciding," Valent told him. He sheathed his sword and took his bow, settling an arrow into it. "I never miss. How many do you think I will kill before you reach me?"

He loosed an arrow and it impaled the shield of one of Steaphan's men. Valent lifted his eyes to his brother and then took in the startled expression on the rest of the McKenzie faces behind him. By his calculation, he would kill ten before felled by his brother's men. The two archers would not be able to strike him right away. They were too high up on the keep.

"Very well. We will exchange all but one," Steaphan said. "We take the murdering McLeod dog with us."

Sidigh leaned to Valent. "We cannot allow them to take him. They will torture him before allowing him to die."

"Then you prefer we lose all of our men over him? He is the reason for all of this."

"All but one," Valent called to his brother. "We agree."

Once the McLeod men were guided to stand in front of the McKenzie men, they did the same. They untied the men's legs so they could walk.

"Archer." Valent motioned for the other archer to position himself next to him. "If they betray us, kill as many of their men as you can."

"Aye," the man replied and lifted his bow.

Valent looked to Steaphan. "We send them forward at the same time."

The prisoners walked towards their clans, the air thick with wariness. Every man focused on the other side awaiting any movement that would indicate they were to attack. The four McKenzie archers exited through the keep and zoned in on him and the one beside him. Interesting that his brother would order him dead so easily after inquiring about an injury. So was the way of his family, he figured. Easily giving up blood.

Once the exchange was completed, the McKenzie and his guard, once again, moved to the front. Valent exchanged looks with Sidigh. "Come, let us see what they want now."

When they came close enough for Sidigh to see

Steaphan's face up close, the blacksmith's eyes widened and he looked from one to the other. Valent, himself, had a hard time not staring at his twin and grasping the familiarity of his brother's features. How ironic for fate to set things up so they were enemies, fighting on opposing sides of a battle.

"A clan war is imminent," Steaphan told him. "You cannot continue to fight with them. You are a McKenzie and the fact that you look so much like me will breed distrust by them. You know as well as I do, it would be best if you come back with me. We are your clan."

"I repeat to you, McKenzie. You are not my clan. If I am to choose a side, then it will be the McLeods." For now, he thought. There was no good reason, other than Ariana, to be in alliance with either one.

"We will meet again, Darach, and we will talk. There is much you need to know."

They backed away from each other. The McKenzie signaled for his men to mount. Beathan was brought forward atop a horse. He was badly beaten, only able to look to them out of one eye. Still, some of the arrogance remained as he spit to the ground. "My men will come for me and you will be sorry for this, McKenzie dogs."

He then focused on Valent and glared. "He is not to be trusted. He should go to hell with the rest of his people."

The men around Valent looked to him as if waiting to hear what he would say. Valent remained silent. Just like the arrogant man, not to know when he was defeated. As good as dead. Beathan would not live much longer. No matter if the McLeods arrived soon or not. He would not be allowed to live after what he'd done.

The newly released McLeods moved behind the horses for shelter and everyone stood by watching the McKenzies leave. There were too many and the McLeods were ill equipped to form any kind of attack that would not lead to all their demises, so there was little choice but to allow them to leave.

Steaphan turned one last time to look at Valent.

Perhaps, it would not be the last time he saw his brother. Valent wondered what kind of message the man would take to the rest of the clan concerning the brother that, according to him, they all thought long dead.

What would Steaphan's reaction be when he found out Valent was amongst the men who attacked the McKenzie hunters.

Chapter 10

"Was the archer the reason you allowed them to live?" Niven, the head of his guard, rode alongside Steaphan, his gaze scanning the horizon to ensure they were not to be ambushed. "It is a costly mistake you will live to regret."

Not used to being questioned, Steaphan ensured to tamp down an angry retort. "I did it to get our warriors back. Your son amongst them. He is but ten and six and should not have fought yet."

"We could have attacked once the exchange was complete. They didn't stand a chance. Although small in number, they will join with the other McLeods upon their arrival and fight," Niven replied, ignoring the comment about his son.

A battle between clans was the last thing he wanted at the moment. Laird for fewer than six months, his father, not too long dead, there was much to learn.

Then there was the fact he was due to marry two weeks hence and begin his life as leader of the large McKenzie Clan. Although the small McLeod Clan was barely a threat to them, if the other, larger McLeod clans decided to join with them, it could prove rather troublesome.

They'd maintained a friendly truce of sorts with the McLeods of Mudduch to the north. The clan was always too busy fighting with the McDonnalls over their eastern border to fight with his. If, however, those McLeods got wind of what happened and joined with the larger clan from Skye, then the clan war could last for a long time.

Steaphan wondered at sending a messenger to the laird of the McLeods of Mudduch explaining the circumstances. Then again, he could visit himself and speak to the man. The McLeod of Mudduch was an older man whom he'd hunted with on several occasions.

"Send half of the men to the keep. You and twenty ride with me to visit the McLeod of the Mudduch," Steaphan told his first, Niven.

After a firm nod, the warrior rode off to give the orders.

Steaphan took the moment alone to consider what to do about Darach. The archer did not trust him and his dislike for him and his clan was evident by the way he looked at them. He did not begrudge his twin's distrust or hatred. If things were switched, it was probable he'd feel the same. But it was important that Darach be given the opportunity to know his family. To become aware of what happened that night twenty-seven years ago.

Neither of them were the same, too many circumstances came between them. Even if identical twins, their personalities were affected by the facets of life. What kind of life had Darach led? He was part of the guard for the McLeod, which meant he'd had a humble life. Unlike he, who'd never suffered for anything, Darach had probably grown up wanting much.

It was only fair that he be afforded the opportunity now to be part of Clan McKenzie and regain all he'd lost.

Steaphan wasn't sure how to go about it, but he'd keep insisting until Darach listened to him.

The next day, upon arriving at Mudduch, Steaphan noted no one seemed at all discomfited by his visit. The gates to the McLeod keep were open. He found it interesting that word had not gotten to them. Or if it had, it did not bother the laird to know his kinsmen were being attacked.

Once inside the courtyard, Steaphan dismounted. When a lad came to take the horse away, he placed a hand on the thin boy's shoulder. "Wait a moment. I may not be staying long."

Laird McLeod, himself, came to greet him. The lanky man emerged from a side entry and looked from him to his guards. "Aye, McKenzie. I didn't know to expect ye."

He motioned for the boys to take the horses. "Go on now. He will remain for the evening meal."

From under bushy brows, McLeod looked to Steaphan. "We have much to discuss. The meal is about to be served and it's best you and your men come inside. I don't want to anger cook as she is quite proud of her food today."

Steaphan walked with the man who limped visibly from an old battle injury. His twisted right leg barely sustained his weight. Yet he moved at a fast pace beside Steaphan.

The McLeod lifted a finger at him. "You fight the McLeods of the south. Very dangerous proposition that. If the clan from Skye decides to declare war, we may have to join with them."

Steaphan nodded. "It was they who brought war to us by killing innocent men who did nothing more than hunt."

86

"Aye. Innocent or not, they should have known the boundaries of the land. It is important the people are aware of them. It never works well to encroach into another clan's territory. Look at my situation. The damn McDonnalls, we are always in some sort of fight or another. They insist on the land on the eastern edge of the loch. I'm of a mind to give it to them just to put a stop to all of it." The McLeod chuckled and coughed to cover it up when entering the great room.

"Let us sit. I have a proposition." With those encoded words, he moved away and went to where his wife sat.

Steaphan bowed at Lady McLeod and then at the younger woman who sat beside her. Upon straightening, he felt his eyes widen at the beauty. She sat straight, her curious hazel gaze taking him in, as well.

The McLeod waited for him to take a seat beside him. "My daughter, Fiona. I don't believe you have met her yet."

"Nay, I have not." Steaphan could not help stealing another look at the woman who spoke to her mother in low tones. Whatever they spoke of seemed to make the fair Fiona unhappy as she huffed in response and pressed her bow-shaped lips together.

Lady McLeod looked toward him and then whispered something to her daughter.

Did they talk about him? If so, why would the conversation anger the younger woman?

"We killed a boar just two days ago. Its meat promises to be plentiful and tasty. Enjoy." The McLeod took two large pieces of meat and placed them on his own plate. The meal was, indeed, quite flavorful. Steaphan noted his men seemed to relax a bit while eating.

His guard, Niven, looked not so at ease as the rest of the men, his gaze constantly traveling the room. As it should be.

Steaphan himself wasn't sure whether to trust the McLeod at this point not to poison his food or attack once his men's guards were down.

"What is this proposition you have?" Steaphan asked the older man who took a healthy drink of his ale.

"That our clans join. We have been on friendly terms for many years. Before you, I hunted with your father many a time. A battle between us would be a pity." The laird waited for him to respond. Steaphan agreed with the man. As much as he loathed the McLeods of the south, Mudduch was like a second home to him. Often, he'd accompanied the older men hunting and, although he'd never met the laird's family, they'd always remained cordial with each other, often remaining neutral over their clashes with other clans.

"I agree. I prefer not to battle against you." Steaphan looked to the older man and noted relief. "How do you propose we join?" Once the words escaped, he immediately knew the answer. The reason for Fiona being there and for the lass being angry. The laird would propose they marry.

His marriage to a woman he'd been betrothed to for years was set to take place within weeks. He stole another look to Fiona, who continued to look straight ahead, her gaze determinedly fixed away from him.

"You know now, do you not?" the McKenzie asked him with a soft smile. "My daughter, Fiona, and you will marry. We cannot waste more time for I foresee the messenger from my kinsmen, arriving within a day or two, demanding we join with them."

Steaphan looked to Niven, whose rounded eyes danced from him to Fiona and then to the McLeod.

"I don't know what to say. I am due to get married."

The McLeod nodded in understanding. "If you can think of a better way, then present it."

Steaphan considered his options. His sibling at the McKenzie keep was a not only female, but already married with a family and his only brother was pledged to the McLeods. Even if he could reach him in time, the male would more than likely slice him down before agreeing to do anything to help his clan. To bring peace to the region.

No, his brother wanted blood and, although seeming to be a leader to the McLeod warriors, he had no alliance.

"I cannot think of another way," he acquiesced. "I will marry your daughter and make her lady over the McKenzie Clan."

"Verra well." The McLeod signaled for a steward to come forward. "Bring the clergyman at once." He stood and the room hushed, all eyes, including his own men, locked to the laird. "There will be a wedding this eve. My lovely daughter, Fiona, will marry Steaphan McKenzie of Gladdaugh."

There were grumbles from the men and gasps from the women. But they all waited to hear what else the laird would pronounce.

"We do this together to keep further war from our clans. We are the friends of the McKenzies of Gladdaugh. They are now to be kinsmen with the McLeods of Mudduch."

Steaphan stood and held up his cup. "Long live the McLeod of Mudduch!"

The clansmen lifted tankards and hailed their chief with louds calls. The laird waited for them to quiet and lifted his. "And long live the McKenzie of Gladdaugh."

A quieter cheer followed. Maids entered with filled pitchers to refill cups and tankards for celebrating. Steaphan looked to Fiona who, at that moment, looked to him and upon their gazes meeting, could barely drag his away. It was hard to decipher her expression. Somewhere between curiosity and wariness. He wondered if it reflected his. As much as he looked forward to marrying the woman back at his homelands, he wondered if fate brought this new woman to him for a reason. Union with her meant the possibility of peace for his people. At least the threat from his northern border would be gone. Maybe, after a time, to the south as well.

He barely tasted the food, his mind turning more to what would happen upon his return home. His betrothed and her family were to arrive within days. He got up and motioned to his first. "Niven, send a messenger to my betrothed's father. Let them know the marriage is off. I'm not sure what excuse to use." He searched his mind. "What say you?"

"The truth. That you are forced to marry to keep peace in our land." Niven looked to the high board. "Yer mother will be angry."

"Aye. I know, but it cannot be helped."

Just then, the clergy was brought, the man looked to be confused by the way he searched the room as if expecting something horrible to happen to him. He stormed toward Laird McKenzie. "What is the meaning of this? You are aware I cannot marry people without banners and such." He lifted his hand and pointed at the man who seemed more amused than angry. "You know better than that, Naill McLeod."

The McLeod peered down at the clergyman. "Would you prefer to see this clan go to war then?"

"It will take time to ensure the marriage is valid. Surely you can wait a fortnight." The clergyman looked about the room as if waiting for agreements from those there. Everyone remained silent awaiting the laird's decree.

Steaphan crossed his arms over his chest upon noticing Fiona also looked to her father with expectation.

Fiona could not believe her luck. A way to get out of marrying a total stranger, a McKenzie no less, came from the vicar of all people. She'd never gotten along with the clergy, but now she wanted to rush to the old, craggy man and kiss him.

If her father agreed to wait, it gave her time to escape, to run away to her beloved. She searched the room for her warrior, but did not see him about. Strange, he'd been there just a few moments ago. Perhaps he was enraged by the announcement. She'd wait to see what happened and then go in search of him.

The McKenzie stood still as a statue, his muscular arms crossed on his broad chest. She'd not seen a man as tall, intimidating, and stoic. She understood why her father would rather join with him than fight. The guards that came with him were battle-seasoned warriors who'd easily mow through their men. At the moment, she hated the lot life dealt her.

"Father, I will not marry him. If he is betrothed, he should marry the woman he made a promise to." Fiona knew her argument would fall on deaf ears, but had to try.

"You will perform the ceremony and that's final," her father said to the clergyman, ignoring her request. He slammed his cup on the table with so much force both she and the clergyman jumped. "Let us get on with it."

"Father, may I first go see about something?" Fiona was relieved when her father nodded.

"Hurry on about it. We have to get you married and

the consummation done before the McKenzie departs."

Her father's words, said without inflection, brought a cheer from the men and her face to blazing warmth.

She hustled from the high board. Everyone suspected she went to relieve herself, but she passed the doorway to the privy and headed down a hallway to the courtyard. Fiona lifted her skirts to move faster. The sooner she got to her warrior, the faster she could convince him they must leave at once.

Moaning from a deep male voice was accompanied by a woman's higher cries. Fiona didn't have to go any nearer to know what happened, but morbid curiosity pulled at her. The couple was so engrossed; they didn't hear her as she moved closer.

A few moments later, she returned to the great room, her spirit dry. It no longer mattered that she was to be used as an object, a pawn in the game men played. She stood next to the much taller McKenzie as the clergyman went through the vows and the proceedings while her mind remained in the hallway.

When her warrior had finally noticed her, he'd barely stopped moving into the woman. His gaze was cold and distant, the message clear. He never meant to take her away.

"Give me your hand." The McKenzie's gray eyes met hers and she had to admit the man was quite handsome. Yet a handsome devil was still a devil.

Their hands were bound, his larger one enveloping hers. The warmth of his touch sent tendrils of heat up her cold arm. She shivered and noticed his eyes go to her face as if assessing what she thought.

"Repeat after me." The clergyman took them through the vows and Fiona repeated the words. The beauty of the promises was not lost on her as one tear escaped and slid down her cheek.

Steaphan McKenzie wiped it away with his thumb. "I hope not to see many more tears from my wife."

Fiona let out a deep sigh and met his gaze. For an instant, she wanted to reassure him, but just as she went to speak, the vicar interrupted, pronouncing them husband and wife.

After a chaste kiss, they turned to face her clan who cheered. She understood the necessity of the marriage; her clan would remain in relative peace from now on. Except for the minor scuffles with the McDonnalls, her union with Steaphan McKenzie was needed. She scanned the faces of her kinsmen and couldn't help but smile at them. They trusted her father's decisions and he was a good laird. Although she'd leave with her new husband, it was comforting to know her clan would be safe and well.

The feasting annoyed Fiona more than anything. Her clansmen celebrated with loud guffaws at crude jokes someone said, while the ale was poured and pitchers passed. It mattered very little to them what they celebrated. More interested in the gossip the union between her and the McKenzie and what their night would be, than actually taking time to consider how she may feel.

She stole a glance at her new husband, who'd yet to speak to her since they'd wed. Instead, he maintained a steady conversation with her father about an upcoming clan issue. It was almost as if he'd forgotten she were there.

"Come, Fiona, we must prepare you for your bedding." Her mother touched her shoulder, her fingers pressing in, in an attempt to reassure her. Fiona stood and followed her. Steaphan's gray gaze went to her at that moment. He looked first to her face and slowly down to her bosom before lowering down the length of her body. Finally, his gaze went toward the hallway to where she'd go and then resumed his conversation with the men.

Breath caught in her throat, Fiona's heartbeat quickened. The effect of his regard confused her. How could a man's gaze alone have so much power? It was probably the culmination of so many emotions in so short a time. Her mind was askew.

Just that morning, she'd woken with thoughts of stealing away with her love, to sneak a kiss and a tender word. Now she had to admit, the warrior never affected her in such a manner. He never looked to her, barely ever met her gaze, so terrified of being found out by the laird. Fiona always chalked it up to him needing to keep the position and provide for his mother and sister, but now she wondered if he'd lied about everything.

Certainly didn't seem too worried about being caught with the maid in the narrow hallway of the keep.

She stumbled and her mother took her elbow. "Fiona, I know this is not easy. I tried to talk your father out of it. More time at least to get you used to the idea. But he said it was best to do so immediately. Time is of the essence."

"Of course, Mother. I understand. It's important to keep our people safe. This is part of being the laird's daughter. To be used as a pawn."

Her mother rushed to the door and closed it. "Do not speak that way. Yes, it is your duty. Just like everyone else in the clan. We each have a role to perform. You may not understand it now. One day you will." Her mother moved behind her to unlace her bodice.

"Do you know how it is between a man and a woman?"

"I've seen it done. Just today, I caught one of the guards tupping a maid," Fiona replied honestly. "The man mounts a woman either from behind or from the front. It may or may not be pleasurable, depending on the circumstances. Since my first coupling with my husband will be public, it will, in most likeliness, not be pleasurable."

Her mother's face reddened. "The McKenzie is a handsome man. He is rather large, so I pray he doesn't hurt you."

She'd not considered his size. The man was rather tall and broad. Would his member be so, as well? Fiona bit her bottom lip in thought. "Mother, how can I ensure it doesn't hurt too badly?"

For a moment, her mother furrowed her brow in thought. "First of all, we'll get you some whiskey. It will help you relax, if you keep your eyes on him. Not on the others in the room. On his face. Breathe evenly and do not clench, but allow your body to remain loose for when he mounts you."

A maid materialized a few moments later with whiskey to which her mother added honey. Fiona drank two large pourings and glad for it when, indeed, her body relaxed. Her lips curved upward and her eyes drooped. "This is so good," she murmured. "I shall have it every single night."

"Oh goodness, perhaps we gave her too much." Her mother leaned closer and peered at her. "Fiona, don't fall asleep. Open your eyes and look at me."

A giggle erupted and she hiccupped at how funny her mother looked. "My eyes are open."

There was a ruckus at the door and her mother motioned the maid over. "Help me get her into the bed. Oh goodness, I hope she doesn't fall asleep before it happens." Fiona pushed away at them to keep the women from fussing so much over her.

"I'm fine." When she swayed, the women caught her and helped her onto the bed.

The door burst open and the men carried a half-naked Steaphan who was just as tussled about as she was. Fiona sat up and peered at him. From the crooked grin and reddening of his cheeks, he, too, had drunk too much whiskey. Fiona covered her mouth with her hand to stifle a hiccup.

Looking to her mother, she leaned over and whispered, "How many people will be present?"

Her mother moved around the bed and to the maid. "Get everyone out except the vicar and the McKenzie guardsman." She looked to her and nodded. "Your father and I will remain as well."

The McKenzie did not seem at all discomfited by the proceedings. Shirtless and with his britches low on his hips, she could only admire his body. Tall and muscular, much more so than the guard, this man was built for battle and war.

She lay back and looked at the ceiling before remembering what her mother said. It was easier look anywhere else but his face. His gaze moved over her, once again, this time slower. He took her by the hips and pulled her lower down the bed until her feet were on the edge of the mattress. Her shift slid up uncovering her bottom half and she squirmed. He then pushed his britches off and straightened.

It was impossible to keep from peeking to note the size of his cock. It was a mistake. Like the man, it was thick and formidable. Fiona gasped and looked back to his face. His eyes had darkened.

The bed dipped from his weight when he climbed onto the bed and over her. He pushed her legs apart and settled between them before looking to the people in the room.

His breath smelled of whiskey and Fiona swallowed when her stomach revolted at the reminder of what she'd already drank too much of.

So intent she was on not throwing up that when he nudged at her entrance, she didn't take much notice except to part her legs wider. It would have been bad form at this point to urge him to move faster as he was taking his time. But she almost did. Of course, she reasoned, throwing up on one's bridegroom was far worse.

She lifted her head and looked down to see that he ran his hand up and down his shaft until it sprung to life. Three mistakes so far. The drinking, the first look and now this. His shaft grew to be even larger.

"I-I don't think it's going to fit at all now." She cleared her throat to hide a burp. Thankfully, it helped somewhat with the nausea. "You shouldna done that."

There were several throats clearing and her mother gasped. Fiona noticed her parents had turned their backs. The clergyman watched with eyes narrowed while her husband's guard paid more attention to her breasts than whatever Steaphan did.

"Ah!" Fiona cried out. When his pushed into her, there was a sharp, quick pain. "You didn't warn me." She attempted to scoot up to get him out of her, but he held her hips fast.

"Don't move," her husband gritted out as if in pain. "Just be still for a moment."

If anyone should be uncomfortable it was she, not him. Or perhaps it hurt the man, as well. The thickness of him filled her completely and her body struggled to adjust. Fiona took a deep breath and fell back onto the bedding in an attempt to force her body to relax.

"What are you doing?" She had to ask since he remained frozen, joined with her.

"Allowing for your body to accept me."

"I do not think it does," she replied.

She thought she heard a man's chuckle before footsteps sounded and the door closed with a firm thud.

Steaphan released a breath and pulled out almost completely. Just as Fiona was about to let out a breath of relief, he moved back in.

"Oh!" She felt her eyes widen as she grasped his shoulders. "You're going to keep going?"

"Aye. I will wife. I will finish and so will you."

He leaned over her and caressed her nipples while his hips moved in a perfect rhythm. Whatever he did was not unpleasant in the least. Fiona closed her eyes and wondered if lovemaking would always feel so good. She lifted her hips to take him deeper, needed him to be totally inside her, to take her completely.

"You are so tight and wet. I didn't expect it," he spoke into her ear, the huskiness of his voice and heat of his breath adding to the pool of sensations. Fiona could only let out a soothing sound as she allowed him to ride her body until she began to float.

She closed her eyes and then opened them again remembering what her mother said. "More!" She dug her fingernails into his buttocks and urged him to move faster, the brink of her coming within reach. Steaphan pulled out and moved down her body.

"What are you doing?" she grumbled at the sudden emptiness and coolness that came at being separated from him.

"I want to feel you more. Be with you in different ways." Steaphan lifted her hips up and reached between her legs. "Open yourself to me, beauty." She started to grumble, but then cried out when his mouth took her. He licked between her folds and then moved his fingers into her sex.

Immediately, she climaxed. Losing all control, she dug the back of her head into the bed coverings and screamed.

When he rolled her onto her stomach and lifted her

behind to enter her again, she could barely function. Any more sensations and she was sure to die. Instead, she began floating back down to him as every inch of his shaft moved into her and slid back out.

"Come again with me," he told her, reaching around to fondle her already swollen nub.

Once again she climbed.

"Milady, wake up." The maid stood over her with a perplexed expression. "Ye has slept much too long."

Fiona jerked upright, sitting up in the bed and looking from side to side. Where was her husband? "The McKenzie?"

"He is downstairs, milady. Preparing to leave."

"Today?"

"Aye, milady. He's returning to Gladdaugh with haste it seems."

She went to the window and could see the guardsmen were preparing their mounts. "But I am not packed."

"Fiona. You're awake." Her mother appeared at the door and came to stand next to her. "I see you know they leave."

"They?" Fiona looked from her mother to her maid. "What is happening? Why am I not accompanying my husband?"

"He feels it will be safer for you to remain here."

"I must speak to him immediately. I do not wish to remain behind. Why did he not speak to me of it?" She rushed about the room and grabbed a robe, which she wrapped around her body as she ran down the hallway.

"Fiona, stop!" her mother called, but Fiona ignored her.

Steaphan was about to leave the great room when she appeared. "Steaphan," she called and rushed to him.

Her father stared at her agape while the other people looked on with curiosity. "I must speak to you at once."

"Fiona, this is not the time," her father started, but she cut him off.

"I wish to speak to my husband, now." She emphasized the word husband between clenched teeth.

"This way." Steaphan took her elbow and walked with her to a side alcove. He looked down at her with expressionless eyes. "What do you wish to speak of?"

"Wha..." Her mouth fell open and she tried to say something besides telling him to go to hell. "I wished to know why you made a decision not to take me with you."

The man was not warm at all. He lifted a brow at her comment. "My clan is at war. You will be a target for them. Being a McLeod who married a McKenzie only keeps your clan safe, not mine."

"But it's only right that I remain by your side," she offered weakly. The last thing she wanted was to remain behind, left to live out her days alone with her family and no husband. Not to mention, facing the guard who professed his love one day and tupped a maid in her home the next.

"I will come for you as soon as possible. Now, be an obedient wife and go back to your room. I will send for you in a fortnight or less."

"In the future, I would prefer if we discuss any matters that affect me prior to you speaking to anyone else. The maid knew more about your decision than I did. Travel well, husband. I hope your horse doesn't step in a hole and toss you over its head." She turned on her heel and headed to the hallway. If she never saw the brute again, it would be too soon.

Chapter 11

Valent entered the dim interior of the McLeod great room.

Everything remained the same, yet utterly different. The same furnishings, wall tapestries and hounds traipsing about, but the entire feel of it changed now. The air smelled of death and despair. Two guardsmen sat at a long table eating without speaking. At another, four men drank ale, their plates ignored.

A serving wench moved about listlessly, barely paying any mind to the fact some food slid off the tray. The dogs rushed over and ate it before he could bring her attention to it. Valent supposed her husband, brother or father must have been killed. Everyone, it seemed, had lost someone close.

"The McLeods of Skye have not responded," Murray, one of the guardsmen at his table and his closest friend said. "Perhaps they are not coming."

"What of the McLeods of Mudduch?" Valent asked.

"They sent notice stating they were kin by marriage to the McKenzies and would not join." Murray shook his head. "I was not aware of there being a union between them.

"'Tis new, I bet," another guard chimed in. "Naill

McLeod has always been friendly with the McKenzie."

"What happens then?" Murray asked no one in particular. "We are weak and easy prey if the McKenzies return."

"They will not." Valent wasn't sure of it, of course. "They could have taken over while here and didn't. I think it was just retaliation they wanted."

"What of Beathan? Should we do something?" the other guard asked, his bread held up to his mouth. "He is our laird's brother."

"He is the cause of all this, if he isn't dead yet, he will be soon. We cannot do much to save him." Valent scanned the room. Ariana had yet to make an appearance. Two days at the keep, they'd buried the dead and the maids had wiped the blood from the floors and walls. Yet he understood that she probably still could see it all. Upon first arriving she looked about to faint at the sight of so much of it. But she'd remained strong.

"Valent, milady would like to speak with ye," Lily spoke to him, her eyes lowered. Like her mistress, Lily had also not quite recovered from the blow of all the changes. As a matter of fact, Lily seemed to assume the role more of Ariana's friend than a maid.

Murray met his gaze. "Upon the arrival of McLeods, your familiarity with Lady Ariana will not be looked upon kindly."

"You do not have to remind me. I know." He stalked off angry at the truth of Murray's words.

He hesitated in the doorway and looked toward the front entrance. If ever there was a time to get away, this was it. Things were about to change, once again, and the last thing he wanted was to serve another McLeod. He owed them nothing and would not give his life in defense of a clan who'd never accepted him fully. Now that he knew where he came from, there was no need to further investigate his heritage.

If anything, no one would question his decision. If he remained just until the McLeods arrived, he would, at least, ensure Ariana was safe. He'd go south, to the lowlands, and offer to work in exchange for food and shelter. He had little need for anything.

"Once the new McLeods arrive, everything will be different will it not?" Lily came up behind him. She closed her eyes and let out a breath. "I wonder how much longer I will remain here. If Lady Ariana marries, I will go with her wherever it is she is to live."

"Perhaps her husband will want to remain here."

"Or Ceardac will return and we will remain almost as before." There was hope in Lily's gaze when she looked to him. "That could happen, can it not?"

"Aye. Anything could. Tell Lady Ariana I will see her later tonight. I must go to see about my cottage before it gets too late." He walked to the courtyard, suddenly needing air. His dog, Arrow, came to him when he whistled and Valent continued on toward the woods.

The cottage he'd lived in since a lad was exactly as he'd left it. He found his bundle of clothing that he'd thrown into the bushes when his plans to leave had been thwarted by the arrival of the McKenzies.

Inside the cottage, he moved about touching the familiar, simple furnishings. The dwelling where he'd lived most of his life already looked abandoned, the air stale as if it prepared for a long slumber. He'd never return. Somehow, Valent knew this was his last time to be there.

The horse made a noise and he looked to see if something was amiss. Everything seemed well. It was probably the wind rustling the leaves that made the animal uneasy. He let the door close behind him and went to the horse. Just then, a man appeared from the forest. From the looks of him, he was a scout prepared for battle. Valent tensed, but didn't reach for his sword. "Who are you?"

"I'm a scout for the McLeod. Are you of that clan?"

"The McKenzies have left. They retreated two days ago. You can go back and assure your laird only the laird's sister, Lady Ariana, and twenty guards remain."

The scout looked past him. "Aye, fine, but I will see with my own eyes before I go back."

Valent shrugged. "Keep is this way." He mounted and urged his horse towards the keep. "I'm headed there now."

Upon arriving, the guards met the scout and invited him in. "Where is the lady?" he asked, not seeming to be at ease.

"I am here. On whose behalf are you here?" In spite of everything that had recently transpired, Ariana held her head high, her shoulders square as she descended the stairs. Her eyes went to Valent first, lingering on his face before moving to the scout. "Is my brother, Ceardac, and my mother with you?"

The scout moved closer to Ariana, stopping only when two guards blocked his way. Regardless of who the man said he was, they would not take his word for it. He understood and didn't attempt to move closer. "Your brother returns with the laird of Skye. They await my return a day's ride from here. Your mother remained at Skye."

Ariana could barely hear the scout's words past the relief that Ceardac and her mother lived. It was also a relief she'd not be forced to marry a stranger in order to keep her home. Just a few more days and her brother could come and take over the reins of lairdship. She waited for Valent to look to her and she motioned to the upstairs. His nod was barely perceptible. "Would you stay the night and leave in the morning?" she asked the scout, hoping to delay the man as much as possible. Hopefully, Valent would agree to her plan and they, too, would leave right after the scout.

The scout agreed only to stay for a meal, but not overnight.

The evening meal was a quiet event. Other than an occasional mumble from the men, everyone ate in silence. Ariana let out a breath and looked to Lily. "We may as well have remained in my chamber to eat tonight. The great room feels oppressive."

"Aye, I agree. 'Tis so much on everyone's minds. But we have good news." Lily's soft smile made her feel better.

"I look forward to Ceardac's arrival, but dread giving him the news about Donall. I know he expects as much, but hearing it will be hard for him."

Lily nodded, her expression pensive. "And there is the matter of the upcoming battle. If the McLeods of Skye come, then they must be planning for it."

Ariana let out a long breath and looked around the room. "Why does it have to be so? The McKenzies retaliated, albeit very harshly, for a wrong my brother committed, but more war does not help matters."

"I don't understand it, either," Lily admitted. "Perhaps you can speak to Ceardac. Convince him not to do it."

"Have no doubt about it, dear friend. I certainly will talk to him and try to get him to offer a truce to the McKenzie and to discuss terms for Beathan's release."

Lily's gaze slid to Valent. "Eerie isn't it how he is the mirror image of his brother?"

It was unavoidable that everyone would question Valent's loyalty after such a revelation. "I wonder what Ceardac's reaction will be. If he doesn't know it now, he will upon arriving. Everyone is talking about it."

"Then you must tell your brother of Valent's refusal to go with the McKenzie."

"I am sure he will learn that, as well, upon arrival. The remaining guardsmen will advise him before I could ever get a moment with my brother alone."

The messenger approached and gave her a slight bow. "Milady, I depart now. Your brother and the McLeod of Skye should arrive two days hence." The slight young man waited for her reply.

"If you are sure you cannot wait, then safe travels. I await their return eagerly." She watched him walk away, her brow furrowed in thought. The sooner she spoke to Valent and convinced him to go away with her, the better.

She looked to Lily and felt a pang of guilt. What of her friend? Would Ceardac allow her to remain at the keep? It didn't seem fair to bring her along on a trek with no destination in mind and not knowing what kind of life she and Valent would be forced to live.

"Lily, do you still wish to marry and have a family? I have not heard you speak about any of the guardsmen lately."

A slow smile stretched across her friend's face. "I do wish for both a husband and children. However, I am not sure if it's possible anytime soon. Especially with all this." She motioned around the room. "Thankfully, none of the guardsmen have taken my notice at the moment."

Hours later, once in her bedroom, Ariana paced. The irrational need to be with Valent overriding anything else. Lily entered the room and took in her bags. "Where do you plan to go?"

The time to tell the first person came. "I am leaving. Once Valent comes to me tonight, I will tell him of my plan to escape. Run away from all of this..." the words eluded her.

"But your brother will come after you," Lily said, wringing her hands. "And what of me, milady?"

"Stop calling me that, Lily, I've told you, you are not my maid any longer." Ariana moved closer and took Lily's hands. "I have thought much about it this evening. You can come with us. Please understand that Valent is my chance at happiness."

Lily attempted a smile. "What does he say?"

She let out a sigh. "That is what I will speak to him about tonight. He has to agree. Has to see it is the only way we can remain together."

"I will prepare my bag then, too." Lily looked ready to cry. "Although, I think it's a mistake. Where will we go?" She placed a hand on Ariana's shoulder. "What of your brother? I'm sure he will allow you to remain here without marrying. He may even turn a blind eye to your relationship with Valent. Allow Mister Ceardac the opportunity before leaving."

"Oh, Lily. He will never allow a relationship with an archer." Ariana knew it was selfish of her. There wasn't a way to explain how she felt without sounding like a spoiled child. "I cannot bear the thought of another man touching me. Or of Valent with another woman."

There was a knock on the door and Lily went toward it. Her eyes remained misty and her lips downturned. "If you leave, I go with you." She opened the door. "I will leave you to it then."

Valent's large, muscular body immediately made the room seem smaller. He moved to her and pulled her against him. "Any moment away from you is torture. I need you right now, Ariana."

They needed to talk, so much to discuss, but she would not deny him the one thing he asked. "Yes." She slid her hands under the rough fabric of the tunic and ran her palms up his chest. "I want you so much, Valent."

He didn't bother with kisses or caresses. Instead, he pushed her bodice past her shoulders and lowered his mouth to her exposed mounds of flesh. His mouth closed over one nipple while his hand squeezed the twin, the pad of his thumb rubbing the pert tip.

"Oh, Valent." Her legs threatened to give way when Valent reached under her skirts and ran his hand up the inside of her thigh. He pushed his palm between her legs and cupped her sex. Slowly at first, he pushed one finger into her, the movements starting between her folds to the entrance of her sex. Each languid caress stirred her body to begin its trek toward the invisible mountain that promised a wonderful fall.

Ariana held on to his shoulders attempting to keep upright as her legs wobbled when a second finger joined the first sinking into her body. "I can't withstand much more," Ariana breathed the words out then gasped when he fell to his knees and lifted her skirts higher holding them up to her waist. His warm breath fanned over her sex sending pools of heat to gather. The motions of his tongue against her pulsing core sent her spiraling to a climax like she'd never felt before. She clung to his shoulders and cried out.

His gaze met hers, his lips glistening. "You are amazing, Ariana." He lifted her and carried her to the bed. "I want to hold this night in my mind for the rest of my life. To always remember you like this. Wanting me. Needing me."

He pulled his tunic up over his head exposing the beauty of his body, hard planes and ripples of muscles with a thin line of hair leading from his stomach to the juncture between his legs. Not taking his gaze from her, he kicked off his boots and removed his britches, freeing his erection.

It was impossible to look away from the perfection of Valent's body. Ariana's mouth watered with anticipation. Valent neared and tugged at her dress. "I need to see you, Ariana. See all of you."

"I can deny you nothing." She pushed her skirts past her hips and Valent pulled the folds of fabric and tossed them aside.

Dress removed, she lay back on the bed. No longer shy with him, Ariana wanted Valent to look his fill. His darkened gaze met hers for an instant before traveling down her length. He pushed her legs apart. Her sex clenched at his perusal. "You are ready, glistening for me."

"Yes." Ariana reached to him. "I want you so much."

He came over her and looked down to meet her gaze. There was something different in the way he looked at her, as if wanting to memorize every inch of her face. Ariana pulled his face closer and kissed him hard on the lips, conveying how much she felt for him, letting Valent know he was the only man she'd ever allow in her heart. "Make love to me, Valent."

His hardness pressed against her entrance and she welcomed him into her body and further into her heart. Every moment in and out was as powerful as him. Valent pushed deeper into her. His neck corded with the exertion of his movements, his throat bared to her when he threw his head back. She lifted and ran her mouth up the side of it, tasting him.

"You are perfect. My match, the woman I'll never forget." He drove in harder, lost in his passion, his climax nearing by the tightening of his body. Ariana wrapped her arms around him, no longer able to crest with him, too consumed by his last statement.

Valent planned to leave. He would not remain and wait for her brother to come. She grappled with what to say to convince him she'd go with him. With a loud growl, he shook as he came, spilling his heated seed into her. When Valent collapsed over her, she held him sliding her hands up and down his back while he settled.

The wonderful sensation of the powerful man undone by her body, laying over her, totally spent, made tears spring to her eyes. She loved Valent. He had to understand how important it was to stay together. She had to make him agree to not allow her family or conventions to pull them apart.

He lifted and kissed her softly. "We should talk."

"Yes, we should." She trembled when he lifted from her, allowing the cool air to touch her skin. Valent must have noticed because he pulled her against him and drew the coverings over them.

"Now that your brother returns, I know you will be safe. Protected," Valent murmured and kissed her temple.

"I do not feel completely safe except when like this. In your arms." Ariana kissed his chest. "Do not leave me, ever."

His broad chest expanded when he took a deep breath. "You know it is not possible."

Would he not fight for them, at least? Ariana tilted her head back to look at him. His gaze was on the ceiling. "What do you plan to do, Valent?"

"I have to leave. I cannot remain and watch you marry another." His jaw clenched. "It would be too difficult for me to know you will lay with someone other than me."

"What about me? I do not wish to remain here without you. I can go with you." Desperation began weaving a heavy net around her body and her heart thudded against her breast. "Please, Valent. Take me."

"I will not. Without a solid place to go and without a name to claim, what kind of life can I offer you?"

"You do have a name..." Ariana stopped when he glared at her. "If you chose it. You can take your birth name."

He did not reply, only frowned. The walls began to form and she lifted to look down at him. "Valent, I love you. Understand me. I refuse to remain behind."

The widening of his eyes was followed by him sitting up. He took her by the shoulders and stared into her eyes. "Do not say that."

"What do you mean? 'Tis the truth. I know what I feel." Ariana clutched his arm. "Surely you care for me if you leave only to not see me remarried."

He nodded relenting. "Aye, I do. That is why I will not take you with me."

"Stubborn man, why must it be your way? Will you at least try to hear what I am saying?" The determination of his expression scared her and she slid closer to him. But Valent slid to the edge of the bed and stood.

He moved about the room completely nude and she devoured the sight of him. His tussled hair fell to broad shoulders giving him a dangerous look. He stood by the hearth and looked to her. "There is nothing you can say to change my mind. As much as I want you with me, I also know how hard my life will be until I find someone who will hire me."

"I have jewels. We could sell them and have gold for whatever we need. It will be a start." Ariana got up from the bed and lifted her coats where she and Lily had sewn jewels into the lining when the McKenzies attacked. "Look, they are ready. I am packed."

Without speaking, he began gathering his clothes and pulled them on. She watched him, not sure what else could be said. If he would not fight for her and gave up so easily, then perhaps his feelings were not as strong. Ariana pulled on her robe and stood idly by watching his jerky movements. "When do you plan to leave?"

Valent looked into her eyes. His lips pressed together in thought. He moved closer and pulled her into his arms. His strength seeped into her and she turned her head and placed it against his solid chest. They remained as such for a long time until he kissed the top of her head. "I will wait until you brother arrives."

"Will you consider us leaving before he arrives?" She looked up at him and lost her breath at his beauty. His gaze was warm, his lips turned up. "If I am stubborn, you are my match in that."

A flicker of hope lightened her heart. "Please, Valent, think on it hard. Take me."

"All right. Aye, I will consider it. I promise." Valent kissed her and stepped away from her. "Sleep well."

Chapter 12

"What are your orders, Laird?" Niven asked Steaphan at dinner the next day. They'd arrived to his keep to find it fortified without incident. "I await news. So far, the scout has not returned. If he does not return by nightfall, I will assume he was killed by the McLeods."

"Aye," Niven was pensive. "It could come to be that the McLeods, however, decide not to fight back. Unless they are joined by others, it would be impossible to beat us."

"Do not be so arrogant in our numbers, Niven," Steaphan told him, looking to the men who ate with gusto, but refrained from drinking too much ale. "Small numbers can sometime win in battle with cunning."

A man walked in from the outdoors. He wore a cape of furs and, from the look of him, had just arrived after a long ride. It was the messenger he'd sent to his betrothed's clan. The young man came forward and waited to be acknowledged.

"What happens?" His mother finally deemed to make an appearance. Steaphan cursed under his breath knowing she'd be very upset at the news of his marriage.

They'd yet to speak, with so much other clan business to tend to. "What is it, young man?" she asked the messenger who looked from his mother to him.

Steaphan motioned for him to speak.

"Sire, Laird Grant takes great offense at you not keeping to the agreement to marry his daughter. He asks for restitution in the form of another groom."

"What is he talking about?" Steaphan's mother gripped his forearm. "Why would you not marry Genevieve Grant?"

The beginnings of a headache, which often happened at his mother's presence, edged into his temples. "We shall speak about it later, Mother." He looked to the messenger. "Eat and rest. I will send you back with a reply in two days."

"Aye, milord," the messenger responded. "There is something else I must inform you of."

"What is it?"

"A large group of McLeods travel from Skye according to another messenger I happened about."

"How many?"

"The man thought about one hundred and fifty, maybe a bit less."

"Go eat."

After a slight bow of his head, the messenger joined the other guards at a long, wooden table.

Steaphan ignored his mother's pointed looks and maintained a conversation with Niven who insisted they go on the offensive and attack the McLeods while they were tired from the travel.

"Not so tired. It's been almost ten days since we attacked. They didn't travel hard."

"What of the laird's brother?" Niven asked looking toward the guards. "He is still alive. Do you plan to release him?"

"Nay. I want to make an example of him. The people need to know they will be defended."

His mother nudged his arm. "Steaphan, we must speak at once."

When he met her blue gaze, he was reminded of his brother. Unlike her, he and his brother had gray eyes closer to his father's. But they'd inherited her nose and full lips. His mother's brow furrowed. "What are you thinking?"

It was not the time to tell her about his brother. She never spoke of him, whether due to pain of the memory or because she wasn't concerned, he didn't know.

"I married Fiona McLeod," he told her bluntly, knowing it was the best way to speak to the harsh woman. "The McLeod suggested it to keep from having to join in any battle against us."

She paled, nostrils flaring. "How could you do such a thing? They are a weak clan, unimportant. To turn your nose at the Grant, an imposing and strong clan is madness." His mother let out a huff. "Annul it at once. Send a messenger to inform the McLeod it was a mistake."

"The marriage was consummated before witnesses," he told her flatly. "It cannot be undone."

She drummed her fingers on the wooden tabletop impatiently. "There is always a way to undo something rash."

"It is done." He slammed both palms on the table and stood. "I bid you goodnight, Mother."

She did not respond, her gaze forward, lips pressed into a straight line.

"And do not do anything. I will ensure things with the Grant are taken care of." He looked to his head guardsman. "Come, Niven, I must discuss something with you in private."

Once inside his large study, he paced the room. "I don't trust my mother. She'll try to do something. Have one of the guards watch her."

Niven walked out to do his bidding and Steaphan turned to look at the fire in the hearth. Immediately, the picture of his wife came to mind. Her beautiful body; curves and plushness like he'd never experienced. The only regret he had about marrying her was that he could not plunder her body further at the moment. Another thing to hold against the damn McLeods. In order to keep Fiona safe, it was necessary for her to remain with her clan. Until the clashes between the McKenzies and McLeods subsided, she would be in danger at his home.

His lips curved at remembering how angry she'd been at his leaving. It could be that the fair lady already felt a tie with him. It was to his liking that she was fiery, with a strong personality.

She'd need to be strong in order to stand up against his manipulative mother.

"It's been done, Laird." Niven returned and poured two glasses of whiskey, handing him one. "What do you plan to do about the Grant?"

"Send a proxy." Steaphan drank the strong liquid waiting to speak until after the fiery path made its way down to his stomach. "I have just the person in mind."

Niven straightened, his eyes fixed on Steaphan's face. "Who could possibly go in your stead?"

"My brother."

Niven threw his head back and laughed. "I wish you luck in convincing him to do so."

"I don't plan to give him a choice. I will send men to take him and bring him here."

"And?"

"I have not figured out that part yet. Mayhap have

the Grant's men come for him. Convince Darach to start anew. Give me time to think on it."

"You are leaving much to probables." Niven rubbed his chin. "What you need is an incentive."

"Like?"

"I do not know, more than likely he has led a humble existence. Silver may convince him. There is the added complication of the McLeod lady. He seemed to be quite taken by her."

"I did find it interesting how he protected her, but it could have been his sense of duty. Send three men to see about bringing Darach home."

"Very well." Niven stood and looked down to him. "Meanwhile, I trust you will come up with a plan of sorts."

Just as Niven walked out, his mother stormed in. "Once again, I demand you annul the marriage with the McLeod lass. Nothing good can come of joining with her clan."

"We are strong and a force to be reckoned with on our own, Mother. We do not need alliances."

"Neither do we need enemies. Especially with the Grants, such a large clan." She settled into a chair. "Besides I cannot abide the thought of having any grandchildren with McLeod blood." She shuddered and looked to his hand. "Pour me some."

Steaphan did as she bid. "Mother, I ask that you allow me to make any decisions that affect the clan. To be at war with two clans, one to the north and another to the south, would mean constant vigilance. Now we don't have to be so worried of our northern border."

"What of the Grant? How do you plan to appease him?"

He wasn't ready to tell her about his brother. Yet he couldn't resist knowing her feelings of late. "If my brother would have survived, it would be easy. I would send Darach in my stead."

Nothing in her countenance changed. She drank from the glass and shook her head. "You speak nonsense. Darach is long dead. Therefore, hoping for him to suddenly appear is not a good plan."

As if without a care in the world, his mother leaned back and closed her eyes. "This whiskey is good. I am going to have to be the one to take care of this circumstance. Trust me to find a way to get rid of the McLeod lass without you having to be involved. It could be that you send for her and on her way here, she happens upon a mishap. Attacked by the McLeods of the south, of course."

He rubbed both hands down his face. Sometimes he hated his mother's penchant toward the dramatic. "No."

Chapter 13

Fiona walked down to the great room when the guard she once considered her love, blocked her path. She refused to think on his name, no longer deeming it important. It was interesting to her that, in looking at his face, her heart no longer skipped a beat. Neither did her stomach quiver in anticipation of his kisses.

"Lady Fiona, I wish a word with you," he told her while his gaze moved past her. "Please, forgive me for what you saw."

For days, she'd practiced what she'd tell him upon having this opportunity. Instead, she let out breath and cocked her head to the side. It didn't matter. "There is no need to speak of it. Although I find the choice of the location for your assignation in poor taste, your actions helped me accept my marriage to the McKenzie."

By his flinch, the words affected him and a small part of her was glad for it. He'd played with her feelings. Yes, he was older and more experienced and she barely a nineteen-year-old virgin, but that did not give him the right to toy with her emotions.

"You are well then?" He lifted his hand as if to touch hers but then lowered it.

Fiona lifted her chin and met his gaze. "Move aside and let me pass, please."

"If you ever need anything."

Why did some people not know when to stop speaking? Fiona's head snapped up to him. "If I need anything, I will ask my husband. Now please, step aside."

He moved, but only enough for her to slip by. When she passed, he touched the side of her face. "I do care for ye, fair lady."

Fiona didn't respond. Instead, she hurried to find the solace of her father's study. She needed peace and quiet away from the women in the keep. All the talk of her marriage and what she'd take when she moved to Claddaugh, how she'd act around her new husband, and what she planned to do first in her new home, was driving her mad.

Her husband had yet to come for her. From what she was told, he was going to battle, which meant there was a chance she'd be a widow before getting to know the man. So all this drivel about the move could all be a colossal waste of time. For some reason, the thought of her new husband perishing did not sit well with her. He was much too young to die. Yes, that was it, what bothered her.

She huffed in aggravation. The situation of remaining there in Mudduch did not do. It did not suit her in the least. Yet at the thought of leaving her home, sadness threatened to envelope her. It was all so aggravating.

"Ah, there you are, darling." Her mother stood in the middle of the great room with cook. Both looking to her with expectation, so she had to change course and go to them.

Her mother smiled brightly and motioned to the

high board. "What a perfect opportunity, it's time we discuss proper hosting. Your husband is laird, therefore, you must be prepared and know exactly where everyone should sit in the case of another laird visiting..."

Fiona sighed and looked towards her father's study. Her opportunity was past.

"...Munro is coming." She heard the name and realized visitors came. The Munros of all people. Fiona groaned at knowing the horrible little man would, once again, visit. At least this time she was married and the visiting laird would not bring up the unpleasant topic of her and his son, who resembled a toad, perhaps marrying.

"Mother, why is the Munro visiting? I thought he was ill and not able to travel."

"It appears he has made a full recovery and wants to hunt with your father."

Fiona frowned. "Now? There is the threat of battle. Would it not be dangerous?"

"Your father plans to keep it very small. It was too late to send word to him not to come." Her mother motioned to two long tables and then looked to the maids. "Join those two together. I would like the Munro's men to sit there."

Finally, after a long while, Fiona sat at a table drinking tea while her mother continued talking about what she needed to know.

"Mother, I have lived here, with you, my entire life. There is no need to go over the minor details of running a household. You have taught me well all these years."

A tear spilled down her mother's cheek and Fiona immediately felt horrible at realizing it was her mother's way of dealing with her impending departure. Fiona rounded the table and hugged her. "I will miss you, too, Mother."

"What happens here?" Her father and his guard entered the room. The younger man avoiding looking at them since both were crying now.

"Just aware that soon our little girl is leaving," her mother replied wiping her face. Nothing to fret about, dear."

It was touching to see her father blink rapidly at seeing them both cry. He cleared his throat. "Yes...well, is everything prepared for the Munro's visit?"

Her mother nodded and began to tell him when a messenger entered.

"Come forward," her father ordered the young man who seemed more cocky than nervous. No doubt, his first time as messenger. "Sire, my laird, Laird McKenzie sends word that he will come for Lady Fiona five days hence."

Her stomach flipped and Fiona grumbled under her breath. Her mother nudged her. The brute was coming for her, was he? Well, she'd not go. Make him wait until she was good and ready. "Tell your laird, I will come to him, instead, in a fortnight."

The messenger's eyes widened and looked to her father who went to the side board and poured himself some mead. "Go on, lad, get some rest. Eat and sleep here tonight and return with the message tomorrow."

Once the messenger left, her father looked to Fiona. "A man like Steaphan McKenzie does not like to be told what to do by his wife. I will not be surprised if he comes regardless and takes you back."

"We'll see about that." Fiona turned on her heel and headed for the stairs. Perhaps in her chamber she could find some peace.

"Lady Fiona. Do you require anything?" Her maid was placing linens by her washing basin. "I can bring you tea, if you wish."

"Mairi, does your husband boss you about?" The

young woman was not long married to one of her father's guardsmen. "Does he become cross if you tell him what to do?"

"Sometimes, milady. But my Firth is so slow about making up 'is mind I have to push 'im along sometimes."

"I can see that," Fiona replied. "What if he wanted you to go somewhere and you said no?"

Mairi thought for a moment. "He would make me do it anyway. Men are that way, milady, not much for allowing us to have our way. Of course, there are certain things we can do to keep them from doing so, but we canna let them know it."

Fiona's eyes went wide and she went to sit, pulling her maid to the opposite chair. "Tell me."

"I'm not so sure it's proper..." the maid looked to the door. "Yer mother may not agree."

"Oh poo. Just tell me." Fiona motioned with her hands for the maid to speak.

"Verra well then, milady. This is what my own mother told me and I find it to be true. Ye see, men are simple creatures. They only want to be strong and brave. They dunna understand feelings or notions and such. But most will do anything and agree to much if they are...well, you know...excited."

"Excited about what?" Fiona asked leaning forward. "Tell me."

"Bedding a woman."

"Oh." Fiona frowned. That would not help her keep Steaphan from coming so soon for her. "What about if said man is far away?"

"Not much ye can do then." Mairi smiled at her. "Yer husband will come for ye soon. He is quite bonnie, is he not? Ye willna have a problem when tryin' to divert 'is attention." Mairi giggled and covered her mouth. "Forgive me for speaking so freely, milady."

"Yes, quite bonnie the devil is." Fiona smiled and then huffed. What was she saying? "But he is a McKenzie."

Still smiling, the maid stood and gathered her basket. "I will see about your tea then."

"No, please, Mairi. I wish to just rest for a bit. I will be down for the evening meal and do not require assistance tonight. Go spend time with Firth."

"Thank you, milady." Mairi hurried out the door closing it softly behind her.

"Bonnie, indeed," Fiona huffed and began to pace. "A pretty devil, he is." A long sigh escaped. Her husband was a very handsome man.

Chapter 14

From atop the keep, Ariana could see the large contingent of McLeods. Although not possible to see individual faces, she searched the lines of horsemen for her brother. "I cannot see Ceardac, can you?" She narrowed her eyes in an attempt to see better.

Lily stood next to her, her hand over her eyes to shade them from the sun. "No, I am trying, we should be able to see him soon, milady. Just wait a few moments." The young woman trembled and, once again, Ariana wondered if Lily cared more for Ceardac than she let on.

Ariana ventured to ask, thinking it would catch her off guard. "What do you feel for my brother?"

It was easy to see the question affected Lily by the blanching of her face. When she exhaled slowly, Ariana knew she prepared to lie. "I care for him, of course. I have known him since we were children. You cannot question my loyalty to your family?"

Somehow, she managed to keep from smiling at Lily's attempt to distract her by the last comment. "Of course, I do not. I would never. It is just that it would be nice to have something exciting, such as a romance in this house, after all the devastation."

Lily's widened eyes met hers. "Ro...romance? That is not possible. Not between him and me."

"Of course, it is. Oh look, they are closer." Ariana watched with a smirk when an expression of anticipation came over Lily as she turned to look. "I would love it if we became family," she told Lily, who pretended not to hear her.

The distraction was gone when the guardsmen appeared on the level beneath her. Valent and nine other archers formed a line, bows held up. Although it was evident the men approaching were friend and not foe, it was best to be safe.

It had been two days since he'd left her bed and had avoided her since. It was understandable to a point. After all, with the rest of the clan coming, Valent would not risk their relationship being found out.

Yet, her heart was broken. His lack of coming to her with a plan meant that, in all probability, he'd not take her when leaving. That he still remained puzzled her. Yet he had affirmed he'd not go until assuring she was well defended. His oath to the McLeod was what kept him here yet.

As if sensing her regard, he turned to look up at her. His face without expression, they locked gazes for a long moment before he turned away. He left the line of archers when a guard came for him and, together, they went to the courtyard.

She let out a long breath of frustration. Social standing kept so many from finding happiness. Unaware Ariana watched, Lily leaned forward from the waist, her right hand over her breast as her gaze scanned the approaching McLeods. There was no doubt. Her friend was in love with Ceardac.

Ariana made an oath. If she and Valent were not to be, then she'd do what she could to ensure Ceardac and

Lily were able to live out their romance. Of course, first she had to find out how her brother felt.

She'd try one last time to speak to Valent and give him the opportunity to fight for their love. Yes, perhaps an unflattering, desperate move, but not trying would be as terrible in her opinion.

Finally, the men came to a stop. A line of three men approached; Ceardac, the McLeod of Skye and another younger man whom she recognized as the younger McLeod. Just behind them, a line of six warriors maintained vigil.

Murray and Valent rode to meet them. The men spoke for a few moments before Ceardac looked up to Ariana and Lily. He lifted a hand up in greeting. Immediately, tears fell from her eyes at the news he was receiving. One brother dead and the other captured and, in all probability, dead as well.

It was comforting to know her mother was well and had remained behind. Although Ariana missed her, it was best not to have her here. It would be one more thing to worry about if the McKenzies returned.

"They speak for a long time," Lily said frowning. "Why are they not coming into the courtyard?"

"I am not sure," Ariana replied stretching forward. "Come, let us go down to meet them once they do enter." The women hurried down the many stairs.

Finally, Ceardac and several McLeods entered the courtyard leaving the rest of the men to set up camp. The guards were immediately dispatched to settle the horses, while Ceardac and two men dismounted. Ariana flew into her brother's arms, thankful for his strong embrace. "You are well. Thank God." She cupped his face with both hands and looked up at him, unable to stop the tears.

Affected as well, by the welling of his eyes, he kissed her forehead. "Aye. I am well enough. Our mother sends her love and insists I send you to her immediately."

The statement set her aback. She'd not considered leaving. "There is much we need to discuss."

"I need to speak with the guardsmen," he replied looking to Murray and Valent. "We must discuss the best way to deal with the current situation. Once all is settled, then we can talk." He was already moving away.

Ariana wanted to kick him. Of course, he'd consider the opinion of men above hers. Instead of arguing as everyone watched them, even Lily who stood near her, Ariana said, "Lily and I have been worried about you."

Her statement affected Ceardac. He stiffened slightly and looked to Lily. "Lily. I am grateful you and my sister are well."

"And she is no longer my maid," Ariana announced, noting his puzzles expression. "Lily is my dearest friend and after all we've been through, she is now a friend of the family and no longer in servitude to me."

Ceardac nodded, his somber gaze flitting between she and Lily. "I agree, sister."

It wasn't until the evening meal that Ceardac and all the men were finally gathered indoors. Ariana had grown tired of waiting to speak to her brother and her mood edged more toward anger than gladness at having one of her brother home safe. They needed to speak. She had to ensure they left immediately to rescue Beathan. The longer they dallied, the more likely her youngest brother was killed. It was of utmost importance she get across to him not to go to battle.

Ceardac settled next to her, his large frame at once making her feel secure. "I am glad to see you faring well, sister." He smiled at her, taking some of the annoyance away. "Be assured that we will leave soon for the McKenzie lands. We need the men to rest. It won't do to show up tired from travel and lose the fight before it begins."

"Each moment that we wait is another moment Beathan could be dead." Tears sprung to her eyes. "If he isn't already."

His arm encircled her shoulders. "I fear we go to avenge his death, sister. Although I mourn for him already, I cannot help but feel angry that he brought all this upon our people."

It was the truth, yet she wondered how much more tragedy would be brought on them if they went at this juncture if Beathan was already dead. Too entwined in her emotions for Valent, she'd pushed any thoughts of what Beathan went through away. It was the only way she could sustain and not crumble at all the loss. "If Beathan is dead, then do not go. It will not do for more men to die because of all this." She looked across the room at the men's faces, some familiar, some not. "Perhaps it is time to let it rest. It is madness to continue to risk the lives of our people for all of this. Please, Ceardac, reconsider going to battle."

The McLeod of Skye sat on the opposite side of Ceardac, his son next to him. He looked to her. "Lass, ye've grown since I last saw you about fifteen years past." His keen green eyes met hers. "Have you met me son, Ross?"

"Welcome to you both," Ariana replied making eye contact with the men. Ross's clear green eyes scanned her face for a moment before he gave her a brief nod. He looked back to his plate and continued eating. The handsome man had dismissed her.

Ceardac spoke to the McLeod. "My sister advises we

do not more forward, but to leave things as they are. What do you think?"

It was surprising to her the men actually discussed her suggestion. Ariana leaned forward to hear what the McLeod would say.

"And not retaliate for what they did? They've killed forty of your men. They've taken your brother. I am sure it will be taken as a sign of weakness to not attempt to rescue your brother."

"To what end?" Ariana could not help but interrupt. "As soon as you appear, they will kill Beathan. If he isn't already dead."

The McLeod leaned forward on his elbow, his gaze now hard meeting hers. "Lass, yer brother is dead or will be soon, in that you are correct. They will not allow him to live for what he did. That is not what matters at this point."

She knew it, of course. Yet hearing it sent a searing pain into her chest. All the days of pushing the thought away came back tenfold. Ariana got to her feet. "I bid you goodnight. I do not feel well." Her legs wobbled as she allowed Lily to assist her away from the great room. Just before leaving the room, she scanned the warriors' table and found the gray gaze on her. Valent's eyes were flat upon locking with hers. Yet it gave her strength to continue on.

Chapter 15

The call to the laird's high board did not surprise Valent. He'd wondered why it had taken so long for Ceardac to ask to speak to him about the McKenzie. Murray stood before the new laird as well as another archer. The men from the tables looked on with interest.

"You are the McKenzie's twin brother, I am told." Ceardac's words were more a statement than a question, so Valent remained silent. "Were you aware?"

"Nay." Valent looked to the new laird feeling a fleeting camaraderie. He'd grown up with Ceardac. That he asked the question was more for the sake of the others present. "I did not know until I came face to face with him."

The McLeod of Skye pinned him with a glare. "And you did not go with him? Did he not offer you an opportunity to go with them? To rejoin your clan?"

Valent inhaled deeply to keep from snapping. "They are not my clan."

Murray interrupted. "If I may intercede. The McKenzie did offer Valent to go with them and he refused."

"How—" the McLeod of Skye started but was interrupted by Ceardac.

"Valent was a foundling. He came to be with us since about three years of age. No one ever came searching for him, that I am aware."

"And yet, it is known blood calls to blood. Can he be trusted to kill his own kin in battle now that he knows? I say he stays behind." The McLeod frowned at him. "I do not trust him in battle against his own."

"I do." Ceardac surprised Valent. Of the three brothers, he'd always been the one he respected the most.

"What do you say, boy?" the McLeod asked.

"I am thirty years of age. Not a boy. I will do as the McLeod wishes." He looked to Ceardac whose eyes widened at being acknowledged as that. A reminder that his eldest brother was gone and he now stood as the laird over the keep.

"You will remain here. Protect the keep, my sister, and...Lily, with twenty men," Ceardac told him his eyes scanning his face. "Is it true you are identical in features to the McKenzie?"

Valent nodded. "Aye." He dared to question the man. "Were you not aware? I am convinced yer father and brother knew, had seen him up close."

Ceardac's brows furrowed. "Nay, I was not aware. As an archer, like you, I remained too far behind to make out the likeness of him."

Valent took Ceardac at his word. The man had no reason to lie. "Now, you will face him and know."

"It would be interesting to kill the man, ye think?" the McLeod of Skye asked Ceardac.

"Aye, it would be." Ceardac studied Valent's face.

The thought of Steaphan being killed jolted him. Although Valent had but a passing acquaintance with his brother, the thought of Steaphan dead was confusing. He maintained a neutral expression and waited to be dismissed.

It was curious that, once again, he was forced to remain at the keep, to ensure Ariana's safety. The last thing he wanted was to stay there and have another opportunity to be near her. Each time made it harder to give her up, to accept they could never be.

The clan going to battle meant he would have the perfect opportunity to leave. The twenty would be good protection. If the McLeod left ten archers, his departure would not make much of a difference.

Just outside the great room in the corridor, Valent stopped and leaned against the wall. Emotions surged through him. On one hand, thoughts of his newly found brother dying and then, on the other hand, the idea that he had to decide when would be the best time to go from the McLeod keep.

He'd already planned to go as far as possible. He'd take only his meager belongings, his dog and horse. One day, he'd start a new life far away, perhaps even marry and have children and this entire portion of his life would be left to be forgotten. The lowlands were a good place to begin anew.

"Valent?" The soft touch on his shoulder was accompanied by the scent of a light fragrance. He closed his eyes for a moment to steel his reaction to her. "You will stay behind. It will give us an opportunity to escape together."

Ariana's beseeching expression tore at him. Her beautiful eyes taking in his face, searching for what he thought.

"You look beautiful today." It was not a reply, but the truth. "If only I could show you how you affect me right now."

Her gaze traveled to between his legs and her lips curved just a bit. "You are avoiding my request."

She was a smart lass, never shirked from the truth.

Valent nodded. "Aye, I am. It is difficult for me to even consider taking you with me. As I told you before, I have nothing to offer you, Ariana. Your life would change drastically and although at first you would not, after sometime, you'd resent it. You should go to your chambers. It would not be a good thing for someone to happen upon us."

The arch of her brow was a sign she was not happy at his words. "Have you considered waiting for all of this to end and for us to approach my brother together? We can ask for his permission to marry. Or it could just be you do not care for me as I do you. Tell me the truth, Valent. I would rather know that I am but making a fool of myself by coming after you."

Her words tore through him. The truth of how many differences stood between them was lost on her at the moment. She remained blinded by romantic notions of what could be. Not seeing the stark truth of what their life would truly be.

"You are not a fool. It is hard for me to fathom that you find me worthy of your love. I do care for you, Lady Ariana. But I am not naïve to the fact that you and I are too different."

She slid her hands flat against his chest, her fingers curling on the fabric of his tunic. When Ariana lifted her mouth in offering there was nothing that could pull him away. He took her tender lips with hunger, teasing the bottom lip with his tongue before delving between them. With a soft moan, she fell against the wall pulling him to her.

The softness of her curves enticed him, called for him to give her everything she asked. The feel of her sent every part of his body to harden in expectation. He pushed his erection into her, the friction of their clothing bringing only a bit of release. Valent reached under her skirts and skidded his fingers up her leg to her thigh before delving between her legs. Ariana suckled and nipped at his throat urging him to continue his exploration, her hand moving to caress his hardness.

When her fingers curled around his shaft, Valent bucked into her hand, needing more. She moved her hand up and down the length until he was sure he'd spill.

Ariana shifted her hips forward into his hand and Valent found the center of her folds and slid a fingertip down the center, flicking it up and down until she moaned and trembled as she climaxed, the nails of her left hand digging into his hip.

She released his hard member and fell against him. "I want to be with you, Valent. Come to my bed tonight."

There was nothing he wanted more at the moment. A part of him wished he could throw caution to the wind and take her then and there and go as far away as possible.

Valent cupped her face and lifted it to his, ensuring to keep the kiss from becoming too arduous. They'd taken enough of a risk already. "I cannot. It is too dangerous. Goodnight, Ariana."

"Valent?" she started, but he placed his finger over her lips.

"I do love you, Ariana."

When she walked away, Valent fell against the wall, his breathing harsh when realizing it would be best to avoid her as much as possible. It would not do for someone to go to the new laird about their relationship. He refused to put yet another burden on the lovely Ariana.

There was too much already on her shoulders.

Perhaps it was true she loved him. Her words

sounded sincere. However, no matter how much he wished it so, it couldn't be. No matter how hard they fought, the road ahead was filled with heartache for them both.

Steaphan's mother stiffened when he entered the study. From the set of her lips, she was prepared to fight him about his new wife. She would try to convince him to annul the marriage by the way she studied the family crest over the hearth, she'd bring up every instance of the purity of the McKenzie clan she could.

Lorna McKenzie rarely exposed her softer side. If there was one. The only time Steaphan remembered his mother ever crying was when his father died. That he recalled, although no more than three years of age, she'd not cried when Darach was taken.

"Mother, you wanted a word with me?" He poured two glasses of whiskey and placed one on a table for her while sitting down with his. "Are you unwell?"

Her keen eyes met his. "I wish to discuss the matter of your marriage to that McLeod creature. After having time to consider and pondering on what you've done, I am sure you cannot continue to be set on remaining tied to a McLeod."

Actually, he had and, each time, his memory of the fair Fiona made him want to return with haste to collect his wife.

"I made an oath and stood before a clergyman when speaking vows to her. So yes, I do plan to remain married to Fiona McLeod, now McKenzie." He sipped, enjoying the heated trail the whiskey left as it traveled down his throat. "There are more important matters to deal with at the moment than my marriage."

She pursed her lips and let out an aggravated breath.

When she opened her mouth to speak, Steaphan stopped her. "I forbid you from interfering or daring to do anything that will harm my wife. Is that understood?"

Her eyes widened slightly. "Do you actually care for her?"

Of course, he didn't. True, he was anxious to see her again. To lay with her and make love until his body could not move. But care, no. It was too soon to feel more than lust. "Of course, I do. She is my wife."

She lifted the glass and studied the liquid. "Nothing good can come of this, Steaphan. It was a foolish, rash decision."

"There is a more pressing topic I must discuss with you," Steaphan told her, changing the subject.

"Whatever could be of more importance than this..." she waved her hand in the air, "...this situation, son? We must at once settle things with the Grant, lest you have a second clan wanting to war."

It was hard at times to keep from losing his temper. It was his right to do as he wished. As laird of Clan McKenzie, he didn't need her agreement to do anything. It was out of respect for her and his deceased father that he gave her consideration. Although truth be told, his patience was running very low.

"Listen to me, Mother." He locked gazes with his mother who leaned back with an apprehensive expression. "I have located my twin brother."

Her mouth fell open and she took a shaky breath. "He is alive, then?"

"Aye. He is alive and very near."

It struck him as interesting when she scanned the room as if formulating her next question. "Did you speak to him?"

"Only briefly. Darach calls himself Valent. He was raised as a foundling by the McLeods."

If possible, her eyes grew rounder and her mouth fell open. "Where is he now?"

"With the McLeods of the south. The clan we are embattled with. He is an archer."

Her hand shook when she brought the whiskey to her mouth. "How can it be? All these years so close."

"I am sending men to capture him and bring him here."

His mother's eyes snapped to his. "No. He is not a McKenzie, but a McLeod. Raised by them, he must hate us. To bring him into the fold now will only open this household to danger. He will be but a McLeod in our midst."

Steaphan leaned forward and studied her. "Do you not want to speak to him, Mother? Meet him and let him know we did not throw him away, but that he was snatched from your arms?"

Lorna McKenzie straightened and looked to him, a look of disdain upon her face. "It was from your hand he was snatched. It is true, a tragedy it was. That your brother was taken from me was horrific at the time. Yet with time, I accepted it was meant to be. A seer once told me I would lose half of one. There is nothing to be repaired now. He is not my son, but a McLeod foundling."

She stood and went to the doorway. "Leave things as they are, Steaphan. Your priority should be to ensure this war between the clans be settled with as little bloodshed as possible and to make amends to the Grant regarding the marriage. Your brother should remain where he is. He belongs there now." Her gaze held his for a long moment. "I am not sure you will ever be happy with a McLeod for a wife, but I tell you this. The last thing you need is your brother here to usurp you. Darach was born almost an hour before you, therefore, by birthright, he is who should be Laird McKenzie."

"How many are aware of this?" Steaphan wasn't sure if he believed her or not. Her penchant for using words to get her way never ceased to astound him. She'd used this to convince him not to bring Darach back. For whatever reason, his mother did not want his brother to return home.

"It was announced at the birthing, of course. Your father made the announcement right after you were both born. So for the first three years of your lives, everyone knew Darach would inherit your father's place." She crossed her arms. "You don't deserve to lose your place after all this time. Think on it, son, you know everyone, have lived here your entire life."

"Is it my brother's fault that he was taken? Did he have a choice in losing everything? You have not even asked how he looks, or if he was hurt. I wonder sometimes what really happened the night my brother was taken. Your reaction is quite astounding."

What was left of her color drained from her face and she gripped the doorway. "Whatever you think of me, I did not willingly give up my child. If I speak so now, it is because I have accepted that Darach is gone forever. This man who was born Darach is now Valent McLeod. He cares naught for us. Would probably kill you if you tried to kill a McLeod in his presence. Did he not kill some of our men?"

It was a useless conversation. Steaphan was sorry he'd told her about his brother. His mother didn't care to know about her own son. He, on the other hand, very much wanted to know his brother, speak to him and find out what his life was like.

"Niven!" he called for his guard, who stood outside the door. The guard entered and looked to Lorna who remained in the room. "When do the men leave for the south?"

"They have already, Laird," Niven replied sliding a glance at Steaphan's mother.

Lorna glared at Niven then looked to Steaphan. "Trust me in this. For once, listen to my counsel. Leave things as they are, son. Nothing can be done to return that boy to us."

It was late when Steaphan finally went to his chamber. He lay in the bed and thought of Fiona. Did she think of him? Had she packed and prepared to come live with him in Gladdaugh? He turned to his side and stilled at hearing footsteps outside his door. With a dirk in hand he waited in the dark for whoever came.

"Laird?" It was Niven. "The McLeods are moving this way and will be on our lands at daybreak."

The morning fog barely lifted over the glen, enough to make out the lines of McLeods. Atop his horse, Steaphan looked to see that a McLeod who resembled his prisoner rode to the front of his men.

Ceardac McLeod, the second born son. He'd seen him once at the games, competed in a timber toss, which he'd won. Although Steaphan had never been close enough to the man to speak to him, he seemed to be very different than the other brothers by the way he interacted with the guards. Almost as an equal. If not for this clash, he would have considered getting to know the man better.

As things were, it would be years before the clans would ever consider charting into any kind of friendliness.

Steaphan scanned the lines of McLeod archers

behind the two ranks of warriors, but at the distance it was impossible to see if his brother was amongst them.

He lifted his sword, signaling for his men to hold steady and wait. The horses pawed at the ground and nickered, the only sounds as both sides studied the other. "McLeod!" Steaphan shouted and moved a few feet forward and the McLeod did the same. "Your men killed my men. We avenged. If you want to fight, we will fight. But if you withdraw, then we shall as well."

"You killed my eldest brother," Ceardac yelled back scanning his face. "Where is the other?"

Steaphan looked over his shoulder to where the young McLeod was held by two men. His head flopped forward, as he'd been beaten and not fed so he barely had the strength to even stand. "He is here. Alive. But not for long."

"Allow him to come forth. Let him go!" Ceardac called out. "We withdraw when he gets to me safely."

"Is that your only offer? I decline," Steaphan replied. "However, I will exchange him for my brother."

"You do not have a brother with us."

Steaphan moved back to where his first line stood and motioned for the men to release the prisoner. The man stumbled until he was alongside Steaphan's horse. By the dazed look, the man would barely be able to walk a few more steps. Steaphan felt no sympathy for him.

With a swift swipe of Niven's sword, his first beheaded Beathan McLeod.

Ceardac released a battle cry and the McLeods rushed towards them.

"Hold!" Steaphan called, forcing his men to wait until they came closer. "Hold!"

When the McLeods were at ten feet he signaled his men forward.

The first lines clashed. The sounds of grunts and swords filled the air.

Soon the smell of blood was thick in the air. Steaphan rushed Ceardac who fought hard, his face raw with rage.

"McLeod!" Steaphan called getting his attention away from his men on the ground. "It is me you are angry with. Face me!"

The loud roar the man released was followed by two slashes of his sword, which Steaphan blocked and returned. Both fought until he cut Ceardac in the side. When the McLeod fell off the horse, Steaphan was forced to retreat as he was too deep into the ranks of the enemy and they could easily circle him.

Arrows rained over them and he held up his shield while moving backwards.

"Retreat!" an older man on the McLeod side called and both sides moved away from each other, grabbing whatever injured they could and dragging them away.

"You are bleeding," Niven scanned the area and kneeled next to a fallen man to check him for signs of life. "Need to see about binding it."

"Why did they call retreat? They were holding their own." Steaphan looked to where the McLeods had gone. "Strange, don't you think?"

His friend looked up at him and then his arm, which now began to throb. "Aye. However, I think he wanted to avoid the last of the brothers being killed. And I doubt he wanted to lose many of his own. They do not have a grudge with us."

"Is he alive?" Steaphan looked to the injured man.

"Aye." Niven motioned for him to dismount. "Help me with Barclay. He still lives."

Steaphan looked across the field. It looked like they'd

fared not too badly in spite of being outnumbered. The McLeods of Skye had no quarrel with them, so they'd fought with restraint. They only came to help their own clan. An attempt to rescue the dead man.

"Do you think the men you sent had enough time to get my brother?"

"Aye, they left two nights past. Probably got their eyes on him now."

As soon as his brother arrived, Steaphan planned to ensure he was confined and then go for Fiona. It was time for his wife to be with him.

The ride home was quiet, solemn. There was always the sad chore of giving the dead one's families the news. They'd have to visit about ten houses before finally going to the keep. The injured would be looked after. The rest who fought would come to the keep and celebrate. It was tradition to drink and eat, appreciate the gift of life.

"I think things are going to be quiet now between the clans." Niven kept his eyes on Barclay who was in the cart next to them. "They retreated and we will not attack again."

"Aye. All is fine for now."

Niven swallowed. "I know this is not my concern. But I agree with yer mother. The archer is not truly your brother. Not anymore. He is a McLeod. Raised by them and lived his entire life with the clan. He will not simply change because you bring him home. Given the chance, he will escape and return to McLeod lands. Why bring him if he will only be held captive?"

He'd thought the same thing, considered that his brother would not be agreeable to being captured and brought to his birth home. But if there was just a chance Darach would want to remain, Steaphan was willing to take it. "He deserves to know where he comes from.

Where his true home is. See firsthand what his life could be again if he chooses."

"And what if he asks about being taken as a child? Questions why your parents didn't search for him? What will you say? Yer mother has never told anyone what happened that day."

"Her handmaid did. Part of it anyway. And my father did send out search parties. Many looked for Darach. Although, I find it puzzling they did not go to the McLeod lands." Steaphan did not say anything else. Instead, he urged his mount to a faster trot.

Chapter 16

"I am sorry, Lily, what did you say?" Ariana looked to Lily who had been rattling nonstop since the men left the night before. When nervous, she tended to talk on and on about different subjects. Although it would unnerve most, to Ariana it was a familiar thing that soothed her.

"I said the guards are lining up, they must have spotted riders coming." Lily ran to the window and peered out. "Should we go up to the roof and look?"

Ariana let out a frustrated breath. "The guardsmen will not allow it. They will insist it is dangerous."

"We should go anyway." Lily surprised her with her new found feistiness. "The lot of them will be too busy guarding to notice us."

"True. Very well, I agree." Ariana went to the corner of her room and grabbed her bow and quiver. "Let us go." They rushed out of the room, down the hallway and to the stairs that led to the roof.

It was clear now that most of the morning misting had lifted. Both shaded their eyes ignoring the young lookouts' glares at them. Finally, one gathered the courage to approach her. "Milady, you cannot be out here. 'Tis too dangerous."

"I will only remain long enough to see if my brother returns. Once I recognize him, Lily and I will return to my chambers."

She turned and once again scanned the distance. "Where are they?"

"There." The young man pointed and she followed to where he looked.

"Oh, I see them. It's them," Lily called out. "Our men." She leaned forward at the waist and attempted to get a better look.

The young guard finally gave up that she'd return into the keep and moved away.

They were too far yet to see if her brothers returned so Ariana looked down to where the guards and archers were lined up. She looked from one end to the other and back again. Valent was not among them. Impossible

She looked back to the lookout. "Did the archer Valent go with them to battle?"

"Nay, milady. He remained." The boy looked down to the archers. "Down there with the rest of them."

Ariana remained quiet. Valent was not there. She was sure of it. If he wasn't lined up to defend the keep, it could only mean one thing. He'd left. Gone and had not taken her.

"I think I see the Laird." Lily got her attention. "Look!" she cried out while pointing towards the mass of men that come closer.

The archers lowered their bows and the warriors sheathed their swords at recognizing the riders. Some hurried down to the courtyard to meet the men. Only a few remaining to keep guard.

"Come, Lily, let us greet my brother." Beathan was not among the riders. She hoped he was in one of the carts bringing home the wounded.

The courtyard was full of people hurrying to gather

the injured and house the horses. Men rushed from one spot to another helping unload the carts. Ariana ran to one cart, the injured man sat up and attempted to move only to groan and hold his side. "Lay back and allow them to assist you." She patted his shoulder and went to the other side of the cart to see who lay there. It was another man. Not Beathan.

"Ariana, go inside." Ceardac's stern command did not bode well. She swung around to look at him only to find he'd dismounted and stood beside her, his hand on her elbow. "Inside, now." He wrapped his other arm around his midsection.

"Are you injured?"

"Aye, cut, but it's been bound, nothing fatal." He managed a shrug.

"Where's Beathan?" She tried to get free of his grasp. "I want to see him."

"He is dead." Ceardac guided her to the great room. "They beheaded him."

Her knees buckled. If it was not for her brother's hold, she would have crumpled to the ground. "Oh God, no. It is too much to bear."

"You should lie down," Ceardac told her and grimaced. She couldn't rest. He needed to be looked after. Her last brother had to recover and she'd see to it.

Once inside the great room, she and Lily insisted Ceardac lay upon a long table so they could administer to his wounds. Once the layers of binding were removed, the angry gash made Ariana's already fragile nerves break and she was not able to stop the tears.

Ceardac's gaze locked to her face. "Lily, can tend to my wounds. Why don't you rest?"

"No," she insisted. "I need to help. This is not the time for sensibilities." Ariana took a cloth and dipped it into the water, then gently cleansed the wound, while

Lily cut more strips and washed off the dirt from Ceardac's face. It was obvious from the looks they exchanged. There was definitely an attraction between them. Ariana was thankful he'd survived. Even if Ceardac didn't marry Lily, it was nice they had this moment without barriers between them.

"Did he suffer?" Ariana had to ask, needed to know the circumstances of Beathan's death. "Did you speak to him?"

Pain reflected from Ceardac's eyes understanding she spoke of Beathan. "Nay, it was swift. I did not speak to him."

"Who did it?"

"The McKenzie's first."

She didn't try to stop the blackness that closed in around her.

"Lady Ariana, will you wake for me please?" The voice permeated the heavenly fog enveloping her and she fought to ignore its pull to the harshness of reality. There in the abyss everything was perfect. No thoughts, only space. The reality of her world was not something she was ready to face again. Here in the swirls of mist, she could float and ignore everything.

"Come now. You can hear me." It was one of the older maids. She recognized the voice. "Ye must eat, milady. Drink something."

She batted at the hand that attempted to pull her head up. "No."

"It's been two days and everyone is worried," the woman persisted.

Ariana pried her eyes open. The room was dim, the window covered with a black cloth of mourning. Beathan. Her younger, brash, handsome brother was dead. If only he'd not goaded the McKenzies with such senseless killings. Tears slipped down her cheeks. "Where is my brother?" She spoke of Beathan, but the maid assumed it was Ceardac she asked about.

"He is probably still abed, milady. It is very early in the morning yet."

"Beathan?"

The maid ignored her question. Instead, she brought the rim of a cup to Ariana's lips. "Drink this. It will help you recover your strength." The broth was flavorful and she drank it down, finding herself hungry.

Once she was propped up on the bed, she looked to the older woman. "Is there any other news?"

"No, milady. Everyone is well, even the guardsman who was hurt quite badly is healing after no one expected him to."

"Lily?"

The maid turned away, but not before Ariana caught the hint of a smile. "Miss Lily will be here to see you shortly. She has been so worried about you."

"I didn't want to wake up," Ariana confessed. "It was wonderful to escape all this." She brush tears away with the back of her hand.

The woman patted her hand. "True, milady, there has been much loss. You, along with many of our clan, have lost loved ones. We should be thankful it seems to be over. The McKenzie sent a messenger to propose a truce between the clans and yer brother accepted it."

It was good news, indeed. Since the woman had not made mention of an archer missing, she hoped Valent remained in the keep. Perhaps he'd not lined up with the others the morning the men returned. For some reason had remained below with the other guard.

"What of my Beathan's burial? Has it been done?"

"Aye, milady. We can go visit the gravesite once you gather your strength."

Ariana smiled at the woman who'd served her family for many years. "I would appreciate that, Clara. Thank you."

The rest of the morning, she remained in her chambers, finally leaving the bed to sit in a chair by the hearth. Each time she considered stepping out, the idea that Valent was gone stopped her.

Lily entered the room. She was flushed and looked pretty as she settled onto the chair opposite her. "I am so happy you are awake." She leaned forward and her lips brushed Ariana's cheek. "It was horrible when you didn't wake. Although everyone said you would recover, I couldn't help the thought that I would lose you as well." Her eyes misted and Ariana smiled at her.

"You fret too much, dear friend."

"It is warranted, I believe." Lily looked to the fire. "There is so much I want to tell you. Unless you heard me when I talked the last two days."

Knowing how Lily would prattle on when upset, Ariana wondered what all her friend had shared. "I did not hear you, so you will have to tell me again."

Lily let out a breath. She seemed to be relieved at Ariana's statement. "Yes, well, first of all, your archer, Valent. He is gone."

A gasp escaped and Ariana's mouth fell open. "Does Ceardac know?"

"Not yet. He has been...preoccupied. The guards have all gone to the village to see about their families and with all that, there were only a few at the evening meal the last two days. Murray himself has gone to see about the village to help with any rebuilding and such."

"Are you sure he has gone, Lily?"

"Aye. I even stole away and went to his cottage. No one has been there in a long time by the looks of it."

Ariana let out a long breath. "I expected he would leave. When Ceardac finds out Valent is gone, he will assume he's returned to the McKenzies."

"If he is with his family, then it is a good thing," Lily pronounced and then flinched. "Forgive me, I misspoke. I know you hoped for him to take you, but if he went to his family it would not do to take you along." Lily covered her mouth with her hand and let out a sigh. "I am so stupid to bring all of this up. You have such deep feelings for him."

"I am the fool for it. It is more than obvious he did not feel the same toward me."

"Nonsense. He cares for you, it was easy to see by the way he followed yer every move. His eyes warmed when lighting upon yer face. Valent loves you; that is why he left."

Lily's words made her feel somewhat better, but when remembering their last conversation, a part of her felt he took the easy route. He'd purposely set her passions loose to avoid her questions.

Valent did not love her. He was not willing to confront her brother and stand up for their love. She'd been willing to leave everything behind and he left without a word.

"Are the McLeods of Skye still here?"

"The older McLeod left yesterday." Lily looked away from her and Ariana knew something else was on her mind. "Ariana...the younger McLeod remains. He is awaiting your recovery."

"Why would he do that?"

"The McLeod asked Ceardac for his son to be handfasted with you." Lily bit her bottom lip and released it. "Yer brother accepted."

"What?" She sat straight up and then fell back onto the chair when the room swayed. "I will speak with Ceardac. How dare he make such a decision without speaking to me?"

Hours later, Ceardac sat across from her in a chair in the study. The clenching of his jaw was the only sign that he was aggravated by her questions. "As your brother and laird, I have every right to decide about your future. You should marry and start a family. Ross McLeod will be a good husband to you, sister." He didn't allow for an argument, holding his hand up when she opened her mouth to protest. "Do not think I am not aware of your interest in the archer. I know something happened between the two of you. I have not said anything, allowing you some leeway with all that has happened. But do not mistake that, dear sister, for allowing you to not do as you are told. The handfast ceremony will be tomorrow. You will leave with Ross two days hence."

There was a knock to the door and Ceardac stood, going to speak to whoever was there. When Ross McLeod entered, she kept her eyes downcast, not wanting to look at him, not now that he was to be her husband. It mattered not to either Ceardac or Ross what she wanted. How she felt was secondary, if that.

Boots came into view followed by the lowering of Ross McLeod. He crouched to look into her eyes. His large hands enveloped one of hers. Eyes the color of a lush meadow were framed by thick lashes. So engrossed she'd been with Valent, she'd not noticed before how handsome this man was. "Lady Ariana, I know it may come as a shock to you that I wish to marry. I have admired you since first arriving."

Ariana slid a glance to the door to find that Ceardac

had left. "I am not ready for yet another change so soon. So much has happened."

"I am aware." Of course he was. Although not related by blood, he, along with his men, had fought for her clan. "But life continues does it not?"

His simple question took her breath. He was right. Valent was gone, had left her, not even saying goodbye. Why did she resist marriage? It was always expected that she'd once again marry a man her brother, Donall, chose.

Ross lowered his head while waiting for her to reply. It gave her the opportunity to study him. His dark brown hair fell to wide shoulders. Ross had strong, well-formed arms and thick thighs.

He looked up when she released a breath and licked her bottom lip. "You are right, we must move forward. I need to ensure you are aware that I am not a virgin. I...I was married before, am a widow. I've had a lover. If it is not to your liking, I understand." Although she maintained a steady voice, her face was hot. "I will not tell you who he was. I will not speak more on it, only that I assure you I am not with child."

"I see." His gaze searched her face. "Then I must admit. I am not a virgin either and hope that is not a problem." His lips curved and she couldn't help but smile in return.

"I suppose I can live with that."

"Ye're quite pensive...Ariana," Lily stated later that day in the sitting room. The hesitation of Lily saying her name was understandable. After so many years of referring to her as milady, it would take some time for Lily to get used to calling her by her first name.

Ariana put her sewing aside. "I cannot fathom the idea of marrying so soon to someone other than Valent. I am not sure what to do." She looked to the cloth she'd held. "I've not put one stitch in. What would you do, Lily?"

Lily let out a breath. "'Tis difficult to say. Honestly, I wish the laird would give you more time. Perhaps you can try once again and ask Ross McLeod for time. What is the hurry anyhow?"

"It is a handfast and not truly a wedding. Yet when I leave with him, it means I am to become his wife, don't you think?"

"Aye, it does." Lily's brow furrowed. "Should I try to talk to your brother? Convince Ceardac that you are in mourning. I could tell him that you need time to get over so much loss before tossing you into yet another situation that will bring you much stress."

Why had she not considered that? Of course, it was too soon. She was in shock from all that happened. No doubt, Ceardac was as well.

As if summoned, her brother appeared at the entrance. "Sister, how fare you?"

Lily blushed and looked to Ariana, giving away they were just speaking of him. "Ariana is not well. She needs more time to recover from all that has transpired." The diminutive woman went to her brother who glowered down at her. Not at all intimated, Lily launched into her speech. "It is not the right time for you to insist she become handfasted and sent away from her home. How could you do this to her at a time of mourning? Both of your brothers are just recently dead. Not just Ariana, but you as well need time to mourn the loss. Think of your mother, she must be distraught over this. She cannot be planning a wedding."

Ceardac's eyebrows rose at Lily's speech, looking to Ariana as if expecting her to help him reply. Lily pushed her index finger into his chest. "Additionally, right now you need her here with you. I am positive your dear mother will want to travel home immediately to see about her sons' proper burial ceremonies and to complete her mourning time as well."

"What you say is true, Lily. I had not considered all that," Ceardac admitted. Ariana noted her brother studied her friend's face for a long moment as if seeing her for the first time. Lily swallowed and moved to sit next to Ariana.

"I will speak to Ross in the morning and ask that we postpone the handfast until after the mourning time has concluded." His green eyes met Ariana's. "Do not take this as me changing my mind. We have accepted his proposal, so you will marry Ross McLeod in the spring."

Chapter 17

The jostling of the wagon made Valent bounce with every dip and rivet they rolled over in the haste of whoever his kidnappers were to get away. He cursed when his shoulder slammed onto the bottom boards. They'd managed to knock it out of its joint and he was sweating from the throbbing brought on by the injury. Once again, he struggled against the bindings, but was not successful in loosening the straps.

Whoever drove the wagon spoke in low tones to another man. Thankfully, the cloth they'd wrapped over his eyes had slipped enough for him to see. They'd knocked him out when they'd overtaken him near his cottage. He'd gone back to look for his bundle of belongings he'd left there and hit him from behind.

He lifted his head to make out whether or not his dog, Arrow, followed. If they'd hurt Arrow in any way, Valent swore he'd kill them.

"Where is my dog?" he yelled so they could hear him over the creaking. "Who are you and where do you take me?"

One of them looked over his shoulder, not seeming discomfited by the fact Valent could see him. "Ye'll know soon enough."

"Did you kill him?"

The men mumbled to each other and one looked past him to the road. "If you mean that one, he's been behind us the entire way."

Once again, he lifted his head to see Arrow keeping pace to the side of the wagon. Valent whistled and Arrow raced to catch up, easily jumping into the back of the wagon before settling next to him.

The same man chuckled upon spotting Arrow. "If yer beastie bites me, I will delight in killing it."

"If you do, then I will kill you," Valent replied, not bothering to look at the man.

They continued on for what seemed forever before coming to high, thick gates, which were opened upon their arrival.

Valent prepared himself for what came next.

A large, muscular man appeared at the end of the wagon and reached for Valent only to stop when Arrow growled. The man moved away. "How am I to retrieve him with a snarling beast with 'im?" the man snapped at the men who'd kidnapped him. "The laird will not be pleased."

For the moment, they left him there. Valent maneuvered himself to sitting, leaned on the back of the cart and studied the surroundings while he waited for the throbbing to subside.

The cart was stopped in a courtyard. It was larger than the McLeod's with neat rows of stables on one side and quarters that he assumed were for the guards along the opposite side. In the center was a well and to the back were gardens. A large fire just outside the guards' quarters warmed whatever brewed in the large pot hovering over it. Several dogs gathered, looking to Arrow with interest. His dog ignored them, too busy sniffing the air and keeping a keen eye on whoever neared.

Instinctively, he knew it was his brother's keep. Why he was brought there was the one thing Valent was not sure of. Why would his brother go to such lengths to bring him back? If he planned to hold him for ransom, he'd be sorely disappointed.

Finally, the laird appeared flanked by two warriors and headed towards where Valent sat. Valent didn't try to move, the pain from his shoulder reaching an unbearable level.

Steaphan neared and barely glanced at a growling Arrow. "Fetch a healer to see about his shoulder." The order was given without looking away from Valent.

"Arrow," Valent whistled softly and the dog moved back, lowering his large head onto his paws. "Why do you bring me here? Release me at once."

Steaphan studied him for a moment before speaking. "As I told you, there is much you must know. We have reached a truce with the McLeods so I do not do this as an affront to the laird, but to allow you a choice."

"My choice is to leave." The gate was closing and, along with it, any opportunity to escape dashed.

"Brother, you are welcome to stay in a chamber or the dungeon. Either way, you will be guarded at all times until we come to an agreement."

"I would prefer to leave," Valent repeated and searched the cart for any sign of his bundle and bow. He was relieved to see them tied to the side of the wagon. "I will require a horse and my weapon. You will never see me again."

Steaphan moved aside. "Get him down from there. Bring him inside." He met Valent's gaze. "Keep your dog under control."

Although Arrow growled softly, he did not snap at the men who pulled Valent from the wagon and untied his feet. They guided him to the interior of the keep.

Truth be told, he almost wished they carried him as the pain was intolerable at that point.

"Come now, bring him to sit here." An old man motioned them forward and without preamble, shoved a piece of leather between his teeth. "Ye will want to bite down on this lad." The man smiled, the few teeth left were dark and yellow. "It will hurt a bit."

Before Valent could prepare, the old man had two men hold him and he shoved at his shoulder. There was a hollow pop and it was set into place. Valent almost passed out, darkness swirled and he let out a groan. He blinked the stars away and spit out the leather. "Whiskey."

A cup was brought to his lips and he swallowed down the fiery liquid, hoping it would take effect soon.

He studied the large room. With bright tapestries on the walls and clean long tables, it was impressive. Large candleholders lit the space and gave it a welcoming ambience. It had a second level along the sides, which allowed for viewing of the space where he sat. The room was completely empty except for him, the healer and three guardsmen.

"Steaphan?" a woman called and hurried into the room. The attractive woman looked to him. "Did you receive a message back from the Grant?"

When he didn't reply, she narrowed her eyes at him and moved towards Valent. The closer she came, the wider her eyes became. "Darach."

It was not a question but a statement. The woman's hands went to her chest and she took a wobbly step back. "It's you, isn't it?" She lifted a hand as if to touch his face, but curled her fingers into a fist and moved away. She looked to one of the guards. "Where is my son?"

The men looked to each of the others. Obviously they

knew Valent was her son as well as Steaphan. From the question, however, it was also obvious she did not consider him such.

"He comes now, milady," one of the men answered and she turned to Steaphan who entered the room and stopped short. "Mother. You have met Valent, I see."

"Valent?" She turned to him. "Is that who you are? Valent McLeod?"

He didn't bother responding. Instead, he studied her face in an attempt to remember her. The woman seemed uncomfortable under his scrutiny and looked away.

"Why did you bring him here?" she asked Steaphan. "You are putting the entire clan in danger."

Steaphan ignored her and came to Valent. "Valent, this is our mother Lorna McKenzie. Do not be distraught at her lack of caring for you. I fear I, too, am treated without warmth. She is not the maternal kind, never has been."

Lorna McKenzie glared at Steaphan. "What are you going to do? Allow him to go free? You must send him away at once."

Valent almost spoke up in agreement, but was still unable to form a word at meeting his mother. His family. No they were not that, perhaps to the young Darach, but to him they were strangers.

Steaphan neared and looked to the healer. "I thank you."

The healer took a long swig of whatever was in a dirty jug. "'Tis a thing, my laird, to see the looks of both of ye at the same time." The old man cackled and bent to pick up the leather. He rubbed it against his tunic and threw it into his sack. "I'll be on my way then. Will ye be at the festival next week, Laird?" The old man looked at Steaphan. "My wager is on ye for the toss."

His brother chuckled. "Aye, Tilam, I will be there. Do

not wager too high. I hear Dugan is tossing it quite far these days."

It was interesting to watch his brother's interactions with the old man. The McLeod would never lower himself to such a conversation. Yet everyone seemed at ease around Steaphan.

His brother waited for the healer to leave before speaking to him again. "Valent, I will allow you to leave after you hear everything I have to share." Steaphan's gaze met his and held it. "I am glad you are here, brother."

The laird looked to the guards. "My men will ensure you remain in your chambers. If you require anything, ask them."

"Did you look for me?" Valent ignored Steaphan and asked the woman who paled visibly. "Or were you the one who sent me away?"

Lorna looked to him. For a brief instant, he saw something akin to hurt, but she quickly recovered and assumed a façade of annoyance. "I will never speak of that day." She lifted her skirts and stormed away from them. "Steaphan, I will not attend the evening meal," she called out as she crossed the doorway.

Steaphan seemed to be used to his mother's ways as he ignored her last comment and spoke to him. "There is something I must do. I will be gone and return in two or three days. At that time I will seek you out and we will speak. Upon learning the truth, you can decide what you wish to do. I will not allow you to go until you are fully aware of the circumstances before making a decision."

"I already know," Valent snarled. "Let me go. There can be no reason for me to remain here." He was surprised the guards allowed him to stand.

There was sadness in Steaphan's eyes when locking to his. "You may change your mind once we speak." He moved closer, his brother's lips to his ear. "It is your birthright that you be laird. Not mine."

The announcement hit Valent so hard, he fell back into the chair. What his brother said should not affect him but it did. It was hard to keep a neutral expression at the knowledge of how different his life should have been.

He did not fight the guards who escorted him to private chambers. Truth be told, he needed the time right now. To be alone with the pain and new knowledge.

Valent was deposited into a spacious set of rooms. He remained by the door taking in the space.

An oversized bedroom with a bed so large, three men could lay on it shoulder to shoulder. He walked around it taking in the intricate word carvings on the bedposts. On both sides of the bed were tables with lamps and across from it a large fireplace with a fire already burning. The window was large, but barred from the outside. Interesting, did the McKenzies always insure their visitors could not escape?

In a small adjoining room there was a table, two chairs covered in thick fabric and another smaller fireplace. On the table was a tray of meats, cheeses, and bread.

Lain across the back of one of the chairs was a McKenzie tartan. The rich blue and green fabric felt thick under his palm when he ran his hand over it. A crest pin fell with a thunk to the floor and he stared at it.

The silver pin, meant to hold the tartan in place would never grace his chest. Valent didn't bother to pick it up off the floor.

Everything was set for someone of high regard, someone who expected the best. This was not for him. Why did his brother insist on treating him with such respect? He did not want this, was not used to this kind of treatment.

A jeweled goblet next to a pitcher caught his attention and he reached for it realizing he was thirsty. Just as his hand touched the cup, he noticed his bruised, labor-marred hand and he snatched it away as if burned.

He moved away from the table and kept walking backwards until his back hit a wall.

Valent closed his eyes when his knees buckled. As he slid to the floor, the first tears streamed down his face. He took a hard, shaky breath that came out as a sob. His head lulled forward onto his knees and in that instant, he felt like that small boy who'd been snatched from his home.

So alone, so scared, not sure what to do or think except to want his father and mother and security of his home. He fell to his side cradling his injured arm and allowed the salty tears to continue falling.

In that moment, he didn't care that someone could walk in. Hurt and sorrow enveloped him and Valent did not fight the barrage of pain that sliced through his heart and soul.

He never aspired to the life of a laird. Would not accept to lead this clan. They were not his family, not any more.

Valent's chest ached with each sob as grief surrounded him, squeezing the air from his lungs. His life should have been so different. All those years of hunger, pain and loneliness, fighting for scraps as a child could have been avoided.

Now, it was too late for him.

He was a man with no one.

Chapter 18

Fiona McLeod pulled weeds from the garden. How had so many sprung so soon? It was only a week past she'd cleaned the entire area where her herbs grew and it was already overrunning with the horrid things.

Horses approached. Fiona shielded her eyes from the sun and looked past to the expanse of the lands. Horsemen rode toward the keep.

The McLeod guards looked on without alarm. Whoever came was not a threat. She tried to ignore the flipping in her stomach at the thought it could be her husband and went back to her gardening.

It annoyed her that whenever she pondered on their one night together, her treacherous body demanded his touch.

One night. That was all they'd had. Yes, it had been wonderful and like nothing she'd ever experienced. But the memory soured at remembering her husband attempted to leave the next day without bothering to say a word to her. She was too angry to consider what would happen between them if he who came now.

There was commotion behind her as the riders were received. She continued about her work, ignoring the voices of the guards and whoever arrived. Once the weeding was completed, she'd feign a headache and hide in her room, avoiding the evening meal.

"Fiona, I came for you. Your message was unreasonable. I will not wait a fortnight for my wife. Are you prepared?" His voice fell over her like a soft, warm blanket. She fortified herself before looking up to the glowering man. Did he have to be so handsome?

"No, I am not prepared. I insist. I must wait a fortnight before I come to your keep then." She continued weeding.

"I can take you, now. With or without belongings matters naught to me."

He stepped closer and she feared he'd pull her up by her hair for daring to speak so freely, so she jumped to her feet and moved away. "You wouldn't dare."

He didn't speak. Instead, he moved closer and closer until he was almost nose-to-nose with her. "You will either pack now or you will leave with me by force." His gray eyes were almost black with anger. The darkness of his gaze reminded her of when he lay with her. She looked to his lips and had to take a step backward.

"Are you always to be so demanding?" she snapped. "I don't understand why the hurry for me to prepare to leave with you. After all, you were in such a hurry to be away."

His gaze swept her face. "You have dirt on your face. Do you always do such work?" Steaphan motioned to the ground.

Did he attempt to distract her? She smoothed her hands down the front of her apron. "Aye, I like being outdoors."

"Then you will enjoy the ride back to my keep tomorrow. We leave at daybreak."

She let out a huff and spoke slowly. "I. Am. Not. Prepared. You will have to leave without me. I will come in a week."

He moved closer and reached for her. Would he punish her? She'd pushed him to lose his temper, perhaps?

Fiona attempted to take a step back but her foot hit her spade and she lost her balance. She flailed her arms out to the sides knowing any second she'd land on the damp earth on her bottom.

Perfect. Just great. She was angering the man and now would fall onto the ground at his feet.

Steaphan grabbed her arms and kept her from falling.

Unfortunately, it meant she fell forward into his hard chest. Fiona pushed away and stepped sideways. Her heart pounded, her breathing in soft gasps.

"Don't push me away." With his hand, he gently lifted her face and frowned. "I cannot stop thinking of you. Of us together." His words were like a caress. "I am anxious to have you in my bed again, Fiona."

Fiona couldn't stand the nearness any longer, she was still angry with him. "You left me."

"It was for your safety." His lips curved, mesmerizing her.

"Of course." It was necessary to move away from him. She needed space in order to think. "If we are to leave so soon, I will see about packing." She pushed his hand away and went toward the entrance only for him to fall in step beside her.

"I will accompany you."

"No need."

"I want to."

"You should visit with Da."

"I wish to visit with you."

"It will take me some time."

"I do not mind."

"I do."

"No, you do not. You desire me as much as I do you."
He took her by the shoulders and, in the next instant,
she was against the wall, her husband's probing tongue
between her lips and her fingers threading through his
hair.

Chapter 19

The Reckoning

The dew was fresh on the grass as Fiona McKenzie paced outside in the garden. The wet hem of her skirts brushed the top of her feet and she shivered at the coolness of it.

It bothered her that no one seemed to be as upset about her upcoming departure as she was. Her mother came outside and rushed to her. "What are you doing out here? You will catch your death." She gave her an incredulous look. "Fiona 'tis time to grow up and act like what you are. A laird's wife."

Her mother was right, but it didn't stop her from letting out a huff of indignation. "I tried to pack, but the oaf kept getting in my way." Her face reddened at the different things Steaphan had done to distract her. He'd gone from kissing the back of her neck to pulling her against him, his hands roving over her body. Thankfully, he'd not spent the night in her chamber as he'd joined her father to discuss whatever men discuss and drinking until the wee hours. As soon as she'd woken and broke her fast, she'd hurried out to the garden to think.

"You leave today, darling girl. I know it is hard to go away from your home. I was young and afraid like you. So I understand completely."

Fiona flung herself into her mother's arms allowing the quiet strength to seep into her. "I am not afraid mother. I am bothered."

"Oh, Fiona," her mother replied with a chuckle. "Poor Laird Steaphan has his work cut out for him with you."

"Fiona!" Her husband rushed outside only to stop when spotting her. He lowered his voice. "I thought you'd run away." He looked to her mother. "Is something amiss?"

Her mother smiled at him. "Not at all. The packing will be done shortly. I will personally oversee it." She skirted around him and went to the side door, turning to give Fiona a meaningful "behave" look before disappearing into the darkened entrance.

Fiona squared her shoulders and slid a sideways glance at Steaphan. In the morning light, she could make out slight creasing in the corners of his eyes. There was light stubble on his jawline and his eyes were a bit reddened. She'd not considered how much the responsibility of leading a clan could weigh on his shoulders.

He met her gaze. "We must leave today. I cannot delay our departure. There is much to do in Gladdaugh."

"I understand you are, indeed, busy with your responsibilities. I planned to come to you once I was prepared. Now it has become a rushed affair that would have been avoided if for just one tiny detail."

He lifted a brow, his gray gaze on her face. "What detail might that be, wife?"

"Listening to me." She moved around him and dashed to the house, not wanting to chance he'd catch and chastise her. Instead, he laughed, the deep sound making her grind her teeth. The man was infuriating.

Each day that passed without Valent was agony for Ariana. Almost two weeks since she'd seen him and, yet, each time she entered the great room it was impossible to keep from searching for his presence. The evening meals had become an ordeal and, more oft than not, she opted to have food brought to her chambers where she ate with only Lily, her constant shoulder to lean on, for company.

It was unfair to her brother Ceardac, who, like her, had just lost their two brothers. She was well aware of it. Yet it was hard to fathom that, forevermore, her life would be as such.

Without Valent.

Ariana kept her gaze downcast and made her way to the front of the great room. Someone reached out and touched her hand and she looked over to see a young child. The boy was a foundling, just as Valent had been so many years before. Ariana had insisted the boy be allowed to live in the keep. Orphaned after the last battle with the McKenzie Clan, as his mother had died at birth and his father was killed when the village fought the attacking damn McKenzies, there was no one left to care for the child.

"Sit with me?" The young lad's innocence made her smile and instead of sitting at the long table with him, she took his proffered hand and pulled him alongside her to the high board.

Ceardac watched with interest, but did not seem at all displeased when she sat the child next to her. "What is your name?" he asked the boy who stared at him with wide eyes, somehow seeming to realize Ceardac's higher position.

"David, like me father," he responded in a soft voice. "I four years old," the child finished proudly.

"A proper young man you are," Ceardac told him and returned to his conversation with Murray, the leader of the guard.

Lily smiled down at the boy and then looked to Ariana. "I see young David has a champion in the laird's sister."

"How could I not? He is simply precious." Ariana let out a long sigh. "Left alone to fend for himself. His father gave his life defending our village. It's the least we can do."

They were both silent watching the boy eat with gusto before reaching for a cup to wash down his food.

"Ariana, I must discuss something with you after the meal." Ceardac's cryptic request put her on edge. What happened now? If Ross McLeod of Skye changed his mind on becoming betrothed, she would be grateful. Perhaps that was it, but from the set of Ceardac's jaw and furrowed brows, whatever it was did not make him happy in the least.

"What do you think it is about?" Lily leaned into her ear. "Bad news?"

Ariana stole another glace at her brother. "I cannot think of what is could be. I am praying to be released from my betrothal to Ross McLeod."

"Aye, that would not sit well with Ceardac. Neither would any news of Valent sit well," Lily added.

Ariana scanned the room and found Valent's usual place at one of the tables. It remained empty as if the rest of the guardsmen expected his return.

"I doubt anyone will ever hear from or about Valent again. He planned to travel very far when he left." Although she spoke with words matter-of-factly, her chest constricted. "It may be nothing of vital importance that my brother wishes to speak about."

Both knew that wasn't true. Ceardac's demands on his time were constant. That he asked her to set aside time meant he had something of importance to discuss.

She admired the way he fell into the role of laird. Taking command with ease, seeming to be fair and equal to the people, while maintaining a good distance. He was tall and attractive, more stoic than easygoing.

"When would you like me to come to you brother?" Ariana asked and waited as he mentally went over his plans for the evening.

"Promptly upon the meal's end," he replied and opened his mouth to say something else but someone came up and tapped his arm. Immediately, his attention was diverted from her.

Ceardac's study had been their father's and his father's before him. It had never been a room to Ariana's liking. The walls were dark and on every one hung a tapestry depicting battle scenes. The laird commanded from a sturdy table that was washed in dark stain. The chair in which she sat opposite it was upright and hard. She looked to the wall behind her brother to a scene of a warrior atop a horse spearing another.

Her emotions rolled and she looked to Ceardac who spoke with Murray, a guardsman, in low tones. There seemed to be a problem between two guardsmen who battled for first position as archer. The one left vacant by Valent.

Her brother's gaze went to her before he spoke to the guard. "Tell the men they will compete tomorrow. Whoever bests the other will have the position. In my opinion, both are good fighters."

When his first left, Ceardac let out a breath and rubbed his temples with his fingertips.

Ariana went to him, placing her hands on his shoulders. She massaged the tightness from his shoulders. "You are allowed to rest, brother. You cannot continue at this pace."

"It helps me not think of so much loss. I prefer to remain occupied," he replied honestly. "Idle time does not suit me right now."

"We start anew. We are no longer at war and the rebuilding of the village is underway. The people admire you and although they come constantly for hearings, I believe 'tis because they want a different decision than the ones given by Donall," she told him referring to their older brother who'd been killed when the McKenzies attacked.

"You are probably correct." Ceardac studied her when she moved away to stand beside his desk. "Your intelligence astounds me at times."

Ariana rolled her eyes and smiled. "Does it? I've always been smarter than you."

His chuckle pleased her.

"Perhaps we can plan a clan festival. Food, music, plenty of ale." Ariana walked about the room. "We have to do something to raise not just our spirits, but those of the clan as well."

"It is too soon, sister," Ceardac told her, his countenance becoming serious, once again. "Have you heard from Valent?"

The question caught her off guard. Ariana fell into a chair and looked to her brother. "No, I have not. Nor do I expect to. He left without saying a word. And although you will probably not like to hear it, I have to tell you that I feel he cared for me. I know there is something special between us. If he left, it was because he did not want to cause any problems for me. He cared not for what happened to him."

She could not make out what Ceardac thought; he maintained a neutral expression. Ceardac raised his glass of whiskey and studied it before speaking. "Some of the men want to mark him as a traitor to the clan. Many think he went to join with the McKenzie."

Her breath caught and she touched her palm to her chest. "That is ridiculous. Valent refused the McKenzie's offer to join with him and go to Claddaugh, in front of me and those present."

Ceardac nodded. "When the McLeod of Skye mentioned killing the McKenzie, I saw something in Valent. For a moment, he was affected by the thought of his brother dying. Although they did not grow up together, it doesn't mean an instant bond was not built."

"I cannot attest to what I did not see, but I refused to think he would join with the McKenzies, regardless of the fact his brother is laird. He does not know them, never knew about the relationship until that day." She searched the doorway for the guardsman, Murray. "What does Murray say? He and Valent were quite close."

"He is one of the few who believes as you do. He maintains that something happened to Valent; that he did not depart of his own free will."

"What?" Ariana wanted to grab Ceardac's tunic and force him to speak faster. "Why would Murray think such a thing?"

Ceardac studied her for a moment as if assessing whether to divulge what he knew or not. Finally, he spoke. "A villager attests to having seen some men tussle in the forest. Claims two men struggled to load up another into the back of a wagon."

"Oh God. We should attempt to rescue him. Valent is probably a prisoner of the McKenzies. Why are we not doing something?"

Ceardac rubbed his hands down his face. "First of all, Valent is a McKenzie from birth. Secondly, the villager is never sober enough to see anything clearly and thirdly, our truce with the McKenzies is tender at best. This is not the time to risk another battle for an archer."

"But..." she began and sank back into a chair, not sure if there was any argument that would work to the truth of what her brother spoke.

"I'm sorry to bring you more despair right now, sister," Ceardac said. "However, I felt it was important that you knew and not heard about it during a meal or some sort of thing. There is another issue I must discuss with you."

She could barely catch her breath. In her mind, she already formulated a plan to get several guards to accompany her to ride to Claddaugh and ask the McKenzie for Valent's release. Surely, he valued the truce as much as they did and he did not intend to harm his own brother.

Ceardac cleared his throat. "I will be married soon. Therefore, it would be best if you began the task of preparing the household for the exchanging of duties to someone else."

"What?" She jumped to her feet and rushed to the table where Ceardac sat. Hands on top, she leaned forward to meet his gaze. "To whom?"

"Genevieve Grant, the laird is quite displeased at Steaphan McKenzie's abrupt cancellation of his engagement with her. His last minute marriage to a McLeod lass meant the Grant had to find another husband for his daughter. He sent a messenger a few days ago and we came to an agreement. This would give us an alliance with a neighboring clan and a good show of force if the McKenzie were to consider fighting us again."

"What about..." She began to say *Lily*, but did not feel at liberty to ask. That she knew of, there was nothing more than innocent attraction between Ceardac and her friend. Besides, Lily had grown up with them, worked as Ariana's maid until the attack when they'd decided it was best if Lily posed as a lady friend of hers. After that, she'd remained in the role.

"Are you sure, Ceardac? Do you not love anyone else?" She peered at his face in an attempt to catch any signs of what he thought

He looked across the room and released a long breath. "Up until lately, I always thought I'd marry someone I loved or cared for greatly. I never expected to be laird. Now it is about the people that I must think of. Not myself."

"I understand." Ariana rounded the table and kissed his jaw. "I will do anything in my power to make Genevieve feel welcome and comfortable. You will be happy, Ceardac, you deserve it more than anyone I know."

"I pray you are right, dear sister."

There was a knock at the door and Murray looked in. "Laird, the guards are ready for you to witness the competition tomorrow at dawn."

Their time, it seemed, had come to an end.

Chapter 20

The knocks at the door made Valent grimace. It was not likely they would leave if he did not reply. He was not a guest after all, but a prisoner. The door cracked open and a face peered in.

It was a woman. Not one of the servants who daily came. Usually, it was either maids with food and drink or one of the guards who came in and searched the room to ensure he didn't have any weapons. His brother had been detained, he'd been told. The reason was not explained, nor did he ask.

Whatever his brother planned did not matter to him except if it affected Ariana. One of the first things he'd ask upon Steaphan's appearance would be if he'd gone to attack the McLeods once again.

The woman looked him over as if assessing if it was safe to enter. "Darach, do you remember me?"

He narrowed his eyes and studied the woman who'd stepped into the room, leaving the door just a bit ajar. "No, I do not know you."

Although her smile was familiar, he couldn't fathom who she was. Her hair was dark like his and her eyes a shade of blue, like the sky on a clear day. "I'm your sister, Sorcha." She waited looking to him expectantly.

Valent wasn't sure what to do, so he motioned to the table and chairs. "Would you like to sit?"

"Of course." She walked ahead of him to the table and he poured some mead, which Sorcha accepted with a bright smile. "I came with my husband and two children to meet you upon hearing of your return. I could not wait to see you as Steaphan's messenger announced you may not remain here long."

Without warning, she got to her feet, rushed around the table and threw her arms around him. Valent stood with his arms to his sides, not sure what to do. Finally, when he heard her sniffle, he patted at her back awkwardly.

A sister. He did not remember a sister. Perhaps there were some vague memories of a girl playing with him. Singing to him.

"Did you sing to me?"

"Yes!" Sorcha exclaimed looking up at him with shiny eyes. "You remember that?"

"Aye, a bit." He was somewhat relieved when she moved away and sat. "I was very young. Do not remember much."

"I understand. I was six when you were taken, so I remember a bit more." She wiped at her face with a kerchief. "I hope you can join us for the evening meal and meet my husband and your nieces. Both of them have your eyes." Sorcha sniffed but smiled.

Valent had not left the chamber except a couple hours a day to walk in the courtyard while under guard. He'd spent the time with Arrow, who seemed to have adjusted well to life there.

"If you wish, I will attend the meal. It would be my pleasure to meet your daughters." Valent kept from calling them nieces, as he did not feel a kinship with the McKenzies.

Sorcha took a dainty sip from her cup. "What about you. Do you have a wife and children?"

Although she claimed to be his sister and he felt it was true, Valent did not feel enough at ease to have a conversation. He'd never been in a situation where he sat with someone and conversed. He cleared his throat and looked past her to the door. It remained open so the guards could enter if Sorcha became alarmed. "No. I am not married. Has Steaphan returned?"

"He should arrive before the evening meal. From what the messenger said, he should have left Mudduch by now."

He recognized the name she spoke. It belonged to a small McLeod clan a half days' ride away. Why had Steaphan remained there for so long? "Does he return alone?" Valent drank his mead attempting a neutral expression.

"Oh, you are not aware?" Sorcha laughed and shook her head. "Of course, you probably arrived just as he left. He married the McLeod's daughter, Fiona. From what I understand, it was a rushed affair."

"Married?"

"Oh yes, our families have been on friendly terms for all of my life. I'm sure it was the only way from being pulled into the conflict with the McLeods of the south."

Once again, he was struck by how much he didn't know about the McKenzies and, for just an instant, he wondered if he should agree to remain. Learn what he could about them. The problem was that he knew, deep inside, that it would not last. Could not last. He was not part of this world.

Sorcha continued unabated, not seeming to be discomfited by his silence. "I always wondered where you were. In my heart, I knew you were out there somewhere. I prayed for you, hoping you were well."

He had not been well. As a foundling with the McLeod Clan, he'd had to fight for scraps of food, barely able to talk and desperate. When Tavish took pity on him and brought him to live in a cottage in the forest, he'd finally had daily meals. The hardships of his life had continued for his entire life. The laird turning a blind eye to his sons constantly beating him. His back was striped with marks from being whipped just a few weeks earlier.

Very rare were the times he was well. Yet when he considered it, most of those times were when he was with Ariana. Admittedly he'd not remained long enough to see what his life would have been like with Ceardac as the new laird, but it was impossible to remain. Daily life, seeing Ariana, would be too hard.

She'd remarry and leave, of that he was sure. As beautiful as she was, Ariana would not be alone for long.

"You are so handsome. I can see the difference between you and Steaphan. Your face is a bit broader. And you seem to be sterner. Of course, it could be you don't know me." Sorcha had continued talking and he'd halfway listened, his mind on Ariana.

Finally, she stood. "I will go and allow you some privacy. I tend to prattle on." She waited for him to stand as well and she reached up and cupped his face. "I know you don't know me, but I do love you, Darach, and am so very happy that you are here. Consider staying. It would mean a lot to Steaphan."

"And your mother?" He didn't know why he said it. Perhaps because the woman seemed cold and distant, he wondered if she was the same with Sorcha.

"Mother keeps her emotions well hidden. I am sure she is relieved you are here as well." Sorcha left and Valent sat back on the chair and drank the rest of the mead.

He wasn't sure he could attend the evening meal. It was not time to face everything yet.

"Sorcha was disappointed when you didn't come to the evening meal." Steaphan entered the room that evening and settled into a chair by the fireplace, ignoring that Valent continued to stand.

Although he'd awaited the day his brother would finally deem it time to make an appearance, he wondered if any information the man gave would make a difference in his decision to travel as far as he could from both the McLeods and the McKenzies.

"I only remained to hear what you have to say. It is doubtful I will stay after that." Valent moved to the chair opposite where Steaphan sat, but stood next to it. "I cannot think of anything that will convince me to remain in Gladdaugh."

"When was the last time you were treated as such?" Steaphan motioned around the rooms with his arms outstretched. "This is what you deserve, what your life should be."

The answer was obvious, so Valent did not reply.

Steaphan's lips curved. "I have pondered a great deal and tried to understand what you feel. How you perceive us here at Gladdaugh. We are strangers. The enemy of your people."

"The McLeods are not my people. I have no clan."

Steaphan got to his feet. "You have made that perfectly clear. You have no clan. To remain without family is your choice at this point."

He pinned Valent with a steady stare. "Have you considered how we felt at losing you? Stop to think a moment of how much Sorcha and I cried at missing you. Father was so distraught he had to be held back from punishing the men who dared to return empty handed after searching for weeks. So much was his grief that he never fully recovered from the melancholy."

Steaphan studied Valent with an angry glare. "Yes, you were left to fend for yourself. And perhaps had a very hard life. But we tried to find you. If you were not found at the McLeods it is because everyone denied any knowledge of a young foundling."

Valent had not considered it. Every word Steaphan spoke painted a picture of a family in pain, hurting for the loss of a child.

His brother was not finished; Steaphan neared and gripped Valent's shoulder. "The reason for your coming here, being brought by force, is not just because I wanted you to know us, but also because we love you and missed you terribly. Yet you come here with an attitude of superiority. Playing the role of the party done wrong. It wasn't just you who suffered Valent." Steaphan swallowed visibly and took a step back. "I must go from the room. I will return if you deem not to come down for the evening meal. Sorcha and her family leave tomorrow." He stormed from the room, slamming the door behind him.

Valent sunk into a chair and covered his face with his hands. What would he do? What did he truly want?

If he was first born, lairdship of the clan was his birthright. Leading the McKenzies was something he wasn't sure he could ever do. Yet, as laird, his station in life would change. And along with it came the possibility of offering a better life to Ariana.

But as a McKenzie? Ariana and Ceardac would never agree to a union between them. His identical twin was the one who ordered both their brothers' deaths.

Chapter 21

Lily walked in the garden. The day was pleasant and she needed fresh air. The keep and its people were still not recovered from all the losses of the McKenzie invasion and, frankly, she found the gloominess oppressing to her spirit. She'd lost both parents as a child, didn't have any family she knew of, so wasn't affected as much as most of the clan's people.

Admittedly, she'd grown up with the laird's children and felt some sorrow at Donall's and Beathan's deaths. Since neither ever treated her well, it was hard to feel more than a passing sadness. More than anything, it pained her to see Ariana and Ceardac hurting.

Had something happened to either Ariana or Ceardac, things would have been horribly different. She loved them both with all of her heart.

At thinking of Ceardac, she placed her palm against her breast and took a deep breath. How could it be that she could barely think of the man and her breath caught?

Although she'd known him most of her life, it wasn't until recently she'd taken more of a notice of how handsome he'd become, how much more sensible he was than the other brothers. He was rapidly becoming popular with the clan as a fair and strong leader.

With beautiful eyes the color of a lush glen and sensual, full lips, Ceardac was a breathtaking man. Days earlier, when she'd been up late, they'd run into each other in a hallway and he'd kissed her. She'd been distraught over Ariana being ill and in bed without responding for two days when Ceardac happened upon her.

He'd held her and when she looked up to him, he'd kissed her. It was soft, sweet and short. Over much too soon.

"Lily, are you unwell?" The deep voice caught her by surprise and she gasped before turning to face the object of her ponderings.

"I am fine. I just need some fresh air. It can be oppressing indoors." She was gratified when he moved closer. "What brings you to the garden?"

"I spied you from up there." Ceardac pointed to the balcony of his bedroom. "I took the opportunity to talk to you alone."

Her heart skipped a beat. "Is something amiss?"

Ceardac raked his fingers through his hair. She recognized this as a sign he was struggling with what to say and her stomach knotted. Whatever it was, it would not be to her liking. "I wanted to apologize for the other day."

"What? ...oh, the kiss." She felt her face heat and let out a huff in frustration. "There is no need. I found it quite pleasant and you helped distract me from my worries."

He nodded, his gaze meeting hers. "We've known each other a long time. I find it strange to not have noticed how beautiful you've become."

His words took her by surprise and Lily cleared her throat, not sure what to say in response.

Ceardac finally tore his gaze away. "I will see you at the evening meal then."

"Wait." She reached for his arm and he immediately stopped and looked to her. Lily wasn't sure what to say to detain him, but she was not ready for him to leave. "How...are you? This has been a horrible terrible time for you. Not to mention all the added responsibilities."

His shoulders relaxed and his lips curved. "It has been an adjustment. Life is certainly not what I expected. But with each passing day, I find it becomes easier."

She looked to the keep. "I will miss my life here."

At her words, Ceardac's brows lowered. "What do you mean?"

"When Ariana marries Ross McLeod, I must go with her. I cannot remain here."

He gave her a curt nod and when he moved away, she did not stop him.

Lily smiled. Good, she'd given him something to consider.

She made her way inside and went directly to the sitting room in search of Ariana. Perhaps it was time to let her friend know how she felt about Ceardac. Ariana had hinted more than once about the possibility of a romance with the new laird. Although she was afraid to aspire to be his wife, she found it refreshing to have a small dalliance of sorts with the handsome man.

Ariana turned from the window when she entered. Her face was drawn and not as vibrant as was the norm for her.

"You should sit," Lily said. When Ariana did not move, Lily joined her and looked to see what her friend spied.

The land expanded for as far as the eye could see. Hills and valleys covered in lush green vegetation contrasted with the brightness of the blue sky. Barely whispers of clouds painted the expanse of the heavens.

"It is a beautiful day," Ariana said, her voice low and soft. "I will miss seeing these lands."

Lily let out a sigh. "I will miss the land and other things as well. My entire life, I have not known more than this."

"My brother? He..." Ariana started, then stopped. A tear escaped down her cheek.

"What is it?" Lily was alarmed and took Ariana's hand to lead her to a settee. "Don't cry, I cannot bear it. You will make me cry, too."

Ariana looked to Lily and sniffed. "I have lost two brothers. I don't want to leave Ceardac so soon, as well. Winter is almost here. The days will be short and nights long. I'm afraid he will suffer melancholy."

Lily wasn't sure what to say to make Ariana feel better. "The way of things is that they constantly change. I, too, feel melancholy at the thought of moving away."

Ariana sniffed. "But there is naught we can do. Things have been decided for us. For me anyway. If you wish to remain here, of course, you can. But I do not think you will upon learning what I am about to tell you."

Her heart thudded against her breastbone and Lily lost her ability to breathe. "What is it?"

Ariana let out a long breath as if fortifying herself. "Ceardac. He is to marry the Grant's daughter."

"Oh." Lily fell back into the chair and could not keep tears from falling. "When did you learn of this?"

"Just earlier today. He informed me so I could prepare for his wife to take over the household duties."

Ariana immediately hugged her. The warmth of Ariana's embrace doing little to console her. Until this moment, she'd not allowed herself to accept how deeply she felt for Ceardac. Just earlier in the garden, she'd hoped he would kiss her. But still, Lily had clung to the idea that it was just an infatuation. By the way her heart constricted, she could not help but acknowledge it. She loved Ceardac and the thought of him marrying another made her want to die.

There was a throat clearing in the doorway. Lily didn't have to look up to know it was he. His deep voice sent another wave of misery over her.

"Is something amiss?" Ceardac asked

Thankfully, Ariana went to him, saving Lily the embarrassment of him seeing her reddened face. "Lily is just emotional over a friend in the village who lost her husband. Is there something you require?"

Lily did not pay attention to the conversation after that. Instead, she took advantage of the distraction to wipe her tears and blow her nose. From the corner of her eye, she caught sight of Ceardac looking to her, but he did not move to come closer.

"Lily," he spoke to her. "We all mourn, do not be distraught. Times will get better."

She nodded. "Aye, I know. Time will help. Perhaps when Ariana and I go to Skye, things will seem better."

"You will meet a handsome Scot and marry. Raise some bairns," Ariana added.

Lily looked to her, eyes wide, noticing Ceardac did the same. "Yes...of course. God willing."

Ceardac entered his study and poured more than his usual amount of whiskey. Ariana's statement disturbed him more than it should have. He did not understand why, but the thought of Lily not being part of his everyday life bothered him.

Whatever possessed him to kiss her days earlier now rumbled in disagreement at him allowing her to leave.

As laird, he had the right to demand she remain, but

to what end? Ariana would be cross at him and Lily would be lonely. Not only that, but he was due to marry Genevieve Grant and it would not do to be distracted by Lily's presence.

From what he remembered, the Grant lass was plain faced and with a contrary personality. There were more than several reasons why the Grant had a hard time getting her married off. It was one thing to put up with an unattractive woman, but another altogether to deal with an off-putting personality.

He let out a deep breath and looked up just as Murray entered. The warrior looked to Ceardac's hand. "Quite early for a drink. Is something weighing on your mind?"

It struck him that he wasn't sure what bothered him more, his future marriage or Lily leaving. "I find myself questioning my decision in agreeing so quickly to marry the Grant lass."

"I wondered at that as well. It never is a good thing to make important decisions during times of chaos and change. However, it is done."

"Aye, it is." Ceardac straightened in his chair. "What brings you, Murray?"

His guard looked down as if pondering how to formulate the words. "How many more guardsmen will we be adding? I have four men outside who wish to join. None archers. Do you think Valent will return? He is missed."

"No. If, indeed, the McKenzies came for him, perhaps it is for the best. He was born a McKenzie after all. What is worrisome is that he knows everything about our clan, the training of our guard. Both the strengths and weaknesses of every man."

"Do you actually believe he would use it against us?" Murray went to the side table and poured a drink before downing it. "I had not considered this. Knowing

Valent as I do, I cannot fathom he could fight us."

"I do not think he would. I find it hard to believe he will remain with the McKenzies. However, if he does, we will have to consider his knowledge if ever we go to battle against them again." Ceardac held his glass out and Murray refilled it. "Murray, you must come up with new training drills for the men."

"What of Lady Ariana?"

"I know of my sister's affections toward Valent, the archer. Fortunately, she is to be betrothed to Ross McLeod. I may have to precipitate this occurring. Although, she surprised me by readily agreeing to the marriage."

Murray nodded. "I knew of it, but did not inform you. My loyalties were torn. I ask you forgive me."

"No need to apologize. As you said, these are trying times. I will have to speak to her and ensure she doesn't plan anything. Now, let us speak about the rebuilding of the village."

During the evening meal, the ambience was lighter than usual. Some of the warriors had hunted and successfully killed a large boar. Their exaggerations of the hunt brought rowdy laughter from their table. The contagious effects of the gaiety spread to the rest of the room. Except for his sister and Lily, who remained subdued.

Ceardac leaned to Murray and mumbled, "The women do not seem to be enjoying the stories of the hunt."

"Perhaps we should attempt to make conversation, speak of something of a softer nature."

Ceardac shook his head at the warrior. Although Murray often tupped the maids and even once proposed to a woman, who later was found to be already married, he had little knowledge of conversing with them. "You go first." Ceardac could not hold back a grin, so he pressed his lips together.

Murray cleared his throat and turned to Ariana. "Lady Ariana, what do you think of boar meat?"

Ceardac spit out his ale with a loud guffaw that had everyone turning to the high board.

His sister looked to him then, ignoring him, spoke to Murray. "I love it. I prefer not knowing how the beast was killed, but it is good to eat."

Murray continued unabated. "And what of you, Lady Lily. Is boar your favorite meat?"

Unable to keep from it, Ceardac watched Lily's face as she pondered Murray's question. "No, sir. I prefer deer or pheasant."

"What about potatoes, do you like them?" Ceardac asked, sliding a look at Murray.

"Yes." Lily looked to him and turned away to watch the guards who were pantomiming how one of them got tangled in a vine.

Murray lifted a brow at Ceardac, obviously failing at keeping the woman's attention so Ceardac persisted. "Lady Lily, what would you prefer? A walk in the moonlight or a stroll along the side of the loch during the morning hours?"

Her widened eyes met his. Ariana gasped and Murray laughed out loud.

The three of them watched, as Lily looked first to Ariana before meeting his gaze. Her expressive, large eyes swept over his face and immediately he regretted the question. Whatever her answer, he would endeavor to ensure to share the experience with her.

"I am quite fond of walks in the moonlight, actually. Your sister and I often steal away after the evening meal to walk in the garden or on the path near the forest."

Murray instantly became a guardsman. "I hope you

alert the guards. It is not safe to go about unescorted during times like these."

Ariana frowned at the man and let out a huff. She nudged Lily and both looked away to the guards' table.

They'd lost the women's attention. Ceardac elbowed Murray and studied Lily's profile. With a small, upturned nose and delicate features, she was like a wee forest Fae. Her graceful neck caught his attention next when she leaned forward in an effort to hear what the men discussed at another table. She had always been inquisitive. He remembered once, when he was about ten, plotting with his brothers to steal Ariana's toys and bury them. They'd caught Lily hiding behind a curtain. She'd kicked him and gotten away, screaming like a wild beastie. She'd gotten his father's attention and both he and his brothers had been punished for hitting her even though none had touched her.

He'd been so angry, until she'd peeked around his father's legs and stuck her tongue out which caused him to giggle.

As if sensing his regard, she turned to him. He must have been smiling because her lips curved in response and his heart skipped a beat. The reaction shocked him so that when she looked away, he pressed his hand to his chest to ensure something wasn't amiss.

"Interesting," Murray drew out the word. "I see now why the hesitation to marry the Grant lass."

Ceardac straightened and picked up a piece of bread. "What nonsense are you speaking, Murray?"

Murray leaned on his elbow, facing him so the women could not see his face. "You are lovestruck with the little miss."

Instead of a reply, he gulped down his ale and motioned for a maid to refill his goblet. Murray did not know what he spoke of.

Chapter 22

Steaphan was astounded when Valent entered the dining room and sat at the opposite end of the table. He didn't acknowledge anyone, but he constantly scanned the faces around the table. Sorcha, being as she was, immediately stood and went to hug him, making a fuss of introducing him to her husband.

Although his mother, who sat on his right, looked to Valent, she did not greet him, but instead turned a harsh look to Steaphan. She'd definitely have something to say on the matter later.

"This is how it should have been all along. I am so happy right now," Sorcha exclaimed and wiped at her tear-streaked face.

Her husband patted her shoulder. "Do not make such a fuss, Sorcha. Eat, go on." Malcolm, her husband, was a quiet, gentle man, the perfect partner for his excitable sister.

Sorcha pushed his hand away and looked from Steaphan to Valent. "My two handsome brothers. Look at you. So much alike, yet I can readily see the differences."

His mother looked to Steaphan and then Valent, her eyes narrowing. "Of course they are different. Steaphan has a leaner face. Always did."

Valent joined the group by looking at Steaphan..
Valent's gaze scanned his face, but he remained silent.

Sorcha shrugged. "Darach has a more angular jaw,
more defined, probably from archery." She mocked
pulling back an arrow and made a stern face.

Steaphan smiled and shook his head, noticing Valent
cocked a brow at his sister's antics. "I prefer to be called
Valent."

"Oh?" Sorcha looked to everyone before meeting
Valent's direct gaze. "I suppose I can do that. Will you
allow me to call you Darach in private? Yes?"

For a long while, Valent studied their sister and
Steaphan wondered at his brother's thoughts. To be
thrust into a new family by force, to know that he could
have lived there and how much his life was changed by
the actions of a man on a night so long ago.

Finally, he nodded.

Sorcha beamed at him and began to eat.

"How long will he be here?" His mother had to sour
the moment as usual.

"Until I tell him what he needs to know," Steaphan
replied. "Do you not have something to say to your son?
We all missed him terribly. Surely, you did as well?"

Lorna McKenzie finally turned to Valent. "Darach,
you were my first born son. I was proud to have given
my husband two healthy sons. But after so many years, I
find it hard to accept your presence. I do not feel you are
the boy who was taken. You are not a McKenzie any
longer in my opinion."

"Mother!" Sorcha exclaimed, slamming her palm on
the table. "Why must you always be so cruel?"

"I am direct. I say what I feel. The truth everyone
else seems to skirt." Their mother glared at Sorcha. "All
of you know it's true. Darach, Valent, or whoever this
person is has no desire whatsoever to be here. This

pretense of a family reunion is just that. A farce." She stood and walked to the door.

Valent spoke up, stopping her in her steps. "Perhaps my trials away from you were not as bad as I thought. That you refuse to acknowledge me as your son is not as bothersome as knowing you didn't grieve for the child who was taken from you."

Lorna gasped and spun on her heel. She stalked to Valent leaning over him, her finger outstretched. "You know nothing of what I felt then. Nor do you know how much that day changed my life." Both studied each other for a moment before their mother let out a sob and stormed from the room leaving everyone in stunned silence. It was the first time in years Steaphan had seen her show any emotion other than bitterness.

Sorcha broke the silence that followed. "I suppose I should to see about her." By her hesitance, it was not her first choice.

"I think it's best you don't," Steaphan told her and then addressed Valent. "We should talk."

They rose and went to his study. Valent moved about the room, studying the items that once belonged to their father. He stopped when spotting a bow and arrow in the corner. "Who does this belong to?"

"It was our father's. He was quite an accomplished archer, as I hear you are."

"Who did you hear that from? I never competed against your clan." Valent reached for the bow and lifted it to inspect it closer.

"Several of my archers were at the games earlier this year. They reported of an archer who looked like me and was a prize competitor."

Valent didn't acknowledge his statement. Instead, he continued to study the bow. "Do you use it?"

Steaphan poured two glasses of whiskey and placed

one on the table next to where Valent stood. "No. I have my own. You may have that one."

His brother held it without response, then placed it back in the corner. "Perhaps it is best if you gift it to someone more worthy in your clan."

"In my opinion there is no one, but I will not argue about it. It is yours if you wish."

Valent drank the whiskey and Steaphan refilled his glass before motioning to the chairs.

They settled and Steaphan looked to the flames in the hearth attempting to formulate how to begin. "The day you disappeared, we returned here. Sorcha and I were hustled to our rooms, but I could hear all the screaming and men being dispatched on horseback. Mother went to her chambers and did not emerge for many days."

He didn't bother looking at Valent, in his mind he was far away. Over twenty-five years away.

"The man who took you came upon us in the town center. He grabbed mother and took her behind the building. She screamed for us to stay put. But you did not listen. You ran after her. I followed and grabbed your hand. You can imagine what the man was doing. I was too terrified to look away. She stared blankly toward us while the man took her. When he turned to look at us, she slammed a rock to the side of his head."

He took a breath and noticed Valent watched him closely, taking in every word. "At the same time, mother's maid showed up. She began screaming. Trying to get someone to help. The man hit mother with his fist and when she fought back, he became enraged."

Steaphan took a breath and let it out slowly. "Everything seemed to happen so fast after that. The man neared us and grabbed you. I tried so hard to hold on to your hand, but you slipped from my grasp. I screamed for you. Over the man's shoulder, you had your arms outstretched to me, your mouth wide open as you called for me. I ran around tugging at everyone's hands, trying to get help, but I didn't speak clearly and they didn't understand me. No one went after you and I could not understand why."

Steaphan took another drink before continuing. "Mother's maid explained to me they thought mother was dead as she lay motionless on the ground. By the time she realized you were not around, you were gone."

Valent finally looked away to the hearth.

"Do you remember any of this?" Steaphan asked.

Valent's hand shook slightly when he lifted his whiskey. His flat gaze met Steaphan's. "Lorna McKenzie is right. I am not the same lad who was snatched from this family. I cannot return and hope to be a McKenzie. There is no place for me here."

"Why must you be so insistent on leaving? Why can you not accept that what happened was none of our faults and that this is your home? We are your family."

Valent seemed to ponder his questions. Steaphan decided to give him one more thing to think on.

"I don't ask that you step in to become laird. But I do ask that you give us some time to get to know each other. I can help you find a post elsewhere. You can join another guard or, if you wish, take one of the McKenzie smaller keeps. It is your birthright as eldest to have whichever you wish."

Valent's gaze met Steaphan's. Valent seemed to soften. Steaphan's words had shocked him. "You are a kind man, Steaphan McKenzie. I am glad to know my twin is an honorable person. I will consider your words."

Steaphan stood. "My wife, Fiona, is here. Another situation at hand. She refused to eat the dinner meal with me because I brought her here and did not allow her to remain home at Mudduch for a fortnight. No one, it seems, wants to live with me at the moment." He rubbed the back of his neck and looked to the doorway. "I will dispense with the guardsmen. If you wish to leave, you are free to do so. A horse will be provided for you. All I ask is that you do not harm any of my people."

By the heavy footsteps, Fiona McKenzie wondered if whoever approached was weary. When Steaphan stepped through the doorway, he met her gaze for a long moment. He sunk into a chair and rubbed his hands down his face. Her anger at him for bringing her here evaporated at seeing his fatigue.

"How are you faring, Fiona?"

"I am well. You, on the other hand, do not seem well at all." She looked to the bed. "I will call for a bath and after, you should rest."

His clear gray eyes met hers and she gritted her teeth at the thumping of her heart. "We should talk."

"Whatever it is can wait."

"You are cross with me."

"Aye, I am. I do not like the ways of men who will not allow a woman to have a say."

His lips curved. "I gave you plenty of say last night."

Her cheeks flushed at the thought and, immediately, she pictured him bereft of clothes climbing over her. "That is not what I refer to and you know it."

"Very well. Can we come to an agreement that in the future we discuss anything that affects us both?"

Fiona's mouth fell open. She was quite enjoying being cross at him. It felt foreign for him to agree to her demands. To talk over things was unheard of. Why was the man being so agreeable? Could it be like Mairi had said? According to her maid, Mairi, a woman could get her way by distracting her husband through bed sport.

"I agree to it," she replied quickly, lest he change his mind. "Let me call for your bath."

Steaphan nodded and leaned back into the chair while Fiona sent the first lad she found to fetch the wooden tub and heated water. She overlooked the preparation of the bath and went to the adjoining chamber to find Steaphan asleep in front of the fire. She contemplated the handsome man for a few moments before clearing her throat to wake him. "Steaphan, your bath is ready."

He stood and stretched, towering over her and she took a step back.

A thousand horses could not drag her away when he began to undress; first his tunic, then his boots and, finally, his britches. Bare as a babe, he went to the adjoining room while she trailed behind him in a trance, enjoying the view of his taut backside.

"Would you like to join me, Fiona?" He looked over his shoulder at her. "I could use company."

She moved toward him and he pulled her against him, his mouth instantly taking hers. It seemed all the air was taken from the room, all sounds were gone and only they existed.

His skin was soft under her palms as she slid her hands up from his chest to his shoulders. Steaphan was already unfastening her dress, pushing it from her shoulders in order to free her breasts.

The only reaction was a loud gasp when he took one tip into his mouth and kneaded the other with his hand. Fiona clung to him, not sure if she could wait to be with him. Her body was alert to every touch, caress, and breath across her skin as well as the solidness of his body.

When he released her, she swayed. "I cannot join you in the water, it's too small. I do not think you alone will fit."

He pulled her hand and brought her closer to the tub. He lowered into the heated water. The steam rising form the heated water crated a surreal atmosphere. His lips curved with invitation. "Come, beauty."

Fiona pushed her dress to the floor, then removed her shoes and stockings. The entire time his heated gaze was on her. She fumbled with her shift and finally approached the tub, feeling disconcerted by his constant regard. When his eyes roamed to her sex, she covered it with her hands. "Must you be so curious?"

He laughed. "I love that you speak what you think. Come, I will help you."

Water splashed over the side of the tub to the stone floor, but she barely noticed as her husband settled her between his legs and pulled her back to lie against him.

His lips grazed her neck while his right hand slid under the water to between her legs.

"Oh!" Fiona gasped when his fingers delved to her center, sliding up and down until she could barely stand it. His left hand moved across her breasts, caressing one and then the other while he continued to trail his tongue on her neck.

She lost all sense and let out a cry when she splintered into pieces. Her hips moved up and down encouraging Steaphan to continue what he did.

"Let's wash and I will finish this in our bed," he told her, his voice husky with want. She could barely think, much less speak.

He, however, seemed to be in full control, reaching for the soap and cloth to wash with. She could only lie against him, too spent to move. Steaphan chuckled as he lifted her arm and washed her side. He continued until they were both well lathered, then helped her to stand.

The cool air of the space brought her out of her dreamlike state. "I'll get the fresh water and pour it over you first." She waited for him to lower and poured the water from a nearby bucket over him. Then did so again with a second one.

He did the same to her and both finally stepped from the tub. Fiona held back the urge to grab his hand and rush to the bed.

She waited while he dried himself and then her, wrapping a large cloth around her shoulders. "Brandy?"

"What?" Fiona wondered how he could drink at a time like this. She looked to between his legs, what had been hardened against her bottom was now semi-flaccid. "I thought we were going to bed."

"We are." Steaphan studied her. "But the lads will be here shortly to collect the tub." As if beckoned, there was a fast rap at the door. The lads entered the room, one of them flushing at noting her state of undress.

Fiona yelped and rushed to the adjoining chamber, while Steaphan chuckled and drank his whiskey.

"I do not find it comical in the least," Fiona admonished him after the lads finished emptying the bath water, bailing buckets out of the window and finally carrying the tub out. "You could have asked them to wait until I was out of the sight."

Steaphan leaned over the bed and kissed her soundly. "I should have, yes. Forgive me." He dropped his cloth and climbed into the bed. "How can I make it up to you, wife?"

Fiona immediately forgot she was cross when he settled between her legs and took her mouth while his sex nudged at her entrance. "Take all of me, Fiona. Let me sink into you and forget all but us."

His words sent her body to burn in want and she softened, watching his beautiful lips part as he slid into her, filling her fully with his body.

Fiona rolled over and stretched. Upon feeling a body against hers, she was immediately awake. It would take some time to become used to sleeping with someone. At the same time, the warmth of his larger body was welcome in the cool chamber. She snuggled closer to her husband.

The unfamiliar soreness between her legs was not overly horrible. As a matter of fact, it brought a smile to her face at the images of the night before.

She stole a glance at the slumbering man. A handsome one he was. In slumber, his face relaxed, he looked less the warrior and more an angel in repose. His dark brown hair was just to his shoulders and upon his cheeks and chin, a light dusting of beard. Not that she could see them at the moment, but he had the lightest colored eyes she'd ever seen, more gray than blue. Although, the night before when he'd plundered her body, taking from her all she could give, his eyes had darkened to a very dark hue.

He stirred and she closed her eyes, then slowly opened one to glimpse him. Good, he remained asleep. Fiona let out a breath and continued to study her new husband.

"I am afraid to ask what you are so deep in thought about," Steaphan opened his eyes and she felt hers widen that she'd not noticed he'd awoken. "You're pondering something." His deep voice was gravelly with sleep and she bit back the urge to kiss his sensual lips. It would not do at all to become besotted so quickly. Not do at all.

"I would like to know more about what bothered you so last evening."

He closed his eyes and let out a breath. "My brother, who was taken from our family over five and twenty years ago, is here..."

Chapter 23

Valent walked the corridor away from his chamber. Still unaccustomed to the large home, when spying a sitting room and another chamber he'd never seen, it was obvious he'd taken a wrong turn.

"Darach?" He turned to find Lorna McKenzie standing in a doorway, her eyes narrowed. "What are you doing? Why are you not guarded?"

Instead of replying, he looked away hoping to spy a maid or servant who could help him get away from the woman.

She neared, her gaze scanning him from head to feet. "I asked you a question. I have a mind to scream for guards."

"You would be dead before you could get out a sound." He looked down on her. It wasn't hatred he felt, that was too strong an emotion. It was more like apathy one feels for a pesky insect that insists on biting. "I am going to the courtyard to see my dog."

"You should collect it and whatever belongings you have and leave. You are a constant reminder of things best left in the past." Her hand shook when she reached for the wall in an attempt to remain steady.

Valent studied the woman. "I find it interesting to

learn I was not the only one to lose their family that day." He walked away, ignoring her calling after him to explain himself. She understood what he'd meant, but just like everything else, preferred to ignore reality.

Arrow dashed to him, his tongue lolling out of the corner of his mouth, his tail wagging. He bent down to rub the animal's flanks then went to pick up a stick. His dog followed alongside. "Steaphan. There you are."

An attractive young woman came to him and threaded her arm through his. Her hazel eyes looked to him and moved quickly away, a pretty blush across her face. She pulled him forward to continue walking. "I was thinking about what you said this morning. I know very little about how it must be for you to have recovered your brother after all this time. But my advice is that you give him time and space. I am sure he cares for you. Especially being twins. Whatever bond was between you, surely a part of it remains." She leaned onto his arm as he attempted to explain he was not Steaphan. With a sigh, she whispered, "I have to admit something. I am beginning to care for you. It is too soon to admit to love, but with time, I think you and I will find it." She looked up to him, her lips pursed and her gaze slid over his face.

Suddenly her eyes widened and her mouth fell open. "Oh!" She moved away, her face instantly red. "You are not Steaphan. I—I..."

"I see you've met my brother," Steaphan said, attempting to keep from laughing by the way his lips trembled when he pressed them together.

Valent cleared his throat. "I apologize for not making it clear. You did not allow me time to speak."

"What?" She jabbed her finger into his chest. "You could have interrupted me. Made it clear who you were."

Steaphan's wife spun on her heel and did the same to Steaphan. "And you. Why didn't you tell me your brother was identical to you?"

Steaphan chuckled before replying. "It didn't occur to me." He yelped and jumped to one foot when she kicked him in the shin and stalked away.

"Your wife is a hellion," Valent grumbled rubbing at his chest. "Has strong fingers."

"Aye, she is," Steaphan replied with a wide grin.

Valent could not help but relax around his brother. What Fiona spoke about suddenly rang true. He did feel a bond with his brother. Being near him was like reuniting with a part of his own body.

Steaphan walked toward the keep gates. "Going for a walk?"

"Aye, I needed time to ponder what I would say to you today. It is hard for me to accept anything you offer. I do not feel part of your family, yet now I understand more how you, our father, and Sorcha suffered my loss. I have made a decision, brother."

Valent and his brother looked to each other for a long moment. It astounded him how easily he could read Steaphan's thoughts. The emotions reflected in the face, so much like his, touched him deeper than anything he'd ever known.

When Steaphan embraced him, Valent lowered his guard and held him. For the first time in his life, he understood what having a family was like.

Although it was an unusually warm day for late in the autumn, there was a chill in her that refused to be dispelled. Lily pulled her wrap tighter around her shoulders as she descended the stairs and walked through the great room, intent on going to the garden to gather herbs to use to make medicinal salve for one of the guards who'd complained about a wound he'd received during practice.

Laughter rung out, the deep timbre could only be Ceardac's. Lily froze in place, looking towards his study. It seemed whatever he spoke of with his ever-present friend, Murray, made him laugh so loud it echoed through the great room. Murray's laughter joined in with whatever they spoke of.

The sound of him having a light moment made her lips curve. Of all people, he deserved to have a good day, after all that he'd been forced to shoulder. Then there was the grief of losing his brothers and many of the guardsmen he'd grown up with. Ceardac, the second born son to the McLeod never aspired to becoming laird. He'd been the most easygoing of the three brothers. He'd always kept an eye on her and Ariana.

She hurried past the study, intent on getting to the garden without being spotted. Her eyes misted at knowing how much she'd miss the sound of his voice and the glimpses of him at the evening meals.

The dry leaves crunched under her shoes as she made her way through the courtyard to the garden, the sun warming her back. Lily let out a breath and looked across the area to where the men trained and spied Ariana with her bow and quiver. Her friend, no doubt, was taking advantage of the warmth of the day to practice.

Lily considered that perhaps she, too, should learn archery or some sort of self-protection. If ever she was faced with an attack again, she wanted to be prepared to defend herself and not cower when faced with someone intent on hurting her.

"Are you considering taking up archery?" Ceardac's voice startled her and she dropped her basket. He bent to retrieve it, which gave her the opportunity to admire the wide expanse of his back and the glimmer of the sun's rays on his auburn hair.

"As a matter of fact, I was. I am going to ask Ariana to help me. If ever I am somewhere that is under attack again, I will join with the men and defend the home." She jutted her chin out to challenge any retort.

Ceardac's lips quivered. "You've always done that. Whenever you set your mind to something and do not wish to be contradicted, you stick out that pointy chin of yours and squint your eyes."

"I do not squint." Lily gasped at the unattractive image he painted. "Do I?" Her eyes rounded and she sniffed. "It does not matter. Do not answer."

When Lily reached for the basket, he held it out of her reach. "I need to speak to you about some news I received just now."

It struck her as interesting that after Murray, she was his choice of who to share the news with. "Why do you share it with me? I heard you laughing. If it is good news, perhaps you should include Ariana as well."

"She is aware and insisted I speak to you."

Lily looked past him to where Ariana stood. She'd stopped practicing and watched them with interest. A tingle of dread crawled up her spine. "What is it?"

"You look as if you are expecting horrible news. Perhaps it is. I am not sure." Ceardac's brows lowered and he seemed to have lost some of his confidence. "The thing is. Well, what happened was..." He raked his fingers through his hair and motioned to a bench. "Perhaps it is best if we sit."

He was sending her away. She'd not considered that in her new position as a friend of the family, he had every right to marry her off in order to make an alliance with another clan. She gripped her hands together in her lap and kept her gaze lowered.

Ceardac let out a breath. "A messenger came from the Grant. It seems my intended has locked herself in the tower and refuses to leave unless the laird acquiesces to her demands."

Damn her curious nature. Lily looked to him, waiting for him to continue the interesting tale. "What does she want?"

"She refuses to wed someone other than her one true love. The Grant sent a profuse apology. The very spoiled chit refused to eat or drink until he agreed to allow her to marry one of the guardsmen. It seems I have been replaced."

He let out a deep breath and held both hands to his chest as if in deep pain. "I must find a replacement for wife who will accept me. What am I to do?"

Lily giggled and shoved at his shoulder. "You are glad for it. Admit it."

His grin made her smile back. "It is for the best, I think."

"I also have made up my mind not to make a rash decision like I did by accepting the Grant's proposal when so much was happening. I almost lost my chance at marrying a much more suitable wife."

The lightness of the moment was gone and Lily's heart sank. She'd not noticed Ceardac speaking with anyone who would be suitable. Perhaps during his visit to Skye he'd met someone. "I am happy for you." Lily stood, prepared to return inside and busy herself in the kitchen to avoid thinking on the matter.

Ceardac took her hand, the warmth of his larger one causing a tingle of pleasure to rush to her chest. "Lily. Will you marry me?"

Her legs gave out and she half-fell back onto the

bench. "Did you just ask me to marry you? Have you gone daft? A laird cannot wed with a maid. No matter what Ariana calls me..."

He quieted her protests by pulling her to him by the shoulders and covering her mouth with his.

In front of everyone in the courtyard, Ceardac McLeod kissed her like no one had ever done and she responded by wrapping her arms around his neck.

When he finally released her, she had to blink in order to see clearly. This had to be a dream. Several of the guards and other people gawked at their open display and she flushed, her face heating.

Ceardac's crooked smile sent new waves of emotion through her and tears threatened to spill. She nodded and laughed, unable to control her emotions.

He pressed a soft kiss on her nose. "I take it your answer is yes?"

"Yes." Lily laughed and hugged him. Over his shoulder she caught sight of Ariana's bright smile.

Chapter 24

Steaphan pulled his tartan up, wrapping a portion of the fabric around his neck. Winter was rapidly approaching and he was behind in visiting his tenants and ensuring they were all well prepared for the colder season.

Niven rode alongside, as well as eight warriors, as they made their way to a small farm community on the southern border of McKenzie lands. This was the community that had lost four men on the day Beathan McLeod ordered his men to kill them for hunting on McLeod lands. The poor men were without hope as they were farmers who'd mistakenly trespassed.

Calum, an older man, waved in greeting as they neared. The farmer who'd farmed his entire life, as his father and father's father, was a friendly sort. He often hosted the other families for meals and such.

"Aye, Laird. Nice to see you. Congratulations are in order. I hear ye got married." The man chuckled and motioned to his wife Jane. "'Tis a good thing to settle down with a good woman, aye?"

"It is Calum," Steaphan replied and dismounted, noticing several farmers gathering at seeing them approach.

Calum pulled a young lad by the arm and pointed a

finger at him. "I give ye great responsibility, lad. Fetch the others and let them know our laird is here. They must come and hear what news he brings."

The boy's chest puffed out at the duty he'd received and raced away, several other boys chasing after.

"Come in. Come in." Calum swept his arms towards the doorway where his wife stood beaming at them. "I have a new jug of mead the wife just made."

Half an hour later, most of the farmers were gathered at the home and Steaphan went out to address them. After dispensing some grain, he reminded them to remain within the borders. Additionally, he granted them permission to hunt further north in the lands surrounding the keep. He set to task and asked questions of each family until being satisfied they would all be fed well during the winter. It was hours later that he and his men prepared to leave.

"There is something I'd like to speak to ye about in private, Laird." Calum's solemn eyes went to Niven and the other guardsmen.

"Of course," Steaphan replied as an unexplainable trickle of apprehension traveled up his spine. They walked a few steps from the others. "What bothers you?"

The man studied his face for a long time as if searching for an answer without having to speak the question. "Laird, when we were attacked by the McLeods, I saw something that has bothered me since. I 'aven't told a soul because no one would believe it."

"Go on."

"The McLeods who attacked, amongst them was an archer. He was identical in features to you. How can that be?"

Steaphan couldn't help his sharp intake of breath. "Did he kill anyone?"

"He pierced poor Ludlow, who was already dead with

an arrow. Here's the thing. I do believe he attempted to distract the others from seeing that our young Ewan was still alive."

"We ensured that every man who attacked you that day paid for what they did."

Calum seemed to ponder what he'd said to him. "Verra well, Laird. I will not speak of it. You know who he is."

It was not a question, but Steaphan nodded. "Aye. I do."

"Yer missing brother then?"

"Aye."

The farmer nodded and wiped a weathered hand down his face. "Strange lots life can deal sometimes."

"Darach followed orders, as a guardsman for the McLeods. He was not aware of his relationship with us. He knows now. It is good to hear he attempted to help in some way."

"What did the farmer have to say?" Niven asked once he mounted and they headed to another area. "It seemed serious."

Steaphan looked back to the farmer who watched them depart. "Darach...er Valent was amongst those who attacked the hunters."

"Old man Calum saw him," Niven deduced. "This could become complicated for Valent."

"Perhaps. Valent has made a decision, which comes at a good time. He will not be in danger of retaliation from our people for the time being. When I see him, I will tell him it is imperative he make amends to these farmers for that day."

"Fiona!" Steaphan entered his chambers and, once again, called for his wife. She was neither in the great room nor in the sitting room. He'd scoured the courtyard and gardens and did not find her. Finally he stalked to his mother's room.

Lorna looked up as he walked in and scowled. "She is not here, either."

With clenched fists he neared the aggravating woman. "What did you do?"

His mother looked out the window and sighed. "Things were much easier when you were younger. You were simpler to manage. Your father, God rest his soul, rarely challenged my requests."

"I asked you a question." He gripped her shoulder. "Where is Fiona?"

"Away. I sent her away." Lorna laughed, the sound without mirth grated at his already tender hold on anger. If she were a man, he would have already smashed his fist into the center of her face.

"Mother, tell me at once where she was taken."

Lorna straightened her back and glared at him. "Never." Spittle landed on his face and he lifted his hand to wipe it. Mistaking that he planned to hit her, she screamed and jumped away. "You will thank me for this, Steaphan. You cannot think I would stand by and allow a McLeod to run my household."

"You are mad." He rushed from the room, stopping the first guard he found. "Go get all the guards into the courtyard at once. Then return here. Guard the doorway and do not, under any circumstances, allow my mother to leave."

"Aye, Laird." The guard ran to do as told.

Steaphan stalked before his guards. "I am laird, not my mother. If any of you followed her direction against my wife, you will be punished and exiled from my lands. Where is my wife?" he screamed.

One guard stepped forward. "I was up on the top, Laird." He motioned to the turrets. "I saw yer wife leaving in a wagon with two men and her maid. I thought, perhaps, she went to the village."

"In what direction?" Steaphan looked to see that Niven was mounted and pulled a horse for him.

"East, Laird."

"Come, you four." He motioned to four guardsmen and then glared at the rest. "You are all restricted to the keep for the next seven days. Train for six hours a day and then another two after the evening meal. God help you all if anything happened to my wife."

Leaving two guards in charge of administering the training, he and the party of five raced east.

The sun was setting and Steaphan was wild with fury at not spotting whoever took Fiona. He imagined the worst and, once again, hated himself for not demanding his mother tell him where she sent his wife.

"I cannot think straight," he admitted to Niven. "I should have insisted she tell me where Fiona was being taken."

Niven scanned the horizon. "Is there a dwelling near here that your mother may be aware of? Or perhaps people she visited on occasion in this region?"

"No..." His eyes widened. "It can't be." Steaphan spurred the horse toward the forest. "Come, there is a place about an hour's ride from here. God help my mother if even a hair on my wife's head has been touched."

Niven finally caught up. "Where do you think she is?"

"There is a group of heretics that live near here. Long ago, my father granted them permission to live at the edge of the forest as long as they remained away from the clanspeople and didn't cause any harm."

He thought for a moment before continuing. "For some reason, after Darach went missing, my mother became interested in them and began visiting them. I followed her once and she became very upset. Demanded that I keep silent."

"As far as I know they are peaceful people," Niven said, attempting to calm him. "Do not rush in with sword drawn. Perhaps your mother threatened them."

They arrived at the quaint circle of cottages. Several women with loosed hair and long, colorful skirts rushed inside the dwellings while the men came out to await their arrival. Steaphan noticed none of them held a weapon.

"Who are you?" a man who was obviously the leader of the group asked, moving forward. "You trespass our circle, which is strictly forbidden."

"I am Laird McKenzie," Steaphan called out. "I come in search of my wife. Is she here?"

The men looked to each other. Steaphan dismounted. "Speak. If you do not, I will forfeit my father's permission to remain on my lands."

The same man closed the distance between them. "The laird's own wife told us we were to host the woman. That she was evil and needed cleansing. She promised to return to witness us perform the ritual in seven days."

Steaphan gritted his teeth. "The woman who spoke to you is my mother. She has no authority to have my wife brought here. Where is my wife?" He glared at the man who moved back and motioned with a hand toward the tents.

A flap lifted and one of the women peered out at him before moving aside.

"I am here." Fiona ran from a tent and threw herself against him, shaking all over.

"Have you been harmed?" He lifted her face and

studied it. Other than her teeth chattering, she seemed unharmed.

"No, just frightened. I was not sure you how long it would be before you found me." She began to cry and he held her against him.

The man shuffled his feet and looked back to the people who'd come out of the cottages and watched with interest. Worry sketched on most faces. "Laird, I beg your forgiveness. We did not know your father had died."

"I should have informed you," Steaphan conceded. "You may remain on the lands. On occasion, it would behoove you to come to court at the keep and remain informed of what happens on McKenzie lands."

"Aye, Laird. I will. You have our gratitude for forgiving this grievous mistake." The man bowed to him and backed away. Silently, the people formed a circle and then began chanting.

"Let us go home." Steaphan wrapped his tartan around his wife and motioned for the guards. They came forward to hold her until he mounted and then assisted her onto his horse.

She lay against him, her trembling lessening. Steaphan kissed her temple. "I will never allow my mother or anyone to harm you. Trust me in that, Fiona."

"I do." Her solemn eyes met his. "I know you will keep me safe, always. As terrified as I was at first, I knew you would not stop looking until you found me. The people back there were different, but very nice. Do not punish them."

"I will not." His mind was already on what he would have to do once they arrived back at their home.

The keep came into view, the majestic, gray stone building presiding over the valleys that surrounded the hill on which it was built. Rather than pride at seeing his home, anger coursed through him. His mother would leave today. Whether she went to live with Sorcha or to a cottage in the village did not matter to him at the moment. One thing he was sure of: she would not spend one more night under the same roof as Fiona.

It was clear he could not trust his mother. She would, in all certainty, try something worse than today. If any harm came to his wife... The thought startled him. He looked down to the dark curls about Fiona's head. He loved his wife. So soon after marrying and already the thought of any harm coming to her had scared him as much as the day he'd lost his brother.

He wrapped an arm around her and pulled her closer, pressing another kiss to her head. "You are precious to me, wife."

She let out a sigh and her hand rubbed up and down his arm. "Thank you for coming for me, Steaphan."

The great room was silent as the assembled guards and servants awaited his mother's entrance. That Valent was amongst them was a good sign.

Lorna entered, her shrewd eyes scanning the room before stopping on Fiona. She gasped, her eyes widening in disbelief. "I see your wife has returned." She met Steaphan's gaze with challenge. "Next time, I will ensure she is removed permanently."

"Have you no remorse?" Steaphan motioned for the guards to stop her from moving to the high board. "Do you honestly believe I will allow you to remain here when you openly admit planning harm to Fiona?"

"You cannot send me away, you swore to your father on his deathbed to care for me."

"I did. But that does not necessarily mean here. Some of your personal belongings are packed and in a wagon outside. You can direct the driver to take you to Sorcha's house or to a cottage in the village that will be prepared for you. Your choice."

The guards who stood beside her did not move, but Lorna McKenzie recoiled in horror from them. "No. No!" She rushed to Steaphan. "I refuse to leave my home. This is my house, where I will die." Before he could stop her, she raced from the room and ran up the stairs.

"Sire, she may lock herself in her chamber. We will not be able to enter," one of the guards pointed out, his gaze toward where Lorna went.

"I had one of the guards posted, just in case."

Everyone began speaking at once. Steaphan lifted a hand and they silenced. "Let it be known. I will not tolerate any disrespect to my wife or anyone in my family. This includes my brother. I send my mother away, but you will not receive as fair a treatment." He scanned the room. "Is that understood?"

"Aye!" the people called out and began to speak again.

"Sire!" An archer rushed into the room. "Your mother is on the roof."

Fiona gasped. "Oh no."

Steaphan, Niven and two men ran up the stairs. Just as he reached the roof, a collective gasp sounded. Lorna leaped to her death. He didn't have to look to know.

Steaphan froze, unable to move.

His heartbeat sounded steady and loud in his ears. Everything disappeared and all he saw was a thick fog swirling around him, clouding his ability to move. Through the haze, a voice penetrated. "Steaphan. Come, love."

Warm hands took his and pulled him. Although he still could not see clearly, he instinctively knew the person that guided him would ensure he did not misstep. Little by little, things came clearer. He found himself in the study with Niven and Fiona. Niven pushed a glass of whiskey into his hand while Fiona held his other.

"Steaphan, look at me." The words didn't make sense at first, until finally he looked into clear, hazel eyes.

"Fiona."

"Aye, my love, I am here. Listen to me. It is not your fault. Your mother, she was not well."

"I drove her to kill herself."

"The consequence of her own actions. She made that choice," Niven interjected. "You've made allowances and have been very patient over the last few years."

His chest tightened. "She is dead, then?"

"Yes," Fiona replied, sympathy etched on her pretty face. "I am so sorry."

Steaphan put the glass down and pulled his wife against him. They rocked in silence. There was light clip of the door closing as Niven left him with his wife to grieve.

Chapter 25

The arrow flew across the expanse landing just outside the center circle. The wind did not help with target practice, yet she was growing exasperated at how badly her aim was on that afternoon.

Ariana lifted her bow and pulled back on the string holding the arrow in place. She let out a breath and closed her right eye. Head tilted to the side, she released the arrow. Much better, just inside the center circle.

Movement at the edge of the wood's line caught her attention. She narrowed her eyes to see Valent's apprentice watching her. She ignored him and moved to the target to retrieve her arrows. The young man went from one foot to the other as if anxious. Ariana motioned him to come closer and he shook his head then looked past her to the other men and quickly motioned with his fingers for her to come to him, instead.

"Of all the things. If he killed a large deer and needs help or permission to take it home, he needs to speak to Murray, not me," Ariana grumbled aloud as she walked to him.

"Milady, I have a message for ye." He swallowed and his face flushed crimson. "I beg yer forgiveness if I offend ye. The archer, Valent, is at the cottage. He asked I tell ye..."

Her heart skipped a beat and her stomach tumbled. "What did he say?"

"Just that he wishes to speak to ye. To not tell anyone else and to let ye know he will only remain this night. He will be gone tomorrow."

Ariana looked over her shoulder. Some of the archers took note of them speaking and looked on with interest. "Walk to the practice area with me and pretend to teach me how to shoot. The others are wondering what we speak of. Let them believe I asked you for help."

They moved to where she'd been standing. Ariana smiled at the boy who would one day be quite a handsome man. "Show me how you shoot."

He stood straight, his face serious as he settled an arrow into the groove of the bow. When he released it, the arrow flew with a much higher speed than hers and, without a sound, landed in the center of the target.

Ariana smiled. "Impressive."

"Thank ye, milady." He beamed at her. "Now you try."

After a few moments, she excused herself and rushed to her chamber. She scribbled a note to Lily asking that she make excuses for her absence at the evening meal and rushed out a side exit near the kitchens to avoid being spotted by her brother.

Once at the stables, she saddled her own horse and headed to the forest. Her breathing was labored, heart hammering against her breastbone as she checked, once again, to ensure she wasn't followed. Why was he back? Had something happened and Valent changed his mind, returning for her?

Her thoughts went in a million different directions as she slowed once in the woods. What would she actually do if Valent came for her?

No, it was not possible. He came for another reason, and besides, now that she'd accepted Ross McLeod's proposal, a sudden departure would make Ceardac appear badly before the McLeods of Skye who'd come to their aid when needed.

The cottage came into view and her heart thundered at the sight of a horse tethered beside it in the small, covered shelter.

As she approached the door, it flew open and she flung herself into Valent's arms. The solid chest and strong arms encircling her made every question and all reason disappear. All she knew at the moment was that there, in his embrace, was the place she belonged. With Valent and no other.

"I have missed ye." Valent's voice was gruff.

He took her mouth with so much need it made her tremble. Valent's body shook as they moved back into the cottage, the door closing behind them.

Both began to undress with urgency and, quickly, he stood totally bereft of clothes, his magnificent body on full display for her. With her gaze, she feasted on the sight of him as he stalked forward and lifted her to the bed.

Once again, his mouth claimed hers as she slid her hand down his back, needing to touch every part of him.

"You are mine," he echoed her thoughts and a shiver of happiness moved through her entire body. "Never again will I be away from you."

"Take me, Valent. I need to know you claim me totally." Ariana cupped his buttocks and pulled him to her.

Valent's breathing was harsh, his lips parted when his darkened eyes met hers. "Yes." He maneuvered his length between her legs and plunged forward, filling her completely.

Ariana gasped and pulled his face to hers so she could kiss him once again. His tongue probed her mouth and she allowed it entrance, enjoying the feel of him entering her body there, as well.

In a steady rhythm, he moved in and out, his slender hips thrusting faster and faster as they both climbed to the precipice from where they'd fall into bliss.

"Yes!" Tremors traveled from where they joined to her very center and Ariana prepared to fall. She tried in vain to restrain the inevitable a bit longer, needing to prolong the moment.

Everything shifted and she fell into a wonderful abyss of warmth, love, and Valent.

He cried out as well, his deep voice penetrating through her dreamlike state and he fell over her.

They clung to one another without speaking in an understood need to convince themselves it was real. With his face between her neck and shoulder, she turned and pressed her cheek the side of it. "I love you, Valent. I missed you so."

Moments later, Valent lay on his back and Ariana snuggled beside him. He'd pulled a blanket over them, which she recognized as one she'd given him months earlier. It seemed so long ago when she'd visited him after her brother, Donall, had him whipped for attempting to save a McKenzie boy from being killed.

"I came for you," Valent finally spoke. "I have a home now."

"With the McKenzies?"

"Yes and no. On their lands, but away from the keep. I was first born." He swallowed visibly and she wondered what had transpired while he was gone.

"You left me." The words brought back the sting of his abandonment. A tear escaped down her neck. "Why?"

Valent wiped her tear way and kissed her. "My brother had me taken by force. I did not leave of free will."

"Something happened while you were there then?"

"Aye, much happened. I learned the McKenzie is a fair, honorable man."

Ariana closed her eyes and fortified herself. "I cannot live on McKenzie lands. He killed my brothers. Perhaps not personally, but he ordered it. I hate him."

"I understand. So does he. I asked that he avoid you and that we would not be ordered to appear at court together."

Valent continued the explanation. "You must understand, Ceardac would have done the same. Your brothers wronged the McKenzie Clan over a simple mistake. Many lives were lost because of Beathan's rash actions."

As much as it pained her, it was true. So much could have been avoided if her brother had not been so intent on making a name for himself. Young and arrogant, Beathan acted without thought. The cruel streak in him had always frightened her.

Valent lifted her face. "I agreed to the land and home only because I wanted to provide for you, Ariana. I cannot fathom taking you with me on a trek without certainty. Accept me. Give us an opportunity to be together as husband and wife."

"What of Ceardac? He has made a handfast agreement with the McLeods of Skye. I am set to marry Ross McLeod."

A deep growl rumbled from him and Ariana could not help but smile at the show of ownership. "We will speak to him at once." Valent slid from the bed and began to dress. "Come, Ariana."

"I cannot agree to this." Ceardac's gaze went from Ariana to Valent. "We have made an agreement with the McLeods of Skye. I cannot go back on my word."

"It is not you, but Ariana who has changed her mind," Valent interceded.

It struck Ariana how different Valent's posture was before Ceardac. The relationship was no longer that of a laird over an archer, but more like equals. Land ownership, a laird in his own right now, Valent shouldered it well and she understood why he needed to accept what was his birthright.

"And with a McKenzie, no less."

She looked to Valent when he didn't deny the clan affiliation. He must have accepted the last name along with the land. Of course, it would be the only way to take lairdship over the tenants of wherever they were to live.

Both men looked to one another for a long time before Ceardac finally held his hand out. "I wish you both well. That you both leave without me knowing is something I cannot help." He gave them a pointed look to ensure they understood the hidden message.

While the men shook hands, Lily rushed in, her face flushed and eyes flying to the others in the room. "What happens?"

"My sister is leaving," Ceardac told her and went to stand beside his new intended and looked to Ariana.

"I have news, as well," he added.

When his arms went around Lily's shoulders Ariana rushed to them, tears already falling. "Are you to be married?"

"Aye," Ceardac replied while Lily turned a bright shade of red. "Perhaps we can rush the ceremony so you can attend." He looked to Valent. "Will you remain for a few days?"

Ariana looked to him willing a yes. She would hate

not being there to witness the new start for her clan. The realization that her marrying Valent would unite their clans and peace would come to the region between them someday. Sure there was much resentment after the recent battles and losses on both sides, but given time, things would settle and, eventually, it would be easier to coexist.

"Of course, we will." Valent took her hand. "Is it possible that the clergyman marry us as well?"

Ariana and Lily clung to each other, happy tears spilling to their wide smiles as they hugged. Both turned to look at the men with expectant expressions.

"How could I say no?" Ceardac replied, his warm gaze on the two women he loved.

The night was cold, but snuggled close to Valent as they strolled outside, Ariana was quite warm. "What are you thinking about?" She looked to the silent man whose arm wrapped protectively around her.

"I am still trying to understand all that has happened. I feel as if I will wake up any moment and be back at my cottage, still in service to your brother, Donall."

If anyone would have told her the story of all that happened, she would not believe a word of it herself. "I can't help but think on the past, as well. I know it was not a happy time for you, but I had my family. My brothers were alive."

Valent lifted her face with a gentle touch and pressed a light kiss to her lips. "Aye, I understand. However, there is much to be happy about now and I will ensure you are always so with me."

"What happened at your brother's keep?" She'd been tentative about asking, but could not keep from it any longer.

They stopped and Valent lifted her to sit atop a

waist-high, thick, stone wall. "I learned my brother is a good man. That we can be so involved in our own circumstance we don't think of the other side of things. I was finally able to see the faces of those who haunted my dreams for my entire life. The woman who gave me life lost herself the day I disappeared."

He bent his head and although Ariana wanted to go to him, she held back, allowing him time to think things through. When his gaze lifted, there was pain. "I am a simple man, Ariana. Selfish to aim so high as to garner you, a laird's daughter."

"Don't say that..." She stopped talking when he shook his head.

"Tis the truth. I can barely read and write. How will I laird over people when I have no knowledge of numbers and such? More than ever, even facing death, I am afraid."

His admission broke Ariana's heart and she opened her arms. "Come, please." He did and she wrapped her arms around him, then spoke into his ear.

"Together is how you will. You have a good heart and are stronger than any man I've ever met. I am not only honored, but feel fortunate that you chose me."

When his shoulders sagged, whether from relief or giving up, she kissed his temple. "If my brother did not consider you worthy, he would have done everything in his power to keep us apart. I know Ceardac enough. He admires you."

"You think so?" In the hope of his gaze, she saw the young foundling looking for acceptance. "Truly?"

"Very much so. Ceardac would not have allowed our marriage unless he found you a man of worth. I stake my life on it."

Valent beamed and, immediately, everything was well. "We should go inside. It's cold."

"Will you come to my bed tonight?"

"Nay. I willna do anything to change your brother's opinion of me. Once we are wed, I will sleep beside you always."

"Except when you go hunting, checking on the tenants, go to war, visit your brother or..."

Valent chuckled and pulled her closer. "You know what I mean."

Chapter 26

The Storm

Arrow wheezed one last breath and went limp. Valent could not breathe. He gulped in an attempt to keep the sob from erupting. The pressure in his chest constricted so tightly, he feared his heart would stop. Frosty wind whipped his hair across his face, the coldness chilling the tears that fell without reserve down his cheeks.

His steed dug into the ground with its front leg, seeming to send a message of understanding, or perhaps the animal was ready for his warm stable and food. They'd been out most of the day searching for the dog, his faithful companion, who'd gone missing the day before. At the moment, Valent didn't care what the horse or anyone for that matter wanted, he pushed his face into Arrow's soft fur and gave his grief free rein.

Through all the hardships, beatings, brutal training, and when Tavish, the old man who'd raised him, died, Arrow had been the one constant source of comfort. Every day, they'd been together and every night the dog had ensured Valent's well-being before sleeping.

In truth, his life was so much better now. He had a

229

home, a wife, and land to call his own. She'd even brought along a young boy, David, now almost ten years old. Everything he never dared to dream of having was a reality.

Yet somehow, Arrow's presence kept him grounded to the humble archer he'd once been, the young boy who'd been abandoned as a child and survived so much.

Ariana would be worried about him and share in his sorrow, of that he was sure. And yet, he wasn't ready to part with Arrow, not ready to face anyone and speak of how deeply he felt the loss of his devoted companion.

The sun was low in the sky by the time he finished burying his dog. He pulled one of the dog's namesakes from his quiver and stuck it into the ground to mark the spot, then went to his mount. Valent closed his eyes and took a deep breath, lifting his face to the starlit Highland sky and fortified himself.

"Laird?" Two guardsmen remained a distance away. They must have caught sight of his grief earlier by the downcast of their gazes. "Are ye ready to return to the keep?" one of the men, Kael, asked. "Your wife, Lady McKenzie, sent us to find ye."

He'd yet to become accustomed to not only being laird, but to men working for him. Crisscrossing his back, the scars of the whippings ordered by the laird he once served made it hard to allow the title for himself at times.

"Aye. Let us make our way back. Go on, I will follow."

The men looked at each other then back to him. "We cannot allow it. You must go before us," the same man responded.

As soon as he walked into the great room, Ariana looked up. So linked they were that one could pick up on the other's emotions. Her eyes welled and she attempted a smile of comfort. Knowing he'd not want her to make a big fuss at the moment, she, instead, motioned for a servant to pour him mead.

She moved gracefully toward him, her eyes never leaving his. "Would you like something to eat?" Her hand rested on his forearm and she leaned to him. "Why don't I order you a hot bath? You can eat in our chambers."

She understood him too well. Chilled to the bone from not only the weather, but the grief that threatened to overtake him any moment, he could not keep from shivering. "I will go upstairs. Please don't come up yet, see about your own meal." He kissed her cheek and left the room.

The fire in the hearth warmed the chamber, but he didn't move to it. Instead, he went to the window and stared into the darkening sky. Things had changed so much since he'd left the McLeod Clan. He was a laird now. Responsible for the small keep and its people, and yet trapped inside him was the archer. The foundling, the one abandoned to fend for himself as a child, never left him. The feeling of not belonging raged constantly.

He'd never admit to Ariana how often he wanted to mount and leave, riding until his horse could no longer carry him. He dreamed of an unknown destination where no one knew him or his past, the degradations, humiliations, and mistreatments.

And yet, one look at his striped back and they'd know. Understand he was a man whose life had been anything but easy.

"Laird?" his male servant walked in. "Your bath is ready in the adjoining chamber." Jules, a younger man who'd served him for almost five years, had quickly become his confidant. Although fair of face and more built for battle than servitude, Jules was forced to serve where he could as he'd lost the bottom of his left leg as a child. The proud male refused to take no for an answer and insisted on completing most of the harder tasks required of him alone, without help.

"Thank you, Jules." He looked down at his attire. He'd forgotten how cold and wet he was. "Stop calling me Laird."

Jules attempted at a smile, knowing how much Valent hated the title. Jules often used it just to poke fun at him. Jules let out a breath. "I will miss Arrow. He was a good companion to me when you were not about."

Valent blinked away the moisture that came so quickly to his eyes, it shocked him. "Aye, he was. I believe he died of old age. Went into the forest to die alone. Proud one, he was." He smiled at how often, as of late, the old dog attempted to keep up with him when he rode. More times than not, he'd had to scoop the animal up and carry him.

"He bit me the first time I met him. I bit him back and we became friends after that." Jules chuckled and Valent joined him, glad for the reprieve from his sorrow. "Aye, he bit Steaphan, as well. I think it was a test for him."

"I know this is not the time..." Jules began, "but I have a request of you."

"What is it, Jules? Feel free to speak. You know more than anyone, I don't consider myself your laird, but more your friend." Valent hoped Jules would not ask to leave; he couldn't take another loss at the moment.

"I wish to compete for archer this year."

Although Jules attempted to seem neutral, there was tenseness to his movements as he went to the adjoining chamber with Valent. He stood by the door, as Valent never wanted assistance with bathing. His hazel eyes met Valent's as he waited for a reply.

"You are a good marksman. I don't see why you can't. I'm surprised you haven't in the past."

"I have never been allowed. Your brother doesn't allow someone like me into the guard ranks."

It surprised him that Steaphan would make such a distinction. Archers, for the most part, fought from rooftops and parapets. They did ride directly to battle, but were the back ranks. But understandably, Jules would be hindered as archers did have to be battle ready in case the front ranks were overrun. "You are a good rider," Valent said more to himself than to Jules. "You will compete."

Jules nodded, his shoulders falling. "I am good with the sword, as well. I train often. Thank you."

"Don't thank me yet. It will be against me that you will compete to gain a position. Kael suggested it and I agreed. It would prove interesting to see how my archers stack up against me."

Jules' eyebrows flew up. Valent was the best archer in the region. To beat him would be almost impossible.

An hour later, Ariana entered the chamber, her beautiful golden-brown eyes going to his face immediately. She came to him and wrapped her arms around his waist and laid her head onto his chest. Within minutes, the front of his tunic was wet from her tears. His wife was plush, an intoxicating blend of sensuality and strength. He pulled her face to his and kissed her salty cheeks, then took her mouth tenderly. "I know you had grown close to him, too. I didn't mean to shut you out earlier."

"I understand. You had him since you were a boy. I imagine your heart is broken." She sniffed and caressed his jaw.

Although married for five years, he never lost his

urgent need to take her, to have her under him, claiming her body over and over. Ariana seemed to understand where his mind wandered as she reached up and began pulling the pinnings from her hair, allowing the auburn tresses to fall past her shoulders.

She moved back and pulled at the ties, freeing herself from the clothing around her waist, the bodice of her dress fell open and her upper body became bare to him.

Valent remained still, not daring to move so she wouldn't stop, his eyes devoured every inch of exposed skin, his arousal already hardening in expectation.

She slipped her skirting away and he allowed his gaze to move from her bare feet up shapely legs to her rounded hips. Her triangle of reddish hair drew his attention next and his mouth fell open with the needed exhalation of breath.

"Come to me, Valent. I need you." She slid her hands down the front of her chest, her fingers splayed and she cupped her breasts. "I want to belong to you fully tonight."

His feet refused to budge. All he could do was stare at the beauty before him, needing more from her than just the physical at the moment. "Continue what you are doing."

At his husky command, her eyes widened, but she obeyed. Her fingers took each puckered tip and she pinched them. Then she closed her eyes and circled them.

"Open your eyes and look at me," he commanded, no longer able to keep from reaching for his own body, his hand sliding under his robing to wrap around his hardness.

Ariana swallowed and her gaze flew to his. Her nostrils flared and enticing lips parted with each breath. She was as aroused as he was. He followed the trail as one of her hands left her mounds and slid down her stomach to reach between her legs. She slid her middle finger between her nether lips and gasped.

"That's it, Ariana." He stroked his rock hard length once and then again. "Lay on the bed so I can see you better."

She moved to the bed and sat on the edge then looked up at him. "Join me, Valent."

"Lay back," he bit out, still not moving. "Open your legs and touch yourself."

She did as he bid, her eyes glued to his.

Her sex glistened with arousal. When her fingers moved through the curls to the center, he let out a moan with her. "That's it." He finally moved closer, pushing his robe open to allow him easier access to continue pleasuring himself.

Ariana's hand moved in a circular pattern. She squirmed and let out a soft moan. "I need you, Valent. Join with me."

"Not yet," he said and looked down at her. "You are so beautiful."

It was apparent she was coming close to desperation, her breasts moved up and down with her harsh breaths and she arched up. "I can't wait."

He pulled her hand away from her core and fell to his knees. She screamed when he covered her sex with his mouth and suckled her tiny nub. Ariana convulsed, her hands clutching the bedding as he feasted on her. When she began to settle, he nudged at her entrance with the tip of his rod, then drove in completely.

Ariana cried out his name and fought to remain with him as he pumped in and out of her, but she was lost in the abyss of her passion. Valent didn't care at the moment that she struggled to regain control, he didn't need her to. He was too lost in his selfish need to take her completely, to lose himself in her.

He pounded relentlessly into his wife until she'd long gone limp, totally consumed by the harshness of her climax. Her only responses to his drives were soft moans and gasps of breath. On and on he continued, his thrusts hard and steady. Ariana attempted to move, but he pinned her down, holding her arms over her head. He couldn't stop, couldn't finish, still rock hard.

Needing more, he pulled out and she let out a sigh and attempted to move away. He wasn't finished, remained fully erect. He rolled Ariana onto her stomach, pulled her up so her round orbs were high and thrust into her again. She mewled and struggled. He wasn't sure if she tried to get away from him or was lost in passion. He held her hips with a grip that would leave marks on her fair skin and continued to drive, the hard sounds of his hips hitting her bottom filling the room.

"Stop, Valent, I can't take any more," she cried out, but he was too blind with need. He continued to pound into her, driving in as deeply as he could before withdrawing almost completely. She was quiet when he finally spilled into her, his climax so hard, he fell over her and still continued pumping, his body relentless.

Drained, he fell off of Ariana onto the bed, his chest heaving. Immediately, regret took over. He hated what he'd just done. He shouldn't have allowed the loss of control.

He looked to Ariana She lay still on her stomach, her eyes closed. Her mouth swollen from his hard kisses. "Ariana?"

Ever so slowly her eyes opened and she looked to him but did not say anything.

"I-I am so sorry." He reached for her and she moved away, not far enough he couldn't reach her, but enough to get her message across. *Do not touch me.*

Her breath was ragged. "I asked you to stop."

The tightening in his chest brought a wince. What had he done? "I could not. I am so sorry." Once again, he went to reach for her, but stopped himself. He moved to the edge of the bed and got up.

She remained on her stomach with her legs draped to the floor. Her bottom already bruising from where he'd held her too tightly.

Guilt assaulted him. He went to the wash basin and returned with a wet cloth. Ever so gently, he cleaned his wife, reverently covering every part of her while she remained limp. While continuously apologizing, he returned twice to rinse the cloth. Once he was satisfied she was thoroughly clean, he retrieved a soft shift and dressed her in it before lifting her in his arms and placing her onto the pillows and pulling the blankets over her. She rolled to her side and curled into a ball. "Leave. I do not wish you in the bed tonight, Valent."

He'd planned to lie next to her, to hold her and continue to apologize. But now he was banned.

"I will remain in the room. If you need anything, please tell me."

She didn't respond. Instead, he heard a soft sniff.

He was an animal. He didn't deserve her. This was the first time he'd taken her so hard. Nothing excused it, not his grief, not how difficult his past was. Whatever it took, he would make it up to his wife. Lying on the floor before the hearth, he made a vow not to touch his wife again.

She deserved better than an animal like him.

Chapter 27

In spite of the chill in the air, the sun warmed Ariana's back as she knelt in her garden. She'd harvested as many herbs as she could to dry in preparation for the winter.

Her mind on her husband, she dug into the dirt with more vigor than necessary. Almost five days since the night he'd taken his grief out on her and they'd barely spoken. Valent was sorry. She understood he was riddled with guilt at having been so rough, taking her until she'd thought to pass out from the brutality of his assault. What had started out as a sensual game between them had turned dark and terrifying.

As much as she wanted to relieve him of guilt, she'd yet to recover from it, her feelings hurt that the one person she trusted the most had hurt her, not stopping when she'd become fearful. Yes, she trusted him and knew deep down he would rather die than hurt her, but the actions of that night made it difficult to sleep and when he reached for her, she flinched without meaning to.

The thumping of horses approaching sounded, the unmistakable pounding of the hooves on the ground accompanied by the creaking of a coach. She straightened to see the McLeod tartan colors on the men who rode toward her home.

Her brother, Ceardac, laird of the southern McLeod Clan, and his wife, Lily, came. She'd missed Lily horribly since moving away with Valent.

Ariana hurried toward the front gates just as Valent came up to stand beside her. He looked down at her, his expression grave. There were lines of worry etched on his face and shadows under his eyes. As much as she wanted to comfort him and reassure him that she'd forgiven his actions, it was hard to muster the words. This was not the moment to speak about it.

Ceardac dismounted and went to the coach, opening the door for Lily, who descended with a babe on her hip, a girl they'd named Ana. A second child, a little boy named Donall, followed.

The women hugged while Ceardac and Valent shook hands. Ariana then went to her brother and fell against him, allowing his strong embrace to comfort her.

"This is a warm welcome, sister," his deep voice echoed against her ear as she lay her head against his chest. "Are you well?"

She couldn't help the bristling of tears. "I am fine. I just miss you, brother. I miss home still at times."

His smile was warm, but his eyes narrowed when going to Valent, who stood back watching them.

They went to the great room and, immediately, maids bustled in bringing drinks and light refreshments. Ariana lifted the babe and admired the chubby girl. "She has grown so much since last I saw her."

Lily beamed proudly. "Aye, she is quite a glutton. Drinks me dry."

The atmosphere became light as both she and Valent entertained the visitors. She noted that Valent never paid heed to children. Seeming discomforted by children.

Although her friend never asked if she was with child, her friend's gaze went to her stomach when she thought Ariana didn't notice. Five years and still no child. She'd never considered that she could be barren.

Although Valent never spoke much about his desire for children, one night he assured her that if they did not procreate, it was probably his fault. He recounted one hard beating he'd received as a young boy where he'd bled from between his legs quite profusely.

Her heart ached for the young boy he'd been, growing up alone, left to fend for himself, with only old man Tavish to look after him.

Yet he'd grown to be a master archer, a formidable, handsome man who should have been laird to Clan McKenzie.

"You seem troubled," Lily said studying her face. "Is something wrong?"

Lost in her musings, Ariana had not noticed the men had moved away to sit by the hearth. "I can't help but wish for my own children when seeing my beautiful niece and nephew," she replied honestly, never able to keep things from Lily.

"Are you sure you are not with child now?" Lily leaned closer. "You have a certain look about you. Something different."

She was unhappy at the moment, not sure how to deal with what had transpired between her and Valent. That was certainly different. The past five years, she had her head in the clouds, so in love with her husband, barely anything other than that mattered. "I do need to talk to you about something." Ariana stole at glance at the men who were now drinking mead and seeming to settle into a comfortable silence.

"Let's take the children up to the sitting room." Lily hoisted little Donall to her hip. "Bring Ana."

"Oh my goodness," Lily repeated for the third time, her eyes round with worry. "I find it hard to believe. Valent has always treasured you so."

"He was not himself, so filled with grief, he was lost."

"Have you spoken to him about it? Are you afraid of it happening again if you join with him?"

Ariana let out a tired breath. "He has apologized over and over. I have forgiven him, of course. A part of me understands, but I am also afraid of him." A tear slid down her cheek and she brushed it away. "What should I do?"

Lily patted her hand and looked to the now slumbering Ana in thought. "Make love with him, Ariana. It is the only way. You have to get over the fear. He adores you and I am sure he'd rather die than treat you in such a manner again."

"When did you become so wise? You are younger than I am, yet seem so much older at times." Ariana hugged Lily. "I miss you."

"As do I, which is why we are here. Ceardac became tired of my bemoaning about you and how much I want to see you." Lily deepened her voice. "We were just here but several weeks ago." She giggled. "This morning he brought the carriage around and told me to pack the children."

"You are certainly my brother's weak spot."

That evening, all through the last meal, Ariana stole glances at her husband. Regardless of his morose mood that evening, he was too handsome for words. With hair as dark as midnight and eyes the color of a morning sky, the contrast was striking. He wore his beard shorn close to his face, which hid the cleft of his chin.

His gaze moved to her and in the depths of the gray pools, she saw regret and sorrow. Ariana reached for his

241

hand under the table. She squeezed it reassuringly and he blinked in surprise. After he let out a breath, he searched her face for a sign of what she was thinking.

She was already in bed when he entered the chamber. From a trunk at the foot of it, he pulled out a thick blanket so he could lay upon it on the floor. No matter how many times she'd asked him to join her in bed, he refused and continued to sleep on the floor before the hearth.

"Valent. Please, come to bed."

He moved to stand closer and looked down at her. "You cringe when I reach for you. I am not certain I can keep from seeking you when I lay next to you."

"Let us try. I miss you."

It was a long moment, but he finally nodded. He went back to the foot of the bed and removed his clothing before sliding under the coverings. He lay on his back and looked up at the ceiling. "I'm glad Ceardac and Lily came. You miss your friend."

"Aye, I do. I cannot wait to spend the day with her and the children tomorrow."

"Ceardac asked me to come with him to the Highland games next month. To compete in archery for his clan."

Ariana slid her hand over his chest and pressed a kiss to his shoulder. "That is cheating. You always win." His inhalation was shaky. It always excited her to see how much she affected her husband.

Valent remained still, not moving toward her, but his voice became husky. "I will go, I think."

Her hand moved down to his flat stomach. "I think you should."

"Ariana," he said turning to her. "What are you doing?"

"What do you think I am doing?" She'd reached his

rigid length and curled her fingers around it. Valent's lips parted and he swallowed. "Do as you wish with me, I belong to you completely."

Of course, he would give her total control. It was the only way she could be reassured. Her heart broke for him, but at the same time, she needed him more than ever. Her body screamed for his.

She climbed over him and straddled his midsection while running her hands down his chest. Valent watched her, his eyes darkening, his breathing fast.

When she leaned over him and took his mouth, he let out a moan of relief but remained passive, his hands to his sides. Her lips traveled over his, nipping at his bottom lip, pulling it into her mouth. He parted and allowed her tongue to delve in. She felt empowered that the warrior would be so passive to her ministrations and became bolder.

She took his face with both hands and moved from his mouth to the side of his face and down to his throat. Licking, kissing, and biting lightly.

Valent moaned and his hips lifted just a bit. By the way he trembled, it was obvious he fought the urge to touch her.

"Do not move." Ariana's words seemed to affect him more as his lips parted and he swallowed before nodding. She trailed her tongue from his throat to his chest, then with it pointed, she twirled it around his taut nipple.

"Ariana," he pronounced her name with desperation. "I love you."

She ignored the silent plea to allow him to touch her. Instead, she continued her trek, moving across his chest to the other nipple.

Reaching between them, she gripped his rigid erection and stroked it, her eyes on his face. His eyes clenched shut, he fought for control gripping the blankets in tight fists and gasping with each slide of her hand.

Her sex throbbed with need and for a moment, she became afraid of what would happen if they joined. Would he lose control again?

No, he would flee before hurting her so. She knew it deep in her soul. His eyes flew open as if he sensed her inner battle. In them, she saw reassurance and longing.

She positioned him at her entrance and slowly moved down, taking him in. He was large, always stretching and filling her fully. Once he was totally entrenched in her, she let out a harsh breath. God how she needed this man, how she loved everything about him. They would overcome this. He shook with restraint, yet didn't attempt to move, seeming to know she had to do this in order for their relationship to move forward.

When she lifted and lowered, both let out a moan. Tonight he would be hers and, without a doubt, he would take all she gave.

Chapter 28

Ariana found Valent in the stables. He'd been gone all day. The day before, he came to bed late and left before she woke. It was obvious he avoided her and she was tired of it. She'd given him time and as much as she grieved for the loss of Arrow, it was strange that he took it so hard.

He was bent over brushing his steed when she walked in. If he heard her, he didn't act like it. "Valent?"

Her husband straightened and looked over his shoulder to her but did not say anything.

Trying hard to keep her famous temper in check, she moved closer and crossed her arms. "Why are you avoiding me?"

"I do not avoid you. I only seek time alone," he replied, not stopping in his task.

Without thinking, she stomped closer and slapped the brush from his hand. "Talk to me."

The emotion in his eyes was overwhelming, anger raged against sorrow in the stormy gray. His nostrils flared, the only outward sign at her action. "Leave me be, Ariana. I will come inside once I finish."

"When? Tonight after you think I've fallen asleep?"

Seeming to realize she would not leave, he took her

arm and walked with her outside to a short rock wall. The chill in the air matched the frostiness in his eyes when he waited for her to speak. It terrified her. Valent had always regarded her with warmth, his eyes usually darkening with want when looking upon her. Today she saw nothing but emptiness.

"Please, tell me what is wrong. Have I done something to displease you? I thought after the other night, things were better."

He let out a breath and bowed his head. "I am not the man for you, Ariana. I should not have come back for you."

His words sliced her heart and, instinctively, she placed her hand flat against her chest. "What are you talking about?"

When his gaze met hers, his eyes were bright with moisture. "I cannot father children, which I know you want. I mistreated you and no matter what happened the other night, it does not remove the stain of it from my mind. I am a simple archer, not meant for all of this. It is all a mistake."

The sound of her palm against his face was loud and it stung, both her hand and in her chest. Rage surged and she could not help but slap him again.

Valent stared at her agog, his mouth falling open, his eyes wide.

"Don't you ever speak of yourself in such a manner," she spat. "I love you and accept you as you are. No one has a perfect marriage, Valent, but when doubt is allowed in, then things become worse. Yes, you took your grief out on me and it took me some time to recover. But my trust in you overtook any fear."

When a tear slipped down the proud man's cheek, her heart went to him, but she refused to soften as he would rebuff any kindness at the moment.

"Now," she said firmly, gaining his attention again. "We may or may not have bairns and as far as I am concerned, it is God's will, not ours."

Once again, he lowered his head, but brought it up sharply when she huffed. Obviously, he feared she'd slap him again.

"If you need to groom a laird, then we can always prepare David for the position. He is like our son and will make you proud. Now, I expect you at the evening meal, husband. Do not be late."

When he pulled her against him and his mouth covered hers, she wanted to cry in relief. But instead, she kissed him back until both were breathless.

"I expect you to finish this tonight," she told him, her gaze locked on his lips. "Will you, husband?"

His lips quivered. "Aye, wife, I will. I agree the boy will make me proud."

Her eyes glistened with tears as she headed back to the keep. Yes, she wanted children, but more than that, she needed Valent. Having him in her life fulfilled her completely.

Fiona McKenzie attempted to get comfortable. She rolled to her side and huffed. Expecting her third child, she wondered how to keep from having another. It was useless to think she'd keep from joining with her husband, the longer they were married, the more passionate their unions became. He was an ardent and prolific lover, which made it very difficult to keep from him.

"Fiona?" His sleepy voice against her ear made her tingle with delight. "Can I join with you?"

She pushed her bottom into him. "Yes."

It annoyed her they had to be so careful and

although the midwife said not to, she never told
Steaphan so. Not only did she join with her husband
often during each pregnancy, somehow the experience
was more alluring.

His thick sex nudged at her entrance and holding her
hips, he thrust in, filling her completely.

"Ah," both exclaimed in union as he began moving,
his length sliding in and out of her in a smooth rhythm.

"I cannot wait until you can do this harder," Fiona
told him reaching around to hold his hip. "Yet, it is so
good like this."

His hand slipped around her to cup her sex and his
finger delved through her folds to her center. Before
long both were lost, his movements coupled with deft
fingers brought her to cry out as he thrust in one last
time spilling into her.

Steaphan bit into her shoulder, the primal act
bringing a mixture of pain and another climb from
which to fall.

"Good morning, husband." Fiona made her way to
the breakfast table.

She couldn't help but giggle at his devilish smile.
"Yes, it is."

The nursemaid entered the room with their other
two children in tow. Both dark-haired boys with their
father's gray eyes. At four and two, they were Steaphan's
pride and joy. He spent countless hours with them at
swordplay with wooden toys he'd made for them.

"Do you wish for another son?" she asked, her hand
rubbing over her swollen stomach.

"Aye, another son would be nice. But a daughter
would make you happy." He leaned over and lifted the
youngest to his lap. "What say you, Ian? Would you like
a brother or sister?"

Fiona laughed when the boy shook his head. "No!"

"Laird, a messenger arrives." One of the guardsmen stood at the doorway. Fiona wanted to follow Steaphan; she was always interested in visitors. But knowing it was best to remain in the small room with the children, she could only look after her husband as he walked away. She couldn't help but admire the strong man. He was not only beautiful to look upon, but his strength came across in his stance and demeanor as well. Both he and his identical twin, Valent, were strong, able men, but in her eyes, Steaphan was without equal.

Steaphan was not sure what to expect, but seeing his father-in-law's tartan on the messenger, he hoped it wouldn't be bad news. He motioned for the messenger to come forward. His master of the guard, Niven, had a questioning gaze, which met his for a moment.

It was Niven who finally questioned the guard. "What brings you here, McLeod?"

The young man seemed ill at ease and Steaphan couldn't blame him, surrounded by McKenzie clansmen, with whom, up until recently, his clan had been at odds. "I bring word from my laird, your father-in-law. The Campbells have attacked the lands to the north. He thought you'd like to know it is possible we may require your help in the matter."

"Damn Campbells, always causing trouble are they not?" Steaphan nodded to a serving wench. "Sit, eat, and rest. I will send men back with you just in case assistance is required. If not, your laird can send them back to me."

The messenger reluctantly agreed and went to sit. Steaphan bowed his head in thought before speaking to Niven. "My brother is north of here. I should send word."

His friend's clear green eyes met his. "I will go. I'll take eight men with me. That will leave twenty here to protect the keep in case it is required."

"Very well. There is something that bothers me." A tingle of apprehension went up his spine. "Keep the messenger here, I will return shortly."

"Aye." Niven was pensive, but did not question him.

Steaphan hurried to his bedchamber. Not finding Fiona there, he went to her sitting room. She looked up as he walked in. It never ceased to please him to see his beautiful wife with their children. Instead of diminishing, her beauty had blossomed with motherhood. He approached and kissed her brow. "Can you come with me for a moment?"

After assuring the children she'd return shortly, he assisted his wife down the corridor toward the great room. "What is it, Steaphan?" Her worried gaze took him in. "What happens?"

"Would you recognize all of your father's messengers?"

"Aye, I think so."

He pulled her closer as they reached the doorway. "Look there at the guard's table. Do you know him?"

She looked at him for a long moment before turning her attention to the great room. It didn't take long for her to spot the messenger and her brows lowered. "He is not familiar to me."

"Interesting." Steaphan shrugged to give her the illusion of nonchalance, but she narrowed her eyes at him.

"Did he say he came from my father's clan?"

Steaphan gave up the pretense. "Aye."

"If he said McLeod, he could be from Ariana's clan. I would not recognize him then."

"No, he specifically said your father."

"Oh." Fiona went to peek again, but he pulled her back. "Return to the sitting room and close the door. Do not allow the children out until I send someone there to let you know all is well."

He returned to the table, noticing the messenger watched him. It took all his acting ability to lift his tankard and drink from it, while looking to Niven with a light smile. "He is not from Fiona's clan."

Following his lead, Niven chuckled. For all intents and purposes, they looked to be sharing a joke of some kind. The messenger returned his attention to the food before him.

"What do you think?" Niven muttered under his breath while allowing a maid to refill his cup.

"I think we will have an overnight guest. I also presume the leader of the guard will get any information we need by morning." Steaphan laughed and slapped Niven on the shoulder when the messenger looked over at them. The young man's eyes sliding around the room to the entrance.

"Quite a bold plan," Niven said. "Sending him into the lion's den."

"Whoever they are, they willingly sacrifice the poor fool."

Steaphan let out a huff. "Whoever they are, the fools should know better than to plan an attack right now. They will freeze their balls off out there. A storm is brewing."

"Who is he?" Steaphan asked as soon as Niven entered his study.

"He is from a band of men who claim no clan. The poor sod admitted that they hoped ye and all the guard would leave to battle and they could come in and pillage the keep. Not a very good plan. They should know a laird never goes to war without first sending scouts." Niven shook his head. "He is balling like a babe, now. Naked and trussed up like a pig. I almost feel bad for the young man." Niven went to the side board and poured a generous amount of whiskey. Whatever he'd done to the boy bothered his friend more than he admitted.

Steaphan went to him and placed his hand on the man's shoulder. "What do you think? I could speak to him, give him the opportunity to remain and work at the stable. He may run away after a time, but it will be long after his companions leave."

Niven nodded, relief apparent. "He'll need a few days to recover."

"Move him into a chamber that can be locked. Have someone see to his wounds."

Steaphan sat back just as one of the guardsmen came to the doorway. "Laird, another messenger arrives."

He met Niven's raised brows. "Who is it?"

"He claims to come on behalf of Laird McLeod."

Immediately, the three of them rushed to the great room only to stop when recognizing the messenger. The man spoke with another of his guards, as they obviously knew each other.

"What say you," Steaphan asked the man who approached at spotting him. "Is all well with your laird?"

"Aye, Laird. I come to give notice that he and Lady McLeod will arrive two days hence to remain and await the arrival of their grandchild."

Steaphan let out a sigh before glaring at Niven, who fought to keep from laughing. "Aye, very well. Make yourself comfortable. Eat...er...drink." He strode from the room to find Fiona.

His wife would be as ecstatic at the news as he was annoyed. The McLeods had a way of taking over. His father-in-law would insist on giving him advice on everything from the training of the guard to the way his crops grew. He let out a breath. In a way, he had to admit his father-in-law had filled the emptiness left from losing his own father.

He let out a resigned sigh. "Fiona!"

Once again, Ariana did not come to the morning meal. She'd assured Valent upon waking to be down shortly, but after a while, it was apparent she would not.

"What happens?" Valent rushed into the chamber to find Ariana abed, her face pale, her eyes watery. When he touched her face, it was cool to the touch. "I will send for a healer. You have been unwell for two days."

She moaned and rolled to the edge of the bed, grabbing for the pail and threw up while he pulled her hair back and soothed her. "I am here." He caressed her shoulders as she dry heaved.

"Oh, Valent, I feel horrible. I don't want to die." She began to cry and he climbed onto the bed, pulling her against him. His normally strong wife's sobs caused an unbearably huge lump to form in his throat.

He could not fathom life without her. After losing everyone that mattered, he would surely die without her. "I will never allow it." He cradled Ariana and kissed her salty cheeks. "Do not cry. You will feel worse."

"It is not possible to feel worse," she attempted to laugh. "All I want to do is lay in bed. I am hungry, but cannot keep food down. I feel so weak. I am so scared." She clung to him and pushed her face into his chest.

For the first time since he was a boy, Valent was truly terrified.

Cook hustled in with a tray. Upon it, a chunk of bread and a cup of what looked like tea. "Mistress, you must eat. I had to see about you meself. The maid said you refused food again." She moved to the edge of the bed and frowned down at them. "Whatever is the matter?"

"How can you ask that?" Ariana snapped at the maid. "I am dying. I cannot eat. I am weak as a kitten. I need a healer, not a hunk of dry bread and watery tea."

To Valent's shock, Cook smiled broadly.

"Do you take this lightly?" Valent glared at the woman. "My wife is very ill."

Cook let out a sigh. "You are not ill, Mistress. You are with child. What you feel is normal for the first weeks of it."

A deadly silence filled the room. Both Valent and Ariana stared wide-eyed at Cook, while the woman moved about the room seeming not to notice. "The bairn will arrive with the spring. Perfect time, if you ask me." She tsked and removed the chamber pot and opened the window. "A bit of fresh air would help. The dry bread will settle your stomach. I also suggest you sit by the window. Sitting up should make ye better. The herbs in the tea should settle things." She came to the bed and pulled back the blanket. "Come, milady, let me help you to the chair."

Valent could not move, he only watched mutely as Cook helped Ariana. Upon sitting by the window with the chilled air upon her, his wife seemed to sag with relief. Cook placed a small blanket across her shoulders then brought a plate with a piece of the bread on it. "Eat slowly." Ariana took a small bite and swallowed, then smiled brightly at Cook. "'Tis staying down."

"Of course, it is."

Valent came up behind the woman and wrapped his arms around her, kissing her jawline while the woman pushed him away.

"Laird, you will make my old heart stop."

He laughed and met Ariana's watery eyes. "We are going to have a bairn."

"Can it be true?" Ariana replied with a wide smile, her eyes misting. "I can hardly believe it."

"Of course, it's true," Cook mumbled leaving the room. "Young people."

Valent kneeled in front of Ariana and took her hands, lifting them to his lips. "Can it be true?"

"Now that I think about it, I have not had my monthly courses. It did not occur to me." She leaned forward and they pressed their foreheads together. "Valent, promise me you will stay with me always. I cannot fathom life without you."

It was difficult to swallow past the renewed blockage in his throat. He let out a long breath and looked into her eyes. "I will love you always and be the best husband to you, a good father to our child, and a fair laird to our people.

"I love you." She took the bread and put it to her mouth. "I am so hungry."

He laughed and pressed his lips to her temple. "I will bring more."

Darac Valent McKenzie was born on a bright spring morning. Valent had stormed into the room at Ariana's first scream and remained steadfast beside her for the entire ten hours it took to bring the bairn to the world.

"He is beautiful is he not?" Ariana asked him for the tenth time. "So perfect our son."

Son. The world vibrated in his chest each time she said it. Valent smiled and nodded as words had yet to form at the sight of the boy.

"He is our little miracle." Ariana's eyes fell and she fought to open them. "I am so tired."

The nursemaid came close. "I'll take the bairn, milady, so ye can rest."

"Nay." Valent finally spoke. "I will remain here with him until she wakes." Somehow he knew. Ariana would not like waking to find her child gone.

"Verra well, Laird." The nurse wrapped the child tightly and placed him in Valent's arms. "I will be back in a bit. I must get rid of some of these cloths and wash up a bit."

"Take yer time," Valent replied. "You deserve it. Eat, I will remain here."

After a relieved nod, the nursemaid shuffled out with a basket of cloths and such leaving them alone.

There was a knock at the door and David peered in. Valent motioned for him to enter. The lad looked to the babe. "A boy?"

"Aye yer brother," Valent replied meeting the boy's gaze. "Ye have a brother."

"Brother?" David blinked attempting to keep from crying. "How can it be? I am but an orphan."

"Nay you are our son and will continue to be treated as such. Now come and meet your little brother. I expect you to help him, protect him and teach him when I am not able to."

"Aye Da." The boy had called him that since four and Valent never corrected him. Now he felt the word sink in. It felt right.

After David left, the babe wiggled, but remained sleeping. Instinctively, Valent rocked to and fro as he moved to the window while keeping an eye the slumbering Ariana.

Through the window, he spied the landscape of his new home. Five and a half years and the view never ceased to fill him with pride. The villagers and farmers had survived winter well and new crops grew well.

Past the village, there was a large loch that provided water and fish. Food was plentiful and, for the time being, peace reigned in the region.

When Steaphan and Fiona came to visit and wish them well in the arrival of their first born, Ariana had joined Valent in hosting them. She and Fiona had become friends and had even visited.

Although his wife would not travel to the McLeods, she looked forward to their visits.

In the distance, a carriage made its way toward the keep. No doubt, it was Ceardac, Lily and their brood. A messenger had been dispatched as soon as Ariana's labor commenced. If Lily was not informed of it, Valent feared she'd never forgive him.

"You are a treasure to many, wee Darac." Valent looked to the babe. "Your life will be better and you will never know hardship. That I vow to ye. Your mother is a great woman who will love you fiercely as will I." Valent swallowed hard.

"You will always know you are loved. I will tell you so. I love you, son." Upon saying the words, a weight lifted from his chest and Valent took a deep breath. He smiled down at the boy who sighed in his sleep. Safe and secure.

Ariana fought not to sniff and let her husband know she overheard his speech. His beautiful words filled the room and, in that moment, she was so consumed with love, she feared her heart would burst from it.

The End.

Excerpt from

The Wolf of Skye

by Hildie McQueen

Chapter 1

The quest to find the well brought Faolan Mackinnon far from his beloved Skye. He'd traveled for many days on the foolish idea that if he found the well and cast his wish upon it, the fair Moira, his true love, would finally be his forever.

As a second born son, he had neither title to offer nor lands and because of it, his father, the laird Mackinnon, had betrothed Moira to his older brother, Ewan.

In a fortnight, the marriage would take place so he'd left prior to the hand fasting ceremony, unable to stomach being present. Faolan rode away on a solitary quest, with his guts churning and heart in pieces.

Now, as he neared a small village just south of Moy in the western Highlands, it was late in the evening and his stomach grumbled in anticipation of a hot meal. He reckoned a warm bed to follow would be quite nice as well. Mentally calculating the coin in his purse, Faolan decided it was worth it. He'd hire a room for the night and a place in the stables for his horse. After all, the well could not be very far from there. According to the stories his grandfather had told to him, he had to be very close to finding it.

The inn was noisy and quite busy. The villagers, it seemed, enjoyed a good drink, lively music and company on cold nights. The din of the conversations over the music accompanied by clinking of tankards lifted his spirits and soon Faolan found himself sharing a table with a local man who introduced himself as Paden Grant.

Paden, who seemed to be about the same age of his eight and twenty, studied Faolan constantly, his gaze full of curiosity at hearing about his quest. "Surely you cannot think that wishing upon that old well will bring the woman to you?" The man lifted his tankard and drank deeply before continuing. "'Tis said it will bring true love, but I do not think it will always be the person of your choosing."

"She is the only woman I will ever love. I am sure of it." The words felt strangely hollow, but Faolan refused to allow the feeling to linger. "Have you wished upon it?"

"Nay, nor have I ever sought it," Paden said with a chuckle. "I have enough on my hands trying to keep my troublesome sister from mischief. The last thing I need is another woman to worry over. It may not exist, but a tale."

"The lass is a feisty one, eh?"

"Quite so." Paden leaned back and scanned the tavern. "She's about somewhere in here. Is refusing to speak to me because I've decided to marry her off."

Faolan looked about the room, searching for someone who favored his new friend. Paden was fair of skin with dark brown hair and light eyes. It was hard to tell in the dimness of the room, but probably a greenish hue.

Clapping commenced and two men assisted a lass onto a tabletop. The musicians began playing a happy tune. People cheered as the lass danced, her arms in the air and feet making quick work. With a riot of red hair and a bright smile, she turned in circles in time to the music.

Faolan could not help notice what a lovely creature she was, with full size breasts, small waist and angelic face.

Still dancing, her bright smile faltered when Paden got to his feet. "She'll be the death of me." His new friend rushed to the table, plucked the lass from the tabletop and set her upon the floor. "Go home, Catriona, and see about that unruly mess of hair." The crowd booed at Paden, but he ignored them.

"I will not." She rushed to the table where Faolan sat and plopped down onto Paden's empty chair. With a pout, she lifted Paden's tankard and drank deeply.

"Catriona," Paden growled, then gave up. He dragged another chair over and sat. "Why do you insist on being foolish?" Her brother took the tankard back while she gifted him with a broad smile.

"I love you, brother of mine, but you are much too serious." She had a melodious voice that matched her beauty perfectly. Instead of sitting upright and still as any lady should, she rocked side to side in time to the music. "I love this tune."

Paden looked to Faolan. "Do you see now why I cannot marry as of yet?"

"Aye," Faolan replied only to garner a glare from Catriona who just then seemed to notice him. Her face reddened and she blinked several times while studying him. "Who are you?"

"Catriona," Paden motioned to Faolan. "This is Faolan Mackinnon of Skye."

"Skye really?" She leaned forward inspecting him as if he were the most interesting thing. "Truly?"

"Aye." Faolan's throat became dry and his heart beat faster. "Have you been there?"

She shook her head slowly and then looked to Paden, who studied them both. "Is this he?"

"What are you referring to sister?" Paden motioned for a tavern woman to come and refill their drinks. "I have no idea what you speak of."

The lass narrowed her eyes at Faolan. "It is you. I know it."

"Who do you think I am?"

"Fine, continue to play this silly game." She huffed and got to her feet. Her gaze on Faolan, she lifted an eyebrow as if in challenge. "Do not expect me to become a wilted lolly who will do every one of your biddings."

"I would never expect that of you lass," Faolan said truthfully. He rather liked her nature and hoped no one would ever try to change her.

She turned to her brother. "Very well then. Bring him along. I'll do it."

Both he and Paden exchanged questioning looks and then waited for Catriona to elaborate. Instead, she laughed at something someone said to her and clapped to get everyone's attention. Someone motioned to the musicians and the music ceased. The crowd quieted.

The slender lass climbed onto the chair and held her

arms out as if welcoming the room. "Attention everyone. My lout of a brother has decided to marry me off." She waited for the hisses and boos to end before continuing. "Hence forth, I will soon be married to Faolan Mackinnon, the Wolf of Skye." She motioned to him with much fanfare and the entire room focused on him with eager expressions. Obviously she'd used the Celtic meaning of his name to garner a reaction from the crowd.

Paden let out a groan and shrugged when Faolan looked to him for help.

The silence lingered until finally Faolan got to his feet and lifted a hand. The room erupted in cheers and tankards were lifted in toasts. A group of men rushed over and lifted Faolan onto their shoulders, carrying him around the room as the music resumed.

When he was brought back to the table and dropped onto the chair, drinks were shoved into Faolan's hands and more than one man clapped him on the back calling him courageous.

Catriona watched with arms crossed and a triumphant look as an older man approached. "Foolhardy if you ask me. No one would marry the lass; she's a good girl but much too strong-willed for her own good. If it were not for the announcement, I'd advise you to run and go as far as possible." The man shook his head and placed a bottle of whiskey on the table. "This may help."

The minx's lips trembled with barely controlled mirth as she eyed the whiskey. "Looks like ye're the townsmen's new hero. This will keep the single men from having to figure out how to tell my brother they will not marry me." She tossed her hair back off one shoulder and cocked her head to the side. "And those who are married are relieved not to have to worry about one of their sons being saddled with me." She leaned forward and peered intently at him. "A silent one are you?"

"Ladies and gents," the old man cried out and the room quieted. "Let us hear from the groom to be." The man motioned for Faolan to come to stand at the bar.

Faolan looked to Paden, whose eyes were round as saucers. "Will you go in my stead and explain the mistake?"

"Come along now bridegroom," Catriona insisted as she tugged him toward the front of the dimly lit room. "Tell these fine people why you're so smitten with me and cannot wait to be my husband." When he met her gaze, just for an instant, he spotted uncertainty. It was barely discernible, quickly hidden by a raised brow of challenge. The minx expected him to come up with an excuse, to rush through the speech, admit it to be a mistake and then run like a coward.

Every eye in the tavern went from her to him as they stared at each other. Faolan wrapped his arm around the woman's waist and brought her against his side. A collective murmur of astonishment sounded.

She felt perfect, as if made for him. Tucked under his arm, her soft curves molding to his harder body, Faolan felt protectiveness take over. He eyed her, noting the green of her eyes reminded him of a lush forest floor.

"I am proud to marry such a beautiful lass. I do not plan to tame her or change her in any way. That she's feisty is true, but a finer heart I dare anyone to find."

The crowd nodded their heads, admitted what he expected. That although Catriona may be hard to control and perhaps a bit too carefree, she cared for the people of the village and they for her.

"You do not know me enough to say that sir," she said softly and pushed away.

The old man raised his cup. "A kiss!"

Catriona's eyes widened and she turned to him. Before she could utter a word Faolan took her mouth, covering it with his and delving head first into an experience like he'd never known.

Desire and innocence combined with madness and heat battled for control, only to be doused by the knowledge that he'd just sealed his fate.

The quest he'd come for could be no more.

– End –

About the Author

Writing is my dream come true. There is nothing I love more than bringing my characters and stories to life and sharing them with you. Writing Highlander and Western historicals is a rewarding and enjoyable part of my life.

I live in a large town in Georgia with my super hero husband and two unruly Chihuahuas.

If you enjoyed *Highland Archer,* please recommend it to your friends and family. And if you have time, I would sincerely appreciate a review.

I am writing another book now, *Highland Laird,* where you will get to know Ross McLeod of Skye much better. The eldest son of Laird McLeod holds a terrible secret that prevents him from seeking a wife. The only way he will marry is if forced by circumstances beyond his control.

I love hearing from my readers and am always excited when you join my newsletter to keep abreast of new releases and other things happening in my world.

Newsletter sign up: http://goo.gl/PH6D00
Website: http://www.HildieMcQueen.com
Facebook: http://www.facebook.com/HildieMcQueen
Email: Hildie@HildieMcQueen.com
Twitter: https://twitter.com/HildieMcQueen
Instagram: @HildieWrites

Manufactured by Amazon.ca
Bolton, ON

34815035R00157